Mystic Pursuit

The Inner Realm

Book One

Mystic Pursuit

The Inner Realm

Book One

Erik Daniel Boudreau

COSMIC EGG
BOOKS

Winchester, UK
Washington, USA

JOHN HUNT PUBLISHING

First published by Cosmic Egg Books, 2023
Cosmic Egg Books is an imprint of John Hunt Publishing Ltd., 3 East St., Alresford,
Hampshire SO24 9EE, UK
office@jhpbooks.net
www.johnhuntpublishing.com
www.cosmicegg-books.com

For distributor details and how to order please visit the 'Ordering' section on our website.

Text copyright: Erik Daniel Boudreau 2021

ISBN: 978 1 80341 034 0
978 1 80341 035 7 (ebook)
Library of Congress Control Number: 2021950006

A CIP catalogue record for this book is available from the British Library.

Design: Stuart Davies

UK: Printed and bound by CPI Group (UK) Ltd, Croydon, CR0 4YY
US: Printed and bound by Thomson-Shore, 7300 West Joy Road, Dexter, MI 48130

We operate a distinctive and ethical publishing philosophy in
all areas of our business, from our global network of authors to
production and worldwide distribution.

For Vanessa & Aili

Prologue

It was a world like our own, in an age lost to time. For millennia, humans co-existed peacefully alongside several orders of enchanted beings, the mystics. Without political division or social hierarchy the world's five known realms were distinguishable only by terrain and climate, with humans and mystics interspersed freely amongst the vast, organic diversity around them.

Aside from a handful of remote island chains, all dry land was limited to a lone continental spread, traversable from coast-to-coast in five days by fleet horse—a lean, powerful breed known for its unrivaled speed and stamina. Despite the land's modest breadth, however, it was endowed with a staggering array of territories, from lush, humid rainforests to barren, sun-parched desert.

Comprising the mystics were three distinct orders, each distinguishable by appearance, ability, and nature.

First were the Masdazii, or matter-mystics. Ceaselessly practical in nature, the Masdazii averaged a head taller than the typical human, though they were most easily recognizable by their girth. Their thick, soft bodies and pale, thin, almost translucent skin belied the coarseness of their disposition. All the same, the Masdazii governed the composition and properties for all inanimate objects, from the tallest mountains down to the infinitesimally minute particles within them.

The second mystic tribe was the Lii-jit, or life-mystics. The Lii-jit contrasted rather starkly against the portly, sallow matter-mystics. Their comparatively compact height and lean, muscular bodies left them ideally suited to a highly agile existence. Also differing from the Masdazii was the Lii-jit's tendency toward impulsiveness and passion. They governed the natural life cycle of all living things, from before birth, through a healthy

1

existence, and into the transition to the next world.

While the life-mystics guided all living things to the next world, on their arrival, they were governed by the final band of mystics, the Ohlinn, or spirit-mystics. The Ohlinn served as a channel between this world and the next, unifying the spirits of all sentient beings whether human or mystic. These tall, slender beings possessed long, dark hair with a streak of silver cascading behind each ear and moved with the grace of a gentle evening breeze.

Together, the three mystic tribes brought order to the world, with each both supporting and relying upon the others.

Overseeing this grand orchestration was a single, all powerful being, the Voduss Grei, more commonly called the Gray Mystic. From a soaring, white, sacred tower, encircled by a jagged volcanic crater deep within the Bray desert, the reigning Gray Mystic sat in quiet contemplation, perpetually in tune with the spiritual and material oscillation of the surrounding world.

When imbalance struck, as tends to happen amidst the machinations of living things, and one domain began overtaking the others, the Gray Mystic would be prompted into action. Silently intuiting his will into his mystic followers, the Gray Mystic would incite whatever response was deemed necessary to avert the crisis and once again restore order. Life, matter, and spirit, in perfect synchronicity.

The noble lineage of the Voduss Grei continued in this manner, uninterrupted for millennia, until the time of Noryssin, the last of the Gray Mystics. For five generations, Noryssin faithfully fulfilled his duty, maintaining and facilitating the balance of all worldly things.

Until a fateful vision spurred Noryssin to unleash a series of catastrophic events, beginning with the destruction of Merrin Ells, an idyllic human village by the sea. It was the first of what came to be known as Noryssin's Three Betrayals, and it thrust the world into chaos.

CHAPTER ONE

In the distance, a flicker of light burst into the night, followed by the faint rattle of thunder. Standing alone in a grassy field littered with tents, wagons and supply crates, the young man glanced up at the cloud-filled sky and forced a breath into his chest. Composing himself, he wrapped his fingers tightly around the hilt of his still-sheathed sword and resumed his watch.

For twelve long nights Hajassin had assumed the duty of evening sentry, wading slowly through the encampment while the other soldiers slept, ensuring the army's safety as they traversed the vast and ever-changing landscape, perpetually assured by those around him that they would soon be at their destination.

Hajassin gazed upon the array of canopies around him, illuminated by the light of the camp's dying central fire. He was surrounded by mercenaries. Warriors. Murderers. The most skilled, ruthless, and loyal fighters from the farthest reaches of the known world. The greatest human army ever assembled.

Hajassin was not like them—that much he knew. The others seemed acutely aware of the fact as well, relegating him to the most menial of chores. Tasks reserved for either the broken-down old soldiers or the uselessly young: cooking, laundering, tending to minor wounds inflicted upon the true warriors during combat training. And night sentry.

Scarcely a month prior, Hajassin had been toiling amidst the drudgery of modest village life when the caravan arrived, searching for fit, passionate recruits. Despite the protests of his mother, his fate was sealed. The allure of participating in a war against a seemingly insurmountable enemy proved too great a temptation to resist. For a young man scarcely beyond the crest of adolescence, it was the promise of glory and adventure.

3

However, the further he ventured from the security of his family and the closer he drew toward the looming specter of war, the more he began to realize he had made a grave mistake. Far ahead, scarcely visible in the haze of moonlight, was their destination. A thick ridge of black jutting up along the horizon. A vast, towering forest containing countless lives the human army aimed to descend upon at first morning light. The enemy.

A second flash of light lit up the clouds ahead as Hajassin made his way toward the settlement's outer perimeter, nerves mounting with every step. A rumbling echoed across the sky, louder than before. Hajassin partially unsheathed his sword at the sound, nervously peering over both shoulders. The crisp, static-laced night air filled his nostrils as he glanced up at the sky. It seemed as though the very weather itself were bristling with aggression. Ever since joining the cursed army, nearly every day had been met with some form of anomalous climate issue, from bitter cold winds to droughts, to sudden, torrential downpours.

Reassured that he was still alone, Hajassin ventured forth, further from the light of the settlement's central fire and toward the posts where the numerous transport and riding animals were kept.

"Almost there," mouthed the young soldier as he passed the final pair of tents, his heartbeat throbbing loudly in his ear.

He was rapidly approaching the point of no return. Abandoning his post would doubtless be met with swift consequences, while the punishment for attempting to defect from his army on the eve of battle would most assuredly be worse. An unfortunate caveat of joining the great human cause was that there were only two ways of leaving the army: death and victory. Hajassin feared the former and cared not for the bloodshed needed to attain the latter. He just wanted to go home.

He weaved through the rows of resting pack mules and

powerful, elegant fleet horses, gently patting their sides as he passed by to keep them calm. For each of the past twelve nights, Hajassin had played his escape over and over in his head. He had even picked out the very fleet horse he planned to take— fast enough to take him far from the army, while small enough to be manageable for a novice rider. Unfortunately, it had taken him the entirety of the past twelve nights to muster both the courage and the desperation to attempt his escape.

But the time had come.

Finding his pre-selected horse, Hajassin thoughtfully loosened the horse's tether and began leading it from the pack. As he did so, a crash of thunder rolled down from above, this time in near-perfect sync with the flash of lightning. The storm had arrived.

Hajassin placed a hand upon the horse's back, on the verge of mounting his ride, when another sound emerged from the settlement behind him.

"Soldier," a voice called out, "I question the value of a sentry who abandons what he has been charged with protecting."

A wave of dread washed over Hajassin.

"My—my Lord—" he stuttered, his legs growing weak as he slowly turned around.

"Unless, of course, you were merely ripe with enthusiasm over our impending attack," smirked the figure. "However, as I made clear some time ago, we strike the mystics with the rise of the morning sun, still several hours yet."

"Lakos—" muttered Hajassin, frozen in place as the figure approached.

"You know you mustn't leave," said Lakos, continuing to draw nearer to the frantic young man. "Not now."

By the light of the dying fire, Hajassin could see that Lakos's normally tied, blonde, shoulder-length hair now fell messily to the sides of his face. Still, the tussled look did nothing to soften his cold, penetrating stare. And while he had, for the evening, abandoned the tarnished metal armor that typically shielded his chest, his omnipresent longsword still clung loyally to his hip.

"My lord... I'm sorry," said Hajassin, tears welling in his eyes. "I'm not a soldier. I can't do this."

Lakos drew closer still, hands held up acceptingly. "My boy—Hajassin, is it? I appreciate that this is all a lot to take in. We stand on the precipice of greatness. We are, all of us, on the verge of becoming legends. Liberating humans from mystic tyranny. It's our time to reign. There is no other place in all the known world where an ambitious young human should wish to be."

"But Lakos, I'm not like you!" cried Hajassin. "I'm just a boy from a simple village. I hold no ill intent toward the mystics."

Lakos's eyes lit up. "But don't you see? You're exactly like me," he said. "I, too, was merely a boy from a simple village. I was younger than you when the Gray Mystic Noryssin and his wretched kind saw fit to destroy my home, my world, and my life." He glanced wistfully up at the night sky. "The night of Noryssin's Three Betrayals, the sky was alight with stars. Far greater than tonight. But once that mystic demon unleashed his fury upon us, everything changed. Every star above suffocated by a blanket of gray. Of course, you were but a spark in your mother's eye at the time, but surely you've heard the tales."

Not waiting for a reply, Lakos continued. "The rains, pelting relentlessly down upon us. The rolling seas, battering our homes with waves the size of the sacred tower itself. And then those cursed Masdazii matter-mystics appearing and joining in the massacre." He looked over to Hajassin, whose gaze had shifted from his accuser to the dark, open field ahead. Taking a step towards the young soldier, Lakos scoffed. "Am I boring you, boy?"

"My lord, not at all," replied Hajassin, returning his nervous gaze to Lakos. "I know the legend very well."

"Ha!" burst Lakos. "A legend. Is that all it is to you? A fantasy, kept safely at arm's length? Might I impress upon you that this is all very real. I feel it as if the past thirty years have been but a heartbeat. The passage of time does not lay its dust upon certain memories. Certain actions. And the consequences of that night plague our kind to this day. And that is exactly why we are charged with this task—why I was chosen by the fates, whoever they may be, to bring the human order to greatness. Why, the villainous Gray Mystic himself knew it was so when he was spurred to attack. And while he succeeded in leaving my cherished home in ruin, he failed to take my life. For no being can alter the course of fate, no matter how greatly he may wish to do so. And as your so-called legend tells, I have spent thirty long years acquiring both the skill and the army to see that future realized." His eyes softened a touch as he edged closer to the young soldier. "Hajassin, my boy, see this fate realized alongside me and future generations will speak of your legend. This is our fate."

Hajassin, his hand still resting upon his horse, glanced briefly back to the dark forest ahead.

Taking notice, Lakos grasped the hilt of his longsword, but kept it securely in its sheath. "Listen, boy," he said sternly. "This discussion is finished. You are a soldier in my army and you will obey my instruction. You will remain with us until we have launched our attack. And then, if you still live, you may return home to your family."

Hajassin shook his head just as a loud crack of thunder burst out from above. The sudden sound caused his fleet horse to jolt a half-stride forward which, in turn, pulled Hajassin slightly off balance. The jarring sequence also served to rob Hajassin of his inhibitions. Like a tightly coiled spring suddenly released, a torrent of thoughts and fears and frustrations came streaming forth. "I'm sorry—but I can't. This is wrong. I can't be a part of decimating an entire mystic order. And why the Ohlinn? The legend says that it was only the Masdazii, the matter-mystics, who supported Noryssin's siege on Merrin Ells. In fact, I always thought that the Ohlinn spirit-mystics actually came to the aid of Merrin Ells during the attack." His tirade complete and the dread of consequence now upon him, Hajassin felt his knees grow weak.

"Aid?" Lakos laughed, the rage in his eyes betraying his composure. "Self-preservation, perhaps, but aid—I think not. The Ohlinn happened to reside in the very forest that borders Merrin Ells. When Noryssin and his oafish Masdazii minions were burning, drowning and battering my people, they merely feared that the attack would spill over into the Valla Forest. They confronted the Masdazii not to defend humans, but to ensure that the battle stayed confined to a human village."

"But is that just cause to decimate their kind?" asked Hajassin, unable to restrain himself.

"The Ohlinn must pay for their selfishness. The Masdazii for their deeds," Lakos replied.

Hajassin felt his fate grow increasingly dim with every adversarial word, yet he couldn't stop. "And the Lii-jit? They were not involved whatsoever in Noryssin's Three Betrayals. And yet if you strive to rid the world of all mystic orders, then they, too, must be eliminated."

"There is blood on the hands of the life-mystics as well, my boy. Failure to act justly—failure to act at all—is as great a violation of morality as the crime itself. They are all guilty, and the time has come for all mystics to pay the ultimate price. And if you, Hajassin, will not be a part of their justice, then I'm afraid that your battle must end tonight." Lakos stepped towards Hajassin, who darted back accordingly.

"And where precisely do you plan to go?" asked Lakos calmly. "Your options are few. The only human village within range is Merrin Ells, and I assure you, they would not be welcoming of a defecting soldier."

Hajassin glanced over toward the forest, and then quickly back to Lakos.

A wide smile stretched across Lakos's face. "I see. You expect to ride through to the Valla Forest and into the waiting embrace of the Ohlinn. Ha!" He laughed heartily. "Those despised spirit-mystics have shown clearly their ambivalence toward human peril. I can only imagine how they would receive a human soldier diverged from the very army set out to destroy them."

Lakos then hastened his approach, coming to within five strides of the frightened sentry. "But all of that is quite irrelevant, I'm afraid," he snarled, "As if you dare alert the Ohlinn to our plans, you had better pray that they protect you from me."

Hajassin could now see several soldiers exiting their tents, roused by the commotion.

"Get back!" screamed Hajassin, unsheathing his sword and waving it at Lakos, struggling to maintain control over its considerable heft. "Don't come any closer, I'm warning you!"

Lakos drew nearer, his face cast in cold stone. "I'm afraid we have moved beyond warnings, young soldier. For my men must know that dissent will not be tolerated. I am truly sorry, but you must be made an example of."

With Lakos almost within arm's reach, Hajassin stepped back, coming up against the now-liberated horse. Startled, he dropped his sword and glanced behind him. Forced into full commitment of his attempted escape, he turned to his horse and, in one fluid motion, mounted it and took off as quickly as he could toward the ominous forest ahead.

"Stop him!" shouted Lakos, waving the other soldiers to mount their horses and take off in pursuit.

Riding low on his horse as he urged it forward, Hajassin could hear the sound of the other soldiers gaining ground. He also began to feel the first drops of rain spotting against his face as the roars of thunder continued to amplify. Then, as the towering border of trees grew nearer, a bright flash of lightning lit up the terrain ahead. In it, he could see a stationary form directly in front of him, blocking his path to the forest.

Following the lightning strike, the path in front of him once again grew dim, save for a faint glow of blue. Hajassin's desperation for escape was quickly obscured by confusion over exactly what lay ahead. A second flash of lightning brought instant clarity to the scene. There was a small wagon, led by a strange animal, the silhouette of which he could not decipher, and a lone figure. The being stood tall but crooked and disturbingly thin, with a sphere of blue light swirling in the air above its cupped hands. The blue was also reflected in the eyes of the being, as it stood calmly in his path.

Hajassin was transfixed by the light. He could not look away. Within moments, the sound of his pursuers drowned out into a murmur of white noise. He had also grown oblivious to the faint mist of rain now descending upon the grassy plain. His focus was completely, inescapably, bound to the soft, blue glow and the slender form projecting it.

His ambition to retreat into the Valla Forest slipped from his consciousness. Hajassin slowed his horse, stopping mere strides from the strange figure.

The group of soldiers racing toward him also stopped to observe from a distance what was unfolding, while Lakos continued ahead.

The mysterious figure glanced up to see Lakos draw near, the swirling blue orb above his hands promptly vanishing into nothingness.

"This does not concern you, stranger," shouted Lakos. "Just continue on your way and leave our business to us."

"I'm afraid it does concern me," replied the figure cryptically.

The weathered old soul stood in front of an equally worn rock leopard, so named for its broad, angular gray-black shoulders. Strung across the animal's shoulders was a round object, roughly the size of a wine barrel, concealed by a tarp and tied tight around the rock leopard's chest.

The figure's sapphire eyes burned brightly, framed by a sallow and mottled complexion. His long, fine gray hair bore the faintest suggestion of contrast against the distinctive light streaks that ran across each temple. The faded, frayed cotton garments identified with his kind hung loosely over his depleted frame, billowing in the cool night breeze.

"You are an Ohlinn!" snarled Lakos, unsheathing his sword while still astride his horse.

"Indeed, I am," replied the figure. "Or at least, was once, long ago."

Lakos's eyes burned as he looked down upon the sorry figure. "In that case, I'm afraid I must agree with you. This does concern you, as it does the rest of your kind. For I have been tasked with ridding the world of every living mystic, Ohlinn or otherwise, and it appears that I will be starting with you. After, of course, we dispatch our mutinous young soldier here."

"Might I suggest an alternate strategy," replied the figure, slowly reaching into his pocket and revealing a small dagger. He tossed it to the ground by Hajassin's feet.

Still seemingly lost in a haze, Hajassin slowly knelt down and picked up the dagger.

"You old fool," laughed Lakos. "The blade will do the boy no good. You do not know who you are dealing with," he remarked, holding his sword high as he brought his horse toward Hajassin.

The strange old Ohlinn merely grinned as he looked down at the young human, his sapphire eyes seeming to glow brighter still.

Hajassin rose, dagger in hand, and looked up at Lakos with eyes wide and forlorn. Before Lakos could strike the boy down, he watched in disbelief as Hajassin plunged the dagger deep into his own chest, falling to the rain-soaked ground.

Lakos looked to the Ohlinn, speechless.

"I know quite well who you are, Lord Lakos," said the

old mystic. "And I come to tell you that there are more ways to defeat an enemy than simple force." The frail spirit-mystic knelt down by the boy and retrieved his dagger, wiping it clean against the grass and sliding it into his pocket.

"Who are you, and how do you know who I am?" asked Lakos. "And why are you helping us when we seek to destroy your kind?"

The old Ohlinn's craggy smile grew wider still. "All answers in due time, my lord. But first, I humbly request entry into your camp. I have traveled across many lands to reach you and my weary bones are in desperate need of warmth. Besides, the longer we stay at the threshold of the Valla Forest, the greater the chance an Ohlinn sentry will grow aware of your presence."

But Lakos sat firm atop his horse. "I will do no such thing. You know of our presence here and our mission. And I know the devious ways of your kind—you could have already warned the rest of your order using Ohlinn telepathy. I should have already killed you."

The old Ohlinn laughed, his voice weak and dry. "Lakos, you are all that I expected. However, you have much to learn of Ohlinn ways. But more importantly, I should impress upon you that I am no longer part of the Ohlinn order, and I have not been for quite some time. I spent my life serving another, until his actions thirty years ago left us all in disarray."

Lakos was dumbfounded. "Gris Hallis," he finally muttered, still in disbelief. "The fallen Ohlinn."

For several tense moments Lakos glared down at the old mystic, scrutinizing him while Gris Hallis stood his ground, awaiting a response.

Seeming to fight against his intuition, Lakos finally conceded, waving the old spirit-mystic forward as he turned and led his men back to the settlement.

CHAPTER TWO

Lakos watched as the old Ohlinn leaned over the settlement's rekindled fire, rubbing the circulation back into his bony shoulders. By this time, the misting rain had dissipated enough to bathe the camp in soft moonlight, as dozens of now-alert soldiers whispered amongst themselves to assess the situation.

"Tell me, old mystic," asked Lakos, gazing into the fire, "how did you stop that soldier? He took his own life, but somehow, you were controlling him."

"There is a depth to mystic ability far beyond that your kind have knowledge of," replied Gris Hallis with a gentle grin. "However, I am here to educate you."

Lakos was perplexed. "Why did you come to me?"

Gris Hallis's eyes slowly shut, savoring the warmth. "I've been waiting a long time for you." He grinned. "For Noryssin's prophecy to come to light." He suddenly turned from the fire, his eyes now affixed to Lakos, alight with their own sapphire blaze. "Following the siege of Merrin Ells, I watched the world both recover and fall to pieces yet again. With the sacred tower, my home, in ruin, I was forced into lands I had seen only in visions. I saw a world without direction, hope or guidance. I saw bonds between beings forged through the ages suddenly dissolve, and it broke my heart."

"Your senility paints a touching picture," sneered Lakos, growing tense. "But the world under Noryssin was far from idyllic. We were prisoners, all of us. Trapped under his ultimate authority. Even you, his... apprentice." The word bitterly left his lips.

"We were instruments in a grand orchestration," retorted Gris Hallis. "Noryssin's role was simply that of the conductor, without whom, our own gifts would be lost in a din of chaos."

"Chaos is a small price to pay for free will!" shouted Lakos.

Unaffected by the outburst, the old spirit-mystic continued. "Following Noryssin's betrayals, through this supposed free will, as you call it, the sacred bond between humans and mystics was fractured. The three mystic orders retreated back to their lands of origin—the Masdazii to their maze of cliff side tunnels, the Lii-jit to the Sani-jai rainforest, and the Ohlinn to the safety of the Valla Forest. I saw it all unfolding right before my eyes."

"And the world was a better place because of it," spat Lakos.

"On the contrary," said Gris Hallis. "Without the Gray Mystic's unifying force, universal balance was lost. Surely you witnessed this happening, the same as I? Lands, long protected by subtly guiding forces, suddenly devastated by an endless string of natural disasters. Dry, desert plains sieged by torrential downpours. Lush, thick forests assaulted by scalding heat waves and battering winds. The world that I so dearly loved had become a disjointed and dangerous place, growing all the more dangerous with each passing day. Of course, I could not expect you, or any other human, to realize that such phenomena were in fact the consequence of a world in chaos. But I assure you, there is no other explanation."

"That still does not explain why you now stand before the very human destined to destroy your kind." Lakos moved directly in front of Gris Hallis, staring into his eyes with barely a stride between them. "I shall ask you one final time. Why did you come here?"

"Following the end of the Voduss Grei lineage, I knew it was only a matter of time before the one prophesized by Noryssin would emerge to restore it. Utilizing one of the few remnants of Ohlinn life I still retained, I would meditate for days on end, desperate for a glimpse of the world's next great leader. And it did not take long for my wish to come true. I saw you, venturing across the realms, absorbing whatever knowledge anyone was willing to pass down to you. You were patient, methodical in your quest, forcing me to do likewise. Over the years, I could see you growing stronger, mastering military strategy, and assimilating volumes of techniques and tricks gleaned from the furthest reaches of the known world. Never before had I seen a human with such conviction, such singularity of purpose. I knew you were the one. And, not surprisingly, so did others. I saw your own following begin, swiftly growing into the impassioned army I now see before me."

"A romanticized vision if ever there was one," replied Lakos, "but your flattery falls on deaf ears." He slowly withdrew his sword and circled the broken-down old mystic. "And so, you've been watching me, studying me. Which means that you know who I am, and exactly what I'm capable of. And yet you, whose former master thrust me to this fate, come to me of your own accord. Surely your great insights have intuited that this encounter will not end well for you."

"It is the actions of my former master that brought me here," replied Gris Hallis. "When Noryssin betrayed the humans of Merrin Ells, he betrayed us all. He took from me the only life I had ever known. But following that night, when he told me that he had no choice but to destroy the sacred tower as well, I could see the fear in his eyes. He knew that despite his savagery, he had failed to kill the one in his vision. The human who would one day assume his throne. And where he saw despair, I saw hope."

"How very astute," said Lakos. "But the fact remains, you were closer to Noryssin than any being. And I am to believe that you are now my ally? I am the chosen one!" he shouted. "I am your master's nightmare!"

Gris Hallis was not fazed. "I do not deny my origin. I was born Ohlinn and left the security of the Valla Forest as a youth to serve Noryssin, the last of the sacred Voduss Grei, from within the sacred tower," he declared, solemnly gazing into the flames. "Nor do I deny my dedication to his rule, or my level of involvement in all actions preceding that fateful night. When

Noryssin took me from my life with the Ohlinn, it was with the ambition of cultivating a successor. You see, he had ruled the five realms for longer than any Gray Mystic before him. He knew that despite his great power, his time in this world was finite. And so great was his love for the world and all life upon it that he wished to ensure its continued prosperity. I, and I alone, was granted access into the sacred tower, and the great many secrets within it. Groomed as his successor, until he determined that I was unworthy to receive this greatest and ultimate responsibility. By that time, Noryssin looked upon me as a son, trusting me completely to serve as his proxy for all affairs taking place beyond the boundaries of the Inner Realm. But, for reasons never revealed to me, I was eventually deemed unsuitable to succeed him as the next Voduss Grei. At first, I was enraged, of course. Convinced that he had grown senile in his old age, crazed and unwilling to relinquish his power. Surely, I was more than fitting to take his place, to do what he had done. To lead, to create, to rule." Gris Hallis turned from the fire to face Lakos, his sapphire eyes glistening in the moonlight. "Or so I thought."

Lakos merely stood and watched the old mystic tell his tale, as the sea of soldiers surrounding him did likewise.

"It took many years and much suffering to realize and accept my place in the universe," continued Gris Hallis. "Noryssin was right. My dear Lakos, I am no more a leader than you are a humble fisherman. But that does not mean that I am without great power. You seek to govern all that you see, all that exists in this world. The ground beneath us, the birds, fish, mountains, the breeze, the rain, the men. The mystics. My dear Lakos, I come to tell you that the breadth of your future kingdom far exceeds that which you can merely see with your eyes. And I come to tell you that in order to see your fate realized, you must first take this fractured world and once again make it whole. Not to blindly destroy those for whom your hatred burns, but to rebuild what has been destroyed. Is the momentary satisfaction of taking the lives of your enemies not inferior to the undying pleasures of ruling over them? There is a great empire at your fingertips, a world of servants laid out before you. It is true that one must know his enemy in order to defeat him. And the powers of the mystic orders cannot be obtained solely through violence."

"Neither I nor my men require any assistance from an old wizard," replied Lakos. "My entire life has been in preparation for the battle we shall soon be engaging in. My men have trained, bled, and sacrificed in anticipation of this moment. If you think that I will cast those years aside to be influenced by you, of all beings, then you severely underestimate both my intelligence and my convictions. My army shall strike the Ohlinn at first light—the dawn of a new age that you shall regrettably not be part of."

"I came to you on this night to stop you from your attack," protested Gris Hallis.

Lakos laughed heartily. "You contradictory old fool. First you profess to aid my quest, and now you have the gall to speak of impeding me. However, if nothing else, you have succeeded in justifying the extermination of your kind. All the same, the boldness of your attempt to sway me did not go unnoticed. And so I will show you this one kindness. I suggest that you return to whatever dark shadow you emerged from, Gris Hallis, and allow me to fulfill my destiny. This world has no further use for you."

"Are you or are you not the subject of Noryssin's great and ominous vision?" asked Gris Hallis bluntly, taking a step back from the fire. "For the last of the Gray Mystics did not envision the mere destruction of the mystic orders, or even their enslavement. He foresaw the rise of a new ruler—a human ruler—taking his place atop the throne of the Voduss Grei. The king of all known worlds. A god. And if that is the fate that you envision for yourself, then there is but one path to take." He paused for a moment, the faintest smirk upon his face. "And only I possess the knowledge to take you there."

Lakos shook his head. "I must admit, old wizard, you paint an intriguing picture. But you make promises that cannot be fulfilled. As appealing as it would be to force the mystics into subservience, I know their kind well enough to know that they would sooner perish than live under human rule. A mortal human cannot assume the throne of the Voduss Grei. It has never been done."

"It can be done," said Gris Hallis, "I have a way."

Lakos paused for a moment, unable to stifle his mounting curiosity. "You have until sunrise to convince me. And if you don't, then this war—and this world—shall move on without you."

At that moment, the object concealed on the back of the rock leopard emitted a groan.

Regaining a spryness in his step, Gris Hallis smiled widely as he loped back to his pack animal, grabbed a corner of the tarp, and pulled it to the side.

Lying atop the leopard's back was a small, muscular figure on its side, curled tightly with its knees to its chest and tightly bound with loop upon loop of rope. It wore dark, well-tailored leather garments stained with blood and a headband of brown and red beads wrapped around messy waves of brown hair that framed a bruised, tan-colored face.

"I must admit, violence does have its place. From time-to-time," said Gris Hallis, pride thick in his voice.

Lakos cautiously approached the figure, which was barely conscious and obviously in pain.

"A Lii-jit," he muttered, contempt on his lips. "Life-mystic. No doubt a challenge to catch, I grant you that. But what are we to do with it?" Lakos grasped the small mystic by the hair and abruptly lifted its head. "One life-mystic? One of these blasphemous creatures is of no use to me. I need them all."

"It starts with one, my lord," said Hallis. "Moths to a flame."

Off in the distance, streaks of electricity flickered across the sky, and the faint rumblings of thunder echoed.

A storm was coming.

CHAPTER THREE

"Where... is your father?" asked Thayliss, struggling to hammer a plank of wood over the broad, open, window as the cold rain blew inside, blinding him. His normally shaggy, light-brown hair was soaked, pasted across the side of his face by the relentless gale. His light, loose-fitting cotton garments also clung to his chilled skin, soaked by the blustering torrent.

"I think he's gone outside again," replied Leysiia. She dashed around the kitchen, retrieving various fruits as they rolled along the wooden floorboards and placing them into a ram's hide bag. Suddenly she stopped and turned to face Thayliss—a panicked look in her shimmering sapphire eyes. "He's been acting strange lately, and he won't tell me why. Thayliss, I'm worried about him."

Hastily securing the board in place, Thayliss went to Leysiia, placed a hand against her smooth, alabaster cheek, and gently swept the soaked, gray-streaked hairs back behind her ear. He leaned close and kissed her tenderly.

"I'm sure he's fine. Your father just wants to keep us safe. He knows what he's doing. After all, like you always say, your father's father was the architectural brains behind this entire settlement. Or was it your father's father's father?" he asked with a gentle smile. A loud crack of thunder raged overhead. "Nonetheless," Thayliss conceded, "I'll tell him he can finish his work after the storm's let up."

Leysiia forced a smile and resumed her activity as several wooden bowls rolled from a cabinet and hit the unstable floor.

Thayliss raced from the kitchen, across the main living quarters, and toward the main entrance, feeling his balance wane with every powerful wind gust. With all the fortitude he could muster, Thayliss ventured past the threshold and out into the bursting gales.

"Leonorryn!" he shouted, squinting through the pelting rain. The screaming wind was near deafening, but he thought he detected a response. "Leonorryn, where are you?" he shouted again, this time hearing nothing.

Thayliss steadied his footing and cautiously edged farther from the cabin's entrance and into the dense thicket one-hundred-and-fifty strides above the ground.

While striking in its ornate carved doorways, arches, and crossbeams, the small wooden treetop cabin was otherwise no different than the fifty or sixty others in the area. Though he could barely see, Thayliss noticed each surrounding abode jostling harshly in the torrents, each home's residents no doubt huddled together in the central room, praying for the storm to abate. For a brief instant, at the mercy of the elements while far above the forest floor, he cursed that his own family had to be the exception to the rule.

"Thay—liss," a voice weakly called out.

It was from directly below.

Thayliss reached for a sturdy branch and, holding on with all his might, lowered himself to the branch beneath. While negotiating precarious treetops had become near second nature to him over the years, sometimes he still felt like exactly what he was: a human who, by the grace of the spirits, found himself stuck up a tree. And this was certainly one of those instances.

Squatting on the lower branch, Thayliss could see the underside of the cabin. At the base of the structure was Leonorryn, hammering a small wooden wedge at the convergence of the cabin's underside and the two thick intersecting branches it rested upon.

"Thayliss," the old mystic shouted, seemingly glued to the small branch his legs wrapped tightly around. "I just need to stabilize the structure. Go back inside. It's too dangerous out here!"

It was just as Thayliss had expected. While the old Ohlinn

had always been fiercely protective of his family, for the past two days his concern had grown to obsession, though neither Thayliss nor Leysiia knew why. Feeling his grasp slip ever-so-slightly, Thayliss again wrapped his arms around the nearest branch. "The structure is fine. We're both fine. You need to come inside!" he shouted, knowing the old man well enough to know that it would be of no use.

Leonorryn shook his head and continued his work. "I'm almost finished. Just a few more beams. Now return to Leysiia. You'll break your neck out here."

Thayliss wouldn't relent. "I'm not going anywhere without you!"

Leonorryn paused for a moment before nodding. "You're right." He leaped from one branch to another toward Thayliss, seemingly impervious to the pelting rain and wind. Before Thayliss could utter another word, the old mystic was next to him, placing a comforting hand on his shoulder. "Let's go inside," he said.

Thayliss was too wet, too exhausted, and too frightened to respond. With the agility of a lemur, Leonorryn sprang up to a higher branch, heading toward the cabin's entrance.

As Thayliss reached up to grab the branch above, a bolt of lightning struck the massive Valla oak. The giant tree recoiled from the blow, and Thayliss's foothold was gone. His hand peeled into the bark of the branch above, desperately searching for traction. But there was none.

He felt himself fall, whipped mercilessly by countless branches as he saw his cabin—his life—up above grow ever smaller.

CHAPTER FOUR

"The Valla Forest awaits," Gris Hallis said, pointing a slender, bony hand through the falling rain toward the dark, ominous thicket ahead.

Lakos called his fleet horse to a stop next to where the old spirit-mystic stood. Behind them, the caravan of rebels and mercenaries seethed in anticipation.

"If this is a trap," warned Lakos, "my horse will wear your spine around his neck—assuming you have one, of course."

"My lord," replied Hallis, "I assure you, I am your ally on this quest. And you forget, my brief time living among the spirit-mystics is but a distant, faded memory. The sacred white tower was my true home. A home to which I dearly wish to return. I want your prophecy realized as much as you do. Once the Ohlinn have fallen and we harness their power, the final two Mystic orders will most assuredly follow suit. But I do respectfully insist that we act swiftly, as the Ohlinn are a most alert breed. Overcautious, suspicious, paranoid. They are as likely to detect our presence, our intent, and vanish as they are to fall into our trap."

"This is your trap," sneered Lakos. "And your one opportunity to prove your worth to me. You promise me infinite power, but take heed—should you fail me, you will feel the same cold steel tearing through your heart as your brethren. I wager that the multitude of loyal soldiers now surrounding you would love nothing better than to see that come to light. After all, you profess to deny them the spilling of mystic blood that I had long promised them."

"Fear not," said Gris Hallis, "I assure you, before your ambitions are fully realized, there will be a great many opportunities for your men to relish the violence they so desperately crave."

"Have at it then, wizard," said Lakos. "Bring me my kingdom."

"As you wish," replied Hallis, walking back to the caravan. One of the larger horses was hitched to a cage wagon, its solid steel bars surrounding the battered Lii-jit. On the floor inside the cage the young life-mystic sat, a ball of muscular tension, breathing heavy, labored puffs of air.

The leather ropes with which he had been bound were now replaced with a lone metal shackle around his left wrist, adjoined to a chain extending outside the mobile prison's bars. The chain terminated in a large spool mounted on the side of the wagon beside a hand-crank mechanism. At the base and the apex of each corner of the cell was a small, irregular fragment of yellowed stone, eight in all, innocuously affixed to the intersecting wooden crossbeams by thin straps of leather.

"First, my lord, we try this the hard way." Gris Hallis turned to the seething Lii-jit and grasped the hand crank. "Now, now, my dear life-mystic, it is time for you to lend a helping hand."

Gris Hallis began slowly turning the crank. With each revolution, the chain attached to the Lii-jit's left arm grew increasingly taut. Within moments, the furious, frightened life-mystic was being dragged across the floor of the wagon toward Gris Hallis. With one final crank, the mystic's left arm was pulled between the wagon's bars, outstretched to its maximum in front of Gris Hallis's eager, glowing eyes.

The small figure writhed in protest, fighting to liberate its arm as it jutted out vulnerably from the wagon and into the rainy night.

Gris Hallis turned to Lakos and slowly withdrew a slender, curved blade from his pocket, scarcely thinner or longer than the willowy hands that wielded it. "They say determining the age of a Lii-jit is next to impossible. That after childhood, the musculature takes on such a gradual progression so as to lead some to believe that these little fellows are in fact immortal.

But just as their silence does not mean they cannot speak, an imperceptible aging process does not preclude death. Or injury."

Lakos grew restless. "You've proved a scholarly point. Now let's have it."

Gris Hallis retained his composure, clearly delighting in the moment. "You see, from my lifetime of experience, I could ascertain that what we have here is a young adolescent male. And herein lies the paradox. As a mystic of any order grows into old age, his powers dissipate. However, it may also be—"

"And what of the mystic elders, and their supposed power?" interjected Lakos.

Gris Hallis nodded gently. "It is true that mystic elders once proved the exception to this rule. However, following the dissolution of the Voduss Grei, the designation of elder is little more than a figurehead. A thinly veiled declaration of senility." The old Ohlinn cleared his throat and continued. "Now, accompanying the enhanced strength and vigor of a mature, adult mystic is increased wisdom and, with it, an understanding of the fragility of life. As such, despite whatever strength or gifts he may possess, an adult mystic is inherently more receptive to gentle methods of persuasion. Meanwhile, a younger mystic—" He jarred the chain still farther, causing noticeable pain on the face of the Lii-jit. "— such as the one we have here, may be too young to appreciate fully the danger he is in. As such, compliance dwindles. He is, however, at an age brimming with unbridled mystical power. Power that we now require."

"The point, wizard!" shouted Lakos, unsheathing his sword.

"The point is this," Gris Hallis replied. "Lii-jit, life-mystic, bring the Ohlinn to me!"

He quickly brought the blade down against the captive mystic's exposed forearm, severing the Lii-jit's hand completely at the wrist. The wounded mystic shrieked, recoiling to the opposite end of the cage and cowering in the corner, now liberated from the chain.

Lakos quickly looked to the forest and surveyed the dim night sky. The harsh winds and descending sheets of rain were all he saw.

"Nothing. The miserable creature did nothing. I told you that mystic witchcraft pales in comparison to human weaponry. You see, Gris Hallis, a sword is always as sharp as you keep it. Whereas a mind, such as yours, will invariably dull in time. My army will proceed into the forest as planned—without you."

Lakos signaled to several of his guards, who began closing in on where Gris Hallis stood, blood in their eyes.

"Wait—please," begged Gris Hallis, pointing back toward the cage. "The demonstration is not yet complete. You see, in a stubborn adolescent life-mystic, persuasion by force will always fail. For reasons soon to become self-evident."

Inside the cage, the disfigured Lii-jit began waving his right hand slowly across the stump of his left wrist, mouthing a silent incantation. Within moments, the bloodied terminus at the end of his forearm began to glow, brightening until it lit up the entirety of the cage around him. Lakos, Gris Hallis, and the surrounding soldiers all strained to watch what was unfolding. Then, even more swiftly than it emerged, the brilliant light vanished, retreating back into its source at the base of the Lii-jit's left wrist, where a new, perfectly formed hand now flexed.

"This, my lord, is why simple force will not get you the power and retribution you seek," said Gris Hallis. "And now for the easy way."

Gris Hallis once again moved closer to the cage and thrust his curved dagger inside it. This time, however, he brought the blade in contact with the small, yellowed stone fastened to the nearest corner of the cell. Muttering a brief prayer of his own, Gris Hallis sent a pulse of energy through his blade and into the stone, quickly retracting his arm and stepping several strides back.

The yellow stone crackled to life as tiny veins of white light surged chaotically across its surface in all directions. Then, an almost imperceptibly thin band of light burst from that stone to one adjacent, in turn igniting that stone with the same electric life. Quicker and quicker, from stone-to-stone the electricity traveled, until the inside of the wood and steel cage became layered with a perfect, pulsing electrical inner frame.

As he sat in the cage, the Lii-jit captive surveyed the display all around him, his initial panic soon washed over with a rigid, unfeeling calm.

"And now, young life-mystic, I once again instruct you, bring the Ohlinn to me," ordered Gris Hallis gently.

Without hesitation, the exhausted young mystic lowered his head and began mumbling inaudibly. Lakos and his men looked around, uncertain what to expect. All they could see was the continued assault of rain, thunder, and lightning, both on the looming forest ahead and on the flat grassland where they now stood.

But then a new sound emerged. A deep, rhythmic rumbling, pulsing from the darkness behind them. A blur of motion up above. It was difficult to differentiate against the blackness of the angry night sky, but it seemed as though a massive object was surging through the air toward the forest. Then another. And another.

"Klacktalli birds," whispered Lakos, his jaw agape.

Huge, black, raven-like beasts, each with a wingspan thirty strides across and a curved, yellow beak capable of severing a man in two. The monstrous birds were normally only seen living among the Southern Cliffs, two days' ride from the spot where Lakos and his band now stood, but it was clear they had been assigned an urgent, unnatural mission as they darted purposefully into the Valla Forest. So vast, in fact, were the birds in both size and number that for two minutes, the entirety of the caravan was blanketed from the rain.

By the time the downpour resumed its assault upon them, Gris Hallis's eyes alone could have lit up the night.

"The power of the Lii-jit, at your fingertips," he said, smiling broadly.

"And should your little captive decide to use his powers against us?" asked Lakos, watching the vast waves of black pulsing high overhead.

"Our little friend is at present no more than a weapon. Our weapon. With as much free will as the sword at your hip," grinned the old spirit-mystic.

"You have yet to convince me that your methods are any better than my sword," replied Lakos.

"Patience," said Gris Hallis softly. "I hold the greatest reverence toward the human military approach, and still more so your personal mastery of it. But I dare say that the mystical, on occasion, can have a certain... utility," he ventured, crafting his words carefully. "Your first steps into your new kingdom, my lord." A thin smile crossed his lips as he gestured toward the forest.

Without another word, Lakos mounted his fleet horse, leading his caravan toward the forest, the captive Lii-jit's wagon one of a hundred that Lakos aimed to fill.

CHAPTER FIVE

As his agonizing descent continued, Thayliss saw the hazy, shrinking figure of Leonorryn suddenly spring into action. The old mystic darted down the tree from branch-to-branch, with speed and fluidity to rival the rain itself. Within moments, he was almost within reach.

For his part, Thayliss fought to slow his fall by grasping wildly at the fragile, slippery branches as they whirred by. Finally, he caught a slightly more substantial branch between his arm and his side, bringing his fall to an immediate, if temporary, stop.

Ignoring the pain and shock of the trauma, Thayliss immediately wrapped his arm around the wet, abrasive branch with all his might. In doing so, he adjusted his position so that he was afforded a quick, and regrettable, glimpse downward. The branch he clung desperately to formed the tree crown's lower terminus, with nothing below but another hundred strides of barren, gnarled trunk followed by the unforgiving forest floor.

The branch had sustained a significant crack on impact, which Thayliss realized as he tried to wrap his legs around it for increased stability. At the site of the crack, Thayliss watched helplessly as splinters continued to pop and fray, the branch growing increasingly disjointed from its base. Thayliss stayed motionless, fearing any additional movement would result in the branch's outright separation. He squinted up above, searching through the falling waves of rain for the old mystic.

He spotted movement amidst the lush green foliage— Leonorryn. The increasing fragility of the lower branches had slowed his progress, but he continued to gain ground. Thayliss felt another burst within his branch as it grew weaker still.

At that moment, the sky above seemed to collapse. A massive blackness lowered down through the trees, snapping everything in its path as it descended.

"Klacktalli…" muttered Thayliss in disbelief.

The giant raptor drew closer, its massive, outstretched talons surging toward him. But in between Thayliss and the rapidly approaching beast was Leonorryn, seemingly oblivious to the massive bird approaching behind him as he laboriously continued his own journey to Thayliss.

"Leo—" Thayliss started to shout, but it was too late.

The klacktalli intercepted the tiring old spirit-mystic, tightly wrapping its thick, leathery talons around his waist. With two beats of its enormous wings, the beast and its captive vanished up through the forest canopy and into the stormy night sky.

Thayliss had scarcely a moment to register the sight of the only father he'd ever known being taken from him. The rush of wind caused by the klacktalli's flapping wings snapped the remaining threads of wood cleanly from the fractured branch he clung to. His aching, bloodied body fell, unencumbered by branches, plummeting toward the unforgiving ground far below.

He closed his eyes and thought of Leysiia. He only hoped that she was somehow spared from this nightmare. He would see her again, if only in the next world.

He waited for impact. But the impact he felt was not what he had anticipated. His descent instantly ceased, and instead, a sharp, vice-like pressure encompassed his torso. Opening his eyes, he found himself clamped in the beak of another klacktalli bird, darting horizontally between tree trunks at speeds exceeding what he'd felt during his freefall. Eventually, the giant predator tilted its head up toward the sky and began to ascend.

Breaking through the forest canopy and into the open air, Thayliss was afforded a clear view of what was unfolding. His heart stopped. Nearly every Ohlinn treetop dwelling that he could see was either demolished or in the midst of being torn apart by a seemingly possessed klacktalli.

Still more of the huge birds circled the sky, many containing small, writhing figures in their talons or beaks. Occasionally, one of the klacktalli would suddenly release its grip, sending its prey to certain death.

Still other, much smaller, figures coursed erratically throughout the treetops. Thayliss could tell by the manner of movement that many of the Ohlinn had eluded the attack and were no doubt seeking refuge.

Accurate to their reputation, the Ohlinn were swift, elusive beings, possessing an innate sense of danger. However, should this intrinsic warning system become circumvented and capture actually achieved, they were more often than not rendered completely helpless. Of the three mystic orders, only the Ohlinn lacked any traditional forms of weaponry, save for their intellect. Which, against the brute, mindless force of a flock of klacktalli was of little use.

Thayliss prayed that Leysiia was among the lucky ones to evade their grasp.

CHAPTER SIX

Thayliss soon realized that the klacktalli birds were not acting of their own volition. One by one, the giant birds deposited the captive Ohlinn onto the grassy clearing on the outskirts of the Valla Forest. They were penned into small groups of five to ten individuals, contained not by cages but by packs of vicious, gray bastik wolves that circled each group, growling menacingly.

Thayliss had been dropped into a pen with three other individuals, two of whom appeared to be adolescent Ohlinn, siblings perhaps, whom he did not know. The two young spirit-mystics huddled tightly together, distraught by whatever was transpiring. The third individual seemed markedly less panicked, though perhaps more deeply troubled. He was Desodorryn, an old Ohlinn, and close friend of Leonorryn.

"Where is Leysiia? Leonorryn? Can you see them? Are they all right?" asked Thayliss as he paced within the savage, living enclosure, his heart aching.

Desodorryn stood at the center of the circle, his head down and eyes shut. Finally, he spoke. "They are alive. In a pen on the other side of the clearing. But we must not grieve what we cannot change." He once again softly dropped his head, lost in deep meditation.

Thayliss could barely see over the dirty, matted haunches of the long-legged wolves as he searched for a way out. Unlike other wolves, the bastiks hunted not by smell but by movement. Their long, thin legs had adapted an increased sensitivity toward the subtlest vibrations in the ground while also granting them the speed and agility to ensnare their prey. While their diet typically consisted of rodents and the diminutive Valla stunted deer, this evolutionary adaptation also made them an ideal prison guard for the mercurial Ohlinn. How and why they had assumed this role, however, was a mystery.

"This is not natural," offered Thayliss, attempting to prompt discussion from the old Ohlinn.

"No, good Thayliss, this is most certainly not natural," Desodorryn replied.

"What do you make of it?"

"There is a power at work here, the likes of which the world has not known since..." He looked at Thayliss, as if assessing him. "Well, since before your time."

The old mystic sighed, observing the growing clusters of captive Ohlinn scattered across the plain. His wandering gaze halted at the sight of a glowing light in the distance. Thayliss struggled to see what Desodorryn had spotted. The Ohlinn were known for their incredibly strong eyesight, which only enhanced their gifts of both foresight and evasion—with neither of which serving them well on this wretched night.

"What do you see?" asked Thayliss.

"A fallen spirit-mystic, one who abandoned our order in both body and in spirit," he replied, before leaning forward, as if not believing his eyes. "And a cursed prophecy come to light."

Thayliss had heard the stories and disregarded them all as myth. The mystic elders, one from each order, convening on the fabled island of Tollos with the start of each new season. It was supposedly the lone occasion whereby the powers of Ohlinn, Masdazii and Lii-jit could be unified without the governance of the Voduss Grei. In fact, so went the legend, on the Night of the Three Betrayals, the collected power of the elders had grown so great that it granted them access to the visions of the Gray Mystic himself. But following the attack on Merrin Ells, the great mystic elders disappeared and both their visions and the very island itself were reduced to the ambiguous haze of myth.

As if reading Thayliss's thoughts, Desodorryn broke the silence.

"On that night, the three mystic elders could see Noryssin's vision as if it was their own," he said. "They foresaw an insurgent human destined to destroy the mystic balance and overtake the world."

"And the Ohlinn residing in the Valla Forest divined this information much later through meditation, long after the human village had been destroyed. I know the story well, Desodorryn," scoffed Thayliss. "But it is no more than that. There was no prophecy, no great human warrior tasked with destroying all mystic life. Perpetuating fairy tales only strays us further from the truth and serves to cloud our judgment now. We must think rationally if we hope to survive whatever is happening here."

"Young Thayliss, the only limits the human mind possesses are those boundaries it affirms to itself," replied Desodorryn softly. "You may have lived under Ohlinn ways for much of your life, but you will always be human. Questioning, doubting. But the truth exists with or without your consent. I was there in the Valla Forest the night Merrin Ells fell to ash. I, alongside Leonorryn and dozens of other Ohlinn, did what we could to stop it, but it was not enough. And as the sun rose the following morning, masked by the smoldering embers of the human village beyond our border, we meditated. Deep in silent reflection we asked the spirits for guidance, for answers. And what we saw, each of us, was the story you find so difficult to believe. But I assure you, despite the loss of the sacred tower, and the fracture of the Voduss Grei lineage, there are those who still fan the embers of the prophecy." The old spirit-mystic's bold blue eyes seemed to dull as he stared blankly ahead, his long, drawn face now ashen. "And those embers now turn to flame."

But Thayliss had heard it all before. As far as he was concerned, the Gray Mystic Noryssin merely grew paranoid governing the world in virtual solitude. Having ruled for longer than any Voduss Grei before him, Noryssin perhaps saw his own time in this world coming to a close and decided that he would rather leave a world in tumult and segregation than relinquish his grand power to another. He saw fit to decimate an innocent village, destroy his own sacred tower, and perish in shame. As much as Thayliss respected and honored the Ohlinn ways, he had no patience for mythology. Their lives were now in danger.

All that mattered was finding Leysiia and Leonorryn. The question was how to do it.

He knew full well that any attempt to break through the circling pack of bastik wolves would prove fatal. But he had no weapons to use, no tree branches to climb. He searched the wet, muddied ground for something—anything—and found a small stone.

He picked it up and, edging carefully toward one end of the perimeter, tossed it to the other side, readying himself to run. The stone soared past the three Ohlinn captives standing behind him and over the dutifully trotting wolf pack, splashing into a puddle of rainwater just beyond the perimeter. The wolves, however, were not deterred, continuing their journey around the circle, mouths agape as thick streams of white froth strained between their sharp, jagged teeth.

Thayliss pondered the situation. Only two possible scenarios could be at play. The first scenario was that the wolves were so focused on the task at hand that they were able to filter out any vibrations along the ground deemed too faint to be attributed to either human or Ohlinn movement.

The second scenario, and the one on which Thayliss was about to bet his life, was that the endless sheets of rainfall hitting the ground were numbing the bastiks' tactile perception, rendering their greatest asset—and greatest weapon—powerless.

It made logical sense. Much like the giant klacktalli birds that attacked the Ohlinn village, bastik wolves were not native to this area. Thayliss had no idea why they were here now, or how they had been coaxed into their present duty, but perhaps, just perhaps, whoever was behind this abomination failed to take the effect of the rain into account.

Thayliss edged closer to the inner edge of the circling pack, feeling like a piece of fruit slipping fatally close to the whirring blades of a hand-cranked blender. Feeling eyes upon him, he turned to see Desodorryn, a despondent look still drawn upon his smooth, long face.

"Be cautious, good Thayliss," he said softly. "We need no more death in these lands."

Thayliss nodded, turning back to the wolves. He tapped his foot lightly against the wet, muddy ground, awaiting a response. There was none. The wolves continued their march, seemingly oblivious. He edged closer still. Given the length of the gap between each wolf—roughly one arm's length—as well as their trotting speed, Thayliss calculated that it was at least conceivable that he could slip between them and out of the circle in time.

As long as he went unnoticed. Should his movement incite a bastik's reflex attack, his body would be half-eaten before the remaining half hit the ground.

He moved closer and closer to the wolves, leaning forward and tensing his body, ready to make his move.

At that moment, a loud CRACK sounded high overhead, almost causing him to lose his balance and slide directly into the wolf pack. He steadied his feet in the mud just in time and looked up.

A bolt of lightning had struck a tree branch high up on the outer edge of the forest, erupting in a cloud of sparks that quickly vanished, doused by the incessant downpour.

Thayliss wiped the rain from his brow as he once again set himself, attempting to gauge the opening and closing of the bastik perimeter. Taking one last breath, he lunged forward with all his might.

At that instant, the severed tree branch hit the ground in the center of Thayliss's perimeter. The wolves that encircled him flew into a frenzy. The ring of bastiks instantly dissolved, collapsing inward, toward the fallen branch and where Desodorryn and the two adolescents still stood.

Free from his captors, Thayliss hesitated for an instant, turning back toward the doomed Ohlinn in a futile gesture. The hesitation proved costly, as one of the wolves turned toward him.

Thayliss immediately froze in place, fully aware that any movement could potentially be his last. The wolf stepped gingerly toward him, its slender legs terminating in broad, leathery feet. The beast sniffed the air and waved its massive head from side-to-side, though Thayliss knew that their sense of smell was far weaker than even that of a human, and its disproportionately small, clouded eyes were largely vestigial, an artifact from a long-vanished ancestor.

Thayliss could hear his own heartbeat pounding in his ears. He fought to restrain his breath into silent, shallow whisps, remaining composed as the animal closed in on him. Through the savage growls and anguished cries echoing nearby, both Thayliss and his pursuing wolf played their game in silence.

Slowly, painfully slowly, the animal cruised past where Thayliss stood, unaware that its prey was literally one stride to its side. Thayliss was almost free.

Unfortunately, a klacktalli soaring above had also apparently spotted the now-liberated captive and began its descent down to retrieve him. Thayliss had to act.

Lacking the luxuries of time or careful consideration, Thayliss leapt onto the back of the bastik wolf, wrapping his arms tightly around its thick, mangy neck. Startled, the beast took off, darting erratically and shaking its head in an attempt to lose its unwanted passenger. Thayliss fought desperately to maintain his hold. They raced past numerous other bastik perimeters, each containing its own group of frightened Ohlinn captives who looked on as the crazed ride passed by.

The journey, however, was short-lived. Just as Thayliss saw that they were approaching the final group of captives, the bastik wolf he rode bellowed a shrill, blood-curdling sound. The beast collapsed to the ground, sending Thayliss tumbling into the mud.

When he finally came to a stop, Thayliss looked up to see the bastik lying dead on the ground, a thick, metallic harpoon jutting from its side. Standing behind it was a man, a soldier, holding a heavy, brass bow cannon in his arms, an arsenal of other weapons strapped to his back. He wore blue paint, streaked across both cheeks and running down the sides of his neck.

Thayliss, his right shoulder screaming in pain, stumbled backwards, away from the soldier. Looking behind him, he saw that he was approaching the final group of captive Ohlinn. The bastik perimeter around them had split open like a gate, allowing Thayliss entry. Once he was inside, the bastik circle restored itself, the grotesque animals resuming their duty.

As he sat in the circle, battered, exhausted, and without hope, Thayliss felt a hand gently fall on his shoulder. He wiped the mud from his eyes and looked up.

Smiling softly down at him was Leysiia, her beautiful, porcelain face framing the brightest sapphire eyes Thayliss had ever known.

CHAPTER SEVEN

From the edge of his caravan, Lakos looked out onto what was unfolding before him and smiled. Across the muddy grassland he saw the beginning of a dream—a prophecy—coming to fruition. The weather itself seemed to signal its consent as the dark night sky and bitter rainfall relented, dissolving into the somber, orange glow of morning.

The last of the klacktalli had deposited its prey onto the prison field and flapped powerfully back to its faraway home, its purpose fulfilled. The cycling rings of bastik wolves, one by one, were also disjoined, replaced by bands of heavily armed human soldiers. As with the klacktalli, the wolves, too, seemed at once cognizant of an unspoken release from duty and scampered off into the bronze horizon.

"Well done, Gris Hallis," said Lakos, his new ally looming beside him. Scanning the masses in front of him, he shook his head. "But I fear we've ensnared but a fraction of their order. How can you guarantee that it will be enough?"

Gris Hallis emitted a subtle laugh. "My lord, as a celestial body to those encircling it, we begin as but a tiny fragment. Like our poor captive Lii-jit chained within that wagon back there. On its own, weak. Not without power, mind you, but hardly possessing the abilities required to restore the universal order. With you at the helm, of course."

"Go on," said Lakos.

"But great enough were his powers, once suitably coaxed, to deliver us these three hundred Ohlinn—perhaps more. Not all of them will prove... appropriate for our needs, but nonetheless, from these, our power—your power—will grow fifty-fold. The others will soon follow or perish resisting us: The remaining Ohlinn, the Lii-jit, and the Masdazii. And once we have them and their power under our control, the sacred tower will rise once again, the Inner Realm pulsing with vital energy, all through your fingertips."

"I must admit, old mystic, there just might be some utility to you after all," Lakos smirked, surveying the conquered masses before turning back to Gris Hallis. "Just never forget that I lead this army." Lakos, still unnerved by his sudden reliance upon Gris Hallis, could not dispute the appeal of what the old Ohlinn seemed capable of delivering.

As they stood in silence, a cloud of tension between them, a guard approached, dismounting his fleet horse with a clear sense of urgency.

"My lord, there was an incident with one of the captives. He broke through the bastiks, but we were able to apprehend him by the forest entrance. A number of the Ohlinn subsequently attempted escape of their own, but they, too, were subdued."

Lakos walked over to his own fleet horse, placing a hand on the saddle. "Wretched Ohlinn. Like vermin, always scurrying to the shadows. Following blindly whomever among them possesses the wherewithal to lead." He brandished a great sword from across his back. "Any so-called protests within their putrid colony must be met with swift and decisive consequence. Co-operation or death."

"My lord—" blurted the soldier. "There's more. Several soldiers overheard whispers among the Ohlinn that the rebel may have been, or was somehow associated with, a human. In all the commotion, it was difficult to tell if this was true or just an Ohlinn ploy. Their kind have been known to rely upon deception and mental trickery when faced with danger."

Lakos grew furious. He moved away from his fleet horse, approached the soldier, and unleashed a backhanded strike. His iron-shielded forearm knocked the unsuspecting soldier to the ground.

"Difficult to tell human from Ohlinn?" Lakos spat at the ground. "Members of my own army, incapable of distinguishing the very race we're trying to liberate from the ones we aspire to enslave? Unacceptable!" He watched as the fallen soldier struggled to his feet. Shaking his head, Lakos returned to his fleet horse. Passing Gris Hallis, who stood dutifully by, he paused. "I will tolerate neither dissension among captives nor incompetence among my own men."

Lakos re-mounted his horse, brought his heels abruptly against its sides, and with a shout, headed off toward the forest entrance.

CHAPTER EIGHT

Venturing past the clusters of apprehended Ohlinn, Lakos felt an almost surreal wave of pride well up within him. The dream he had stoked since that dreadful night thirty years ago was finally on the verge of becoming reality. While he'd always envisioned the events unfolding as a simple act of brutal, savage aggression, there was a certain elegance to using the mystics' own powers against them. Gris Hallis was right. Lakos could already feel his power building, feeding off of the despicable mystics all around him. He rejoiced at the sight of every anguished, frightened Ohlinn civilian he rode past. Parents torn from their children, families, and friends. A society in ruin. Soon, all mystics would feel his pain. He smiled, riding on toward the other end of the plain.

When Lakos finally arrived to the site of the apprehended escapee, he was disappointed by what he saw. He had envisioned some fierce, defiant Ohlinn warrior, if there was such a thing, ranting about justice and freedom. On the other hand, should the rumors of an interfering human turn out to be true, Lakos would have most likely come upon an overzealous, mystic sympathizer, not unlike poor Hajassin. A poor, misguided fool, either pleading for compassion or ready to die a martyr for his so-called cause. Lakos's still-unsheathed sword seemed to beg for such a sight, a chance to lash out and draw blood through his own hand and not through the emotionally devoid actions of hypnotized beasts. The bloody, savage battle he had envisioned those countless nights before.

What he saw instead was as starkly opposed to either scenario as one could imagine. Huddled on the muddy ground were two figures, embracing each other tightly as an aged Ohlinn stood nearby, seeming to insinuate himself between them and the bloodshed around them.

Lakos left his fleet horse and approached the prisoners. He raised his mighty sword above his head. "Insurgent, show yourself!"

Dozens of other Ohlinn captives watched the scene unfolding, a sea of bright blue eyes looking on, mouths agape in anticipation and dread.

Surveying his audience, mystic captives and loyal human soldiers alike, Lakos seized the opportunity. "I am Lakos, Lord and ruler of this world. There is word of a human in your midst. A traitor to his kind. If this is so, I urge the rest of you to reveal him to me so that he may be dealt with. By sacrificing him, you will be assuring your own safety, you have my word. But whether human or Ohlinn, I ask the one among you who dared defy me to step forward lest every Ohlinn before me suffer the price of your defiance. Now I repeat—insurgent, show yourself!"

Hearing Lakos's words, Thayliss attempted to push away from Leysiia's desperate embrace, but could not. Her beautiful eyes, filled with tears, begged him to remain close.

"Thayliss—please, no," she cried softly in his ear.

Leonorryn, standing beside the huddled couple, stepped forward. "I am your insurgent. You have my word, there are no humans among us. These two are innocents. They want none of this war. But I know of your maniacal quest. A villain, born from the ashes of that seaside tragedy so long ago. I pity you for the pain you must have known and the still greater pain you seek to create." His eyes were blue granite, unfazed and unwavering. "But I see your future, and it is wrought with failure and death."

Lakos laughed richly as he neared the old Ohlinn, his arms limp by his sides, his long, steel blade dragging along the ground behind him. "Ah, the Ohlinn clairvoyance. Or, rather, mind control. Trading physical capability for parlor tricks, lies, and illusion. However, I do grant you this—I see death in my future as well." His grasp grew firm upon his sword, swinging it back in front of his body as he moved slowly toward his target.

Thayliss fought to break from his embrace with Leysiia but there was now a greater force keeping him still. He was paralyzed—completely unable to move. Panicked, he looked at his one great love, whose slender, delicate hands pulsed with a soft, white light as they rested on Thayliss's immobile legs.

"Leysiia," he whispered breathlessly, "I must stop him! I must save your father!"

"I'm sorry, my love," she whispered. "This is the way it must be."

Lakos laughed. "Old mystic, I must admit—there is much to admire in you. Relinquishing what little remains of your own cursed life to save two of your shamelessly cowering brethren. You know, that may be one of the bravest acts I've witnessed from your cowardly, contemptible kind." He held his sword up high above his head, his wild eyes aglow. "Unfortunately, you're just too damned old to be of any use to me."

He lashed his sword across the old mystic's chest, striking him down and killing him instantly.

He then turned toward the two figures kneeling upon the ground, interwoven tightly together.

Within their embrace, both Thayliss and Leysiia wept. "Leysiia," pleaded Thayliss, "you must release me or he'll kill us both."

Leysiia gave Thayliss one final, desperate kiss and relented. "Very well."

But before her hands left his thigh, she sent an even brighter wave of white energy surging throughout his body, forcing the two captives apart. The impact threw Thayliss five strides from where he'd knelt and shook him deeply.

When his wits returned, he saw Leysiia lying in a heap before Lakos's menacing figure.

"No!" shouted Thayliss, attempting awkwardly to lunge

toward him as the sensation gradually returned to his body. Before he could take another step, he was held back by several armed guards who stood behind him. He was powerless.

Thayliss cried in protest as Lakos turned the fallen Leysiia onto her back with his steel-shielded boot. As he did so, Thayliss noticed that Leysiia had changed. Her hair, once brilliant black with its Ohlinn streak of gray, was now a lusterless, uniform brown. Lying supine on the muddy ground, she slowly opened her eyes and turned her head weakly to Thayliss. Her eyes were still blue, but they now seemed lifeless, dull... human.

"I love you," she said, looking only at Thayliss as Lakos brought his bloodied sword down upon her.

Thayliss felt his heart tear from his body. He was an empty vessel, devoid of emotion or thought. The pure agony of seeing the love of his life slain was as boundless as it was merciless. He could only hope that he was next.

"Well then," said Lakos, clearly savoring the moment. "It appears that the old spirit-mystic deceived me. It seems that humans and mystics can co-exist peacefully after all. Such a pity." He wiped his sword clean against Thayliss's leg.

Thayliss's knees gave way but his body remained upright, held tight in the unrelenting grip of the soldiers behind him.

"Go ahead. I beg you. Do it. No man could ever cause another more pain than you've already given me. Now please, show me compassion and kill me," he pleaded.

Lakos laughed. "How truly sad. Merely associating yourself with this human female does not make you any more a man than any of your cowering cohorts around us." He leaned close to his distraught prisoner, holding his sword vertically between Thayliss's face and his own. "I'm afraid that you are not one of us."

Thayliss slowly raised his head and gazed into the sword. He recoiled in shock as reflected back in the cold steel were the sapphire eyes and gray-streaked hair of an Ohlinn. His breath left him.

Lakos paused, infatuated with running his thumb along the length of his sword. "Still, I must say Ohlinn, there is something intriguing about you." He leaned in close, his cheek nearly against Thayliss's ear, and whispered, "You know my story, so now let me tell you yours. You tried to escape, which takes bravery and strength uncommon to your people. You could have then vanished back into the trees like so many of your cowardly brothers, but instead returned to your love, no doubt well aware that doing so would seal your fate. Strength, bravery, loyalty. Without fear of death. I may have use for you. You'll need to be broken first, of course, but there will be plenty of time for that. Or, as you so passionately plead for death, perhaps keeping you alive is no more than a means with which to serve my own devious nature, as there would doubtless be more pleasure in watching you suffer than in watching you die. Either way, you're mine now."

Lakos brought his sword's tarnished ivory hilt up before striking Thayliss flush against the temple, dropping him to the muddy ground, unconscious.

CHAPTER NINE

By the time he regained consciousness, Thayliss had no idea how much time had passed or where he was. The surface he was lying on jostled and bumped incessantly, sending pangs of discomfort through his aching head. Slowly he opened his eyes and looked around. The bright, stark daylight showed no mercy, making him once again seek comfort in the dark crook of his arm.

"Alas, our fair prince awakes," a voice called out, its tone rich with sarcasm.

Thayliss once again struggled to open his eyes, fighting against the brightness until the pain gradually subsided. The brilliant light of day was cut into a series of vertical segments, split between columns of shimmering metal bars. He craned his neck to see that the bars wrapped completely around him on all sides. He was in some form of mobile prison.

"Tell us, Ohlinn, how you plan to save us from this predicament," the voice continued contemptuously.

"What?" Thayliss slowly rose, barely getting to his feet when the unstable flooring once again shook violently, knocking him against the bars and back to the floor.

When he recovered, Thayliss grasped one of the bars behind him and pulled himself to his feet. Looking around the cell, he saw seven figures surrounding him, all wearing expressions ranging from despondency to rage as they sat staring back. An eighth figure, smaller than the others, huddled in a far corner alone.

Staring into the eyes of the seven Ohlinn brought two images surging back to Thayliss's consciousness. The first fleeting thought was that he, too, had somehow become one of them, if only on the outside. That swiftly led to the second, infinitely more anguished memory of his dear Leysiia. He felt his knees weaken and stomach drop, and grasped the bar all the tighter to remain upright.

The pain was too much to bear. Why had the human— Lakos—not just taken his life as well? He didn't know where he was now being taken, and he didn't care. His life had ended back on that rain-soaked field when the only love and only family he had ever known were mercilessly taken from him.

"Leonorryn was the last of the Ohlinn elders," another spirit-mystic spoke. "The final great leader of our kind. Following the tragedy on the island of Tollos years ago, that torch was passed to him. And because of your weakness, that torch has been forever extinguished. You allowed him to be taken from this world. His blood is on your hands."

Thayliss was outraged. "Leonorryn was like a father to me! I loved him!" Tears flowed from his sapphire eyes. "I tried, the spirits know that I tried! But I could not stop it!"

The Ohlinn seated around him could not be swayed.

"Speak not of the spirits, human, for they neither listen nor speak to you," voiced another. "Through some dark illusion, you wear the face of the Ohlinn, though it is but a shell. A mockery of the sacred order that so trustingly embraced you. Behind that mask is the soul of a human, like all others. Wrought with deceit, cowardice, and greed."

Still another Ohlinn spoke, this one with eyes bearing the faintest hint of compassion. "Thayliss, my boy," he said, "this night, and undoubtedly many to follow, are surely of a most regrettable nature. I knew Leonorryn well, as I did his fair Leysiia. They were cherished in this world, and most assuredly will be in the next. Their loss pains us all, as does a tree without its roots." His expression grew firm. "But your fate will henceforth deviate from that of the Ohlinn. You are stricken from our brotherhood, no matter the face you wear. Instinct is ingrained and unchanging. Regrettable though this may be, it is the manner of all nature. We Ohlinn will patiently await our fate with quiet dignity. But you, a human, cowered selfishly while the great Ohlinn leader who pitied you, took you in and raised you as his own, fell victim to one of your own kind. You merely acted within the confines of your nature. A primitive instinct toward personal survival above everything else. And everyone else."

"I lost my life last night!" shouted Thayliss in desperation, striking the metal bar beside him with his clenched fist. He stared blindly at the ragged leather canopy above, tears stinging his eyes.

He could not betray Leysiia's memory by divulging her mystical intervention during their anguished, final embrace. Assuming that they would even believe the truth. The fact that they seemed unaware that such a thing could be achieved suggested to Thayliss that Leysiia had somehow divined some secret process known only to a select few. Like her father. All the same, it pained Thayliss that he could not tell the Ohlinn how he tried, how he ached to intervene. To defend Leonorryn. To protect Leysiia, and the whole of the Ohlinn brotherhood. He would have died for them last night, knowing that it would have made no difference. That Lakos and his army would have taken the Ohlinn with or without his resistance. But nonetheless, he would have done it, for it was all he had to give.

But none of that mattered now. As was written in the ancient Ohlinn texts, every moment gone by, every word spoken, every experience, was another mark, chiseled into the great stone of the past. Readable by all, changeable by none, and growing ever longer.

Thayliss pushed off from the bar behind him, struggling to retain his balance as he staggered past the spiteful glares of the Ohlinn and toward the other side of the cage. Once there, he took hold of two sun-heated, metal bars and looked out at the scrolling horizon.

The blazing yellow sun shone brilliantly in a cloudless

sky. The plains by the Valla Forest were replaced by terrain unfamiliar to Thayliss. A sea of small, jagged rocks layered the ground, seeming to burst into puffs of gray smoke as the wheels of the countless wagons surrounding him barreled forth. In the distance, a herd of malnourished, long-legged ungulates swarmed between and around sparse thickets of thornberry trees.

Thayliss had never before seen such creatures, but they called to mind a memory of being served a peculiar meat stew during an Ohlinn light season festival. As the Ohlinn rarely consumed meat, his young eyes had lit up at the sight. But before he could lunge into the exotic meal, Leonorryn, seated to his left as always, had stopped him.

"Now, Thayliss," he had said, in his composed, paternal voice. "This meal, as all others, must be respected. This animal is not a mere novelty. It was a living, breathing entity, from a faraway land."

Leysiia, seated to the right of her father and herself but a child at the time, snickered.

Leonorryn calmly turned to the girl. "Very well, ni-Leysiia, seeing that you fancy yourself an expert on the matter, please inform Thayliss of the meal we have before us."

Without hesitation, and with much pleasure, Leysiia had told the tale of a faraway deer, living off thornberries and sparse water pools rich with volcanic minerals. She went on at some length, speaking of the fearsome, grotesque ash trackers that typically preyed upon the deer. Nearly twice the height of a fully-grown Ohlinn, the ash trackers were said to be giant, troll-like beings, with legs thick as tree trunks and a ghostly white complexion dotted with tufts of thick, wiry hair. So vivid was her description, in fact, that Leonorryn saw fit to conclude the lesson and begin the meal before all parties involved lost their appetite. After which, Leysiia peered across at Thayliss with a mischievous, self-satisfied smirk.

The prison cart rattled especially violently as the terrain roughened, snapping Thayliss from his daydream. The sweetness of the memory became embittered by the painful reality that she was gone. They both were gone. His whole world, gone. Now but a memory, chiseled in stone.

As he stared through the bars, fighting to retain his composure, he felt a slight but aggressive tugging on his pant leg. He glanced down to his side.

A weary Lii-jit life-mystic anxiously rocked beside him, looking up as he leaned against the bars. "In a bad way, I see? You're in a bad way. I know it." His head darted quickly toward the group of Ohlinn seated at the other end of the cage, and then back to Thayliss. "But there's a secret. I have a secret. Do you want to know it?" he asked, his eyes fluttering eagerly.

CHAPTER TEN

Lakos surveyed the brutal landscape before him—the ground cover of small rocks and pebbles growing deeper and the hot, dry winds more searing as they approached their destination. "The great Bray Ridge," he muttered as his fatigued fleet horse valiantly negotiated the difficult ground.

Riding beside him atop his rock leopard, Gris Hallis nodded. "Your new home, my lord."

The massive volcanic crater up ahead jutted out from the otherwise flat, barren terrain, its high, jagged rim seeming to pierce the sky. As they neared the glistening, gray mountain, its sheer size blocked out half the sun as well as much of the horizon ahead. The caravan rode under its colossal shadow for an eternity, the coolness of shade granting the weary travelers a welcome respite from the scorching heat.

The sight of the great mythic volcano sent a shiver down Lakos's spine. While he'd pictured exacting his revenge upon the mystics countless times before, not once did he fathom riding up to the Inner Realm, his future palace.

Lakos gazed upon the glory of the great Bray Ridge, enthralled. True to the legend, the sacred tower was gone. But the sheer wall of rock itself seemed to radiate a solemn majesty.

Nearing the great ridge, Lakos felt the sparkling wall of stone begin calling out to him, urging him forward. The closer he drew, the stronger the sensation. He knew, beyond reproach, that this was his quest. His kingdom. That he was the chosen one.

Gris Hallis pointed up ahead. "It appears out of place, does it not, in this barren desert? Some have called this place an aberration. A mistake of nature. But this is not true. It is in fact the perfection of nature. You see, despite its rugged exterior surface, its inner wall forms an exact circle." His voice rang with pride.

"It is perfect," replied Lakos, unable to take his eyes from it.

The caravan made its way closer to the range, with Gris Hallis leading the way. "Only I know the entrance to the Inner Realm. This way."

Leading the charge, Gris Hallis and Lakos ventured toward a path of white stones, conspicuously cleaner than the surrounding ground cover. The path snaked toward the base of the volcano, disappearing into the shadows between the massive ridges of stone.

Gris Hallis intersected the path and continued on.

"I see the path, it's right there," Lakos called out, incredulously.

The old mystic shook his head. "My lord, this realm possesses many secrets. Through the eras, the lineage of the Gray Mystic is wrought with paranoia, littering the outer walls of the Bray Ridge with dark energy, lies, and treachery. Be ever cautious and stay with me. We will soon be there."

Lakos felt his better judgment pulling him toward the white path. However, he could not conceive of Gris Hallis bringing him so far only to mislead him now.

Riding alongside the volcano's outer ridge, Lakos glanced up the sheer, vertical mountainside. What had been imposing from a distance was simply astonishing up close. It was as if half the sky had been removed, replaced with an endless wall of stone. As he rode, his fleet horse began to slow, edging closer to the radiant, gray mountainside beside it. Gris Hallis, lost in the nostalgia of returning to his former home, was oblivious.

Lakos had gotten so close to the wall, in fact, that he was able to touch it with his outstretched hand. His fingers dragged serenely along the cold, damp stone as his fleet horse slowly marched on. The gray-black stone was alive with twinkling light, sparkling against the few sun's rays to reach it. The stone's rich, mildly acrid smell filled Lakos's nostrils with each breath, instilling in him the satisfaction that he had truly come home.

His mind growing murky, Lakos glanced up ahead to see a solitary, bright red flower, jutting out from the rock face. As he neared it, he was enthralled by its beauty. It was the boldest, most striking color he had ever seen. How had it gotten there? It was as though the mountain itself were humbly presenting a gift to its new master.

Lakos reached out his hand, his fingers desperately stretching forward to grasp it. As his fingertips touched the base of the stem, he leaned forward on his fleet horse to finally extract his gift from the mountainside. But before he could fully grip the flower, a sudden, sharp pain darted through the back of his hand, causing him to release his grip and recoil as the flower passed him by, intact.

Lakos looked up in shock to see Gris Hallis holding a wooden staff extended toward him. Lakos was livid.

"You dare strike me!" he uttered, dumbfounded. "What madness possesses you, wizard? I have run my sword through countless souls for lesser offenses! Speak now, or else I fear our time together has come to an end. I'm certain that my men and I can quite capably locate the entrance to the Inner Realm without your assistance." Lakos unsheathed his sword, and recoiled his arm, awaiting a response.

At that moment, a scream bellowed behind him.

He spun back to see one of his soldiers holding the brilliant red flower tight in his hand, it's stem broken free from the wall. The soldier's mouth lay agape, his eyes protruding slightly from their sockets. The flower's bold red petals quickly browned, as did the soldier's skin. Within seconds, his face grew sallow and dry, utterly devoid of moisture. As the first of the dried petals broke off and fell to the ground, so too did one of the soldier's fingers. The grotesque dehydration continued until both the soldier and the flower crumbled to dust, swirling into nothingness in the warm, abrasive wind.

The broken stem, still jutting out from the wall of glittering stone, thrust further out into the open air, a new bulb forming and splitting open, revealing a flower still more vibrant and beautiful than the one preceding it.

"As I said, these are perilous parts. I implore you, my lord, to follow my lead."

With that, Gris Hallis resumed his journey, Lakos following closely behind.

CHAPTER ELEVEN

Unable to tolerate the Lii-jit's mania, Thayliss returned his attention to the scenery beyond his cage. The sky had darkened considerably as the stifling air grew cooler. His visibility was limited to clusters of pack mules on all sides, each pulling a metal-barred wagon like his own. He estimated that there were at least fifty such wagons around him, each containing five to ten prisoners. From what he could see, every wagon seemed to contain only Ohlinn, with the exception of his own, which housed seven Ohlinn, the annoying Lii-jit, and whatever he, himself, had become.

The small Lii-jit was not deterred. "I was just thinking, because there's really little else to do at a time like this than think, about how we all got here. Here, in this cage. All of us."

Thayliss couldn't take it anymore. "Lii-jit!" he bellowed down at the diminutive mystic. "I have no patience for this. Why on earth do you infernal creatures have such a reputation for timidity when once you start talking, you never shut up?"

The Lii-jit quickly turned to look outside, his shoulders hunching slightly.

Thayliss was still riddled with guilt over the loss of Leysiia, convinced that there was something—anything—he could have done to intervene. Looking down upon the small, derided prisoner cowering before him, he felt yet another wave of remorse.

Obviously the little Lii-jit was subjected to torment of his own. Where was his family? Was he the only survivor? Thayliss knew that as elusive and mysterious as the Ohlinn were, the life-mystics were in many ways even more so. They were energetic, boisterous creatures that thrived on flittering about, at one with nature. He surmised that being stuck in a filthy metal cage in a smoldering, ashen desert must be at least as challenging for the

Lii-jit as it was for him.

"I'm Thayliss," he offered, glancing down at the lean, muscular figure.

"Nahlin-tiig," the Lii-jit replied, nodding an appreciative smile. "But Tiig is fine. Often, we Lii-jit abbreviate our names when speaking with kin for the sake of convenience—though you are clearly from an Ohlinn order and not the Lii-jit order, as I am. All the same, we mystics are, in a sense, a common brotherhood, are we not?"

"What was your secret?" asked Thayliss, still unsure if encouraging the life-mystic was a wise idea.

"Secret? Oh yes, my secret. Two secrets, in fact. Isn't it strange—don't you find it at all strange—that those who managed to contain us all within these rolling prisons did so in spite of our innate mystic abilities? My kind governs all that is alive. To a lesser degree, we may also exert some measure of control over such life. So, then, did I just allow myself to willingly be captured and enslaved by these criminals? Could I not just utilize my gifts to summon those who could help me? Of course, the answer is no. But the question is why?"

Thayliss, struggling to keep up with his frenetic little companion, simply nodded.

Tiig continued, "And what of your kind, the Ohlinn? Powerful spirit-mystics, your kind. Possessing gifts of persuasion, no doubt capable of dissuading our captors from their diabolical aim. Communicating with past and future ethereal entities, seeing into the future, forever one step ahead." He snorted obnoxiously. "Well, certainly this was not the case. Again, why?"

Thayliss could not hazard a guess. Fortunately, the Lii-jit did not wait for one to emerge.

"The secret involves those little yellow stones up there, do you see? Up in each corner of our cell—up there, there, there, there and down there, there, there, there."

Thayliss nodded. He had noticed the stones earlier but thought nothing of them at the time.

"Sacred stones, salvaged from the ruins of the mystic tower, still pulsing with the collective energy of all mystics. Once used to ensure proper balance and flow in the universe while under control of the Voduss Grei. But now exploited for sinister purposes by the one who now aids the villainous, prophesized human."

"Who?" asked Thayliss, looking up at the innocuous stones in disbelief.

"The fallen Ohlinn, Gris Hallis."

Thayliss knew the name well—a ghastly, lecherous character tied into the Betrayals of Noryssin. Thayliss, like most, had assumed that the old Ohlinn outcast perished alongside his Gray Mystic master with the destruction of the sacred tower.

"Gris Hallis lives?" he asked, pondering the implications.

"In truth, it is so," replied Tiig. "And so long as he harnesses the power still residing within the fallen temple, he will exert over us the very power we were created to wield."

Thayliss looked over to the group of Ohlinn across from him, each staring dejectedly to the floor or bleakly through the prison bars. "Do they know?" he asked Tiig.

"They know that their powers have left them," he replied. "Though it is doubtful that any of them know the reason why. You see, the logic is circular. For them to know the reason for their loss would necessitate the very clairvoyance taken from them. A most sorry state of affairs indeed."

"And how did you come to possess these insights?" asked Thayliss, his eyebrow raised.

"I feigned loss of consciousness for a time. Rather intriguing what one may overhear through somnolence. Humans do love their talking, do they not? Especially when presenting themselves as brave, intelligent, and on and on and on. Anyhow, the rest I figured out while being forced to exert my abilities to draw a flock of klacktalli birds and packs of wild bastik wolves upon your home in the Valla Forest. Regrettable in the most to have played some small part in your tragic loss," he said, his voice lacking any semblance of sympathy.

Thayliss grew ill once again. The steel bars of the cage seemed to close in on him. A hot flush rose up from within as his footing grew unsteady. He pushed away from the Lii-jit and toward the only unoccupied corner of the cell.

Truly, and insufferably, alone.

CHAPTER TWELVE

"Just a little further," assured Gris Hallis, leading Lakos and his men farther along the mountainside. The massive gray wall teemed with ribbons of deep inlets and crevices, occasionally suggesting a way in where there was none.

In Lakos's estimation, the only perceptible change in the terrain had been the white stone path they'd passed many strides ago. Both before and since that time, their journey yielded the same bleak view: sheer rock face to the right, dusty, ashen desert to the left, and a varied smattering of volcanic ground cover beneath them. The fact that they had not again ridden by that same white path provided the only tangible evidence that they were not traveling in circles around the great volcanic ridge.

Finally, to Lakos's great relief, Gris Hallis pulled his ride to a halt. Glancing over his shoulder toward Lakos, his thin, pale lips curled into a grin. "We have arrived."

To Lakos, the thrill of coming upon the entry to the great and sacred Inner Realm was tempered by the complete absence of any perceptible way in. He scrutinized the vast section of rock before him but saw not even the prospect of an inroad. To the contrary, this particular section of rock face was completely flat, lacking any of the cracks or inlets they had seen previously.

"My lord," Gris Hallis continued, "we need an offering."

The groundswell of affirmation that Lakos felt on first arriving at the volcano now degraded to suspicion. His years of advanced tactical training gave him both a heightened sense of danger as well as the conviction to allow himself to be led by it. Something was awry.

"An offering?" he asked, incredulous. "I see no entrance. I see only rock. And now you tell me that we need an offering to be granted entrance into this realm? I suggest that you offer yourself, mystic."

Gris Hallis smirked softly, as if to acknowledge the incredulity of his request. "I assure you, my lord, that this is no ruse. The Inner Realm concealed within these volcanic walls does not merely attract and concentrate the world's energies, it feeds on it. During my apprenticeship with Noryssin, I was his ambassador to the outside world. I wanted more, but that was the role he granted me. Such that it was, it afforded me many years of experience with the secrets and intricacies of the Bray Mountain you see before you. It is but rock, forged from the very core of our planet, thrust outward toward the sky through some prehistoric calamity. But, as such, it also serves as a direct link to the beating heart of our world. Through it, we can feel its pulse. Its energy. That's why all of the world's great energies return here, drawn back to its very core, only to be released yet again. The eternal circulation of our living world."

Lakos was not swayed. "Spoken like a true mystic. Now, as for the offering?"

"Following Noryssin's Three Betrayals and the energetic discord that followed, the steady influx and rhythm of energy circulating between all life and the planet itself was disrupted. Our world grew disjointed and weak, no longer able to sustain itself. But now, an offering, a voluntary return of life—of energy—back to the world will grant us entry into its domain. The Inner Realm has been starved of its vital energy for far too long—it, too, grows desperate. As evidenced by that poor soldier, lured in by the red flower. Upon absorbing his relatively meager life energy, the flower re-grew all the brighter."

"I am not about to sacrifice another one of my own men just to see if your story is correct," Lakos protested, still unable to fathom where along the sheer, unrelenting wall of gray an entrance might be hidden.

Gris Hallis lowered his head, the slightest hint of a smirk returning to his face. "In the past, when the Inner Realm pulsed with universal energy, I was routinely granted re-entry through these walls with little more than a hog, or a crate of fowl. But now, in these weakened, desperate times, with no disrespect to you or your valiant soldiers," he said, "it will take much more than a human life to be granted access."

Lakos glanced back at his caravan, through the waves of mounted soldiers, and toward the sea of prison wagons peppering the barren landscape.

"A mystic then," offered Lakos, seeming to detest the implied power differential more than the thought of sacrificing one of his men.

"The life-mystic," Gris Hallis replied. "As all life is both bound by matter and infused with the spirit, the Lii-jit serve as a link between the Masdazii and the Ohlinn. They unify all three orders, and by virtue of their innate vitality, the Lii-jit wield more energy than the others."

"And greater energy means a greater offering," surmised Lakos.

"I believe it will prove sufficient, with minimal loss of assets for us. Besides, I do believe our Lii-jit's purpose on this quest has already been served, my lord." Gris Hallis bowed his head in reverence.

Lakos once again scanned the wall of rock before him, glanced back to the throng of wagons in the distance, and signaled his nearest soldier.

"The life-mystic, bring him to me," he ordered.

CHAPTER THIRTEEN

Thayliss stood in silence, his hands gripping the metal bars on either side of his face as he gazed blankly at the world beyond.

A while back, his wagon, like all the others, had slowed to a halt. He could see many of the Ohlinn occupying the other wagons pacing and fretting, with others seemingly lost in serene meditation. As swiftly as he had taken to many of the Ohlinn ways and customs in his youth, the act of meditation had always eluded him. Through his childhood and into adolescence, Leonorryn had tried on countless occasions to instill in Thayliss the meditative stillness so ingrained in their kind. More than any trait, it was what truly defined the Ohlinn—the opening of a sacred channel to the other world. Providing guidance, affirmation, and a link to spirits long past.

Thayliss knew the instructions verbatim: remain still, seated on the shins, back arched, head forward, hands on the knees. At times, while attempting the exercise with Leonorryn on the floor of their dwelling high in the Valla treetops, he would feign achieving a meditative state. Then, he would slowly open one of his eyes just enough to watch Leonorryn. It was amazing. Thayliss would watch as the great old mystic grew increasingly still. His breath regulated and slowed, almost to the point of becoming as rigid and wooden as the walls around him. But then, just as Thayliss began easing his own body, the frozen Leonorryn would bellow, "Be still, Thayliss, be still," before returning to his own meditative bliss.

But no matter how hard he tried, what came naturally to so many Ohlinn seemed perpetually just beyond Thayliss's reach.

Finding himself trapped in a mobile prison, forced towards an unknown destination, Thayliss could use those meditative gifts now more than ever. He caught his distorted reflection in one of the metal bars in front of him and looked away in grief.

He didn't know how long the curse would last, but he begged for its end. The Ohlinn features projected upon his face were a constant reminder that he had lived a lie, and that the bright sapphire eyes staring back at him were those of the family he left behind. The family he let die. In spite of a heart that yearned otherwise, he inescapably harbored the soul of a human. Flawed, weak, plagued with sin and vice. Perhaps this was his penance for ever having thought otherwise.

Thayliss heard a murmur wash over the captive Ohlinn around him. Word traveled fast amongst their kind, so much so that it often blurred into the telepathic tendencies they also displayed on occasion. Before he had a chance to register what was about to happen, Thayliss heard the seven Ohlinn crouching behind him suddenly sequester tightly against the far wall of the cage, distancing themselves as much as possible from where Thayliss and the Lii-jit silently stood.

He then heard the sound of footsteps—several pairs—growing louder. Within moments, a cluster of armed soldiers swarmed his wagon, forming three distinct layers. Thayliss observed that, save the lone soldier closest to them, the innermost layer of soldiers each wielded some form of close-range weapon, knives or daggers. Behind them was a row of soldiers brandishing longswords. Finally, the third, outermost layer of soldiers each held a crossbow at the ready. Whatever their objective, reasoned Thayliss, such weaponry to harass a small cluster of Ohlinn and a weary Lii-jit seemed excessive.

The soldier at the front slowly gestured the Lii-jit toward him. Thayliss watched as the previously animated little life-mystic stood perfectly still, eyes affixed on the soldier, a coiled spring, tense and ready for action. For reasons he did not know, Thayliss also found himself standing his ground as the soldier gestured more deliberately to his intended target, this time pointing toward Tiig's clenched fist. The surrounding soldiers all leaned forward in unison, their weapons drawn and at the ready. The Lii-jit's quivering right arm slowly extended toward the soldier's outstretched hands.

Then, just as the soldier reached into his pocket, the Lii-jit sprang into action, pulling back his arm before bounding frantically around the cage. Several of the soldiers in the outer circle, thrown by the display, fired their crossbows into the cage. Their deadly arrows soared toward the wagon, some deflecting harmlessly off the metal bars, others driving deep into the wagon's thick hide canopy.

Thayliss dropped to the floor, shielding his head from both the incoming projectiles as well as the blur of crazed fury smashing against the walls of their shared confines. The other Ohlinn captives, previously silent and stoic, yelped in fear, uncertain what to do.

Finally, mercifully, the Lii-jit settled his outburst, landing in the very spot he had been standing. His chest throbbed like a battered drum, his breath expelling in small, quick puffs.

Undeterred, the soldier once again beckoned the small life-mystic forward. Reluctantly, the Lii-jit edged toward the soldier, extending his small, powerful arm through the bars. Slowly, deliberately, the lead soldier removed an object from his pocket. Thayliss strained to see what it was but could not. Tiig's arm quivered as it jutted out of the wagon, his eyes shut in anticipation.

The object was a bracelet seemingly fashioned from the same yellowed stone adorning the eight corners of the mobile prison. With one, swift motion, the soldier wrapped the adornment around the Lii-jit's wrist and locked its hinged clasp in place. Thayliss saw Tiig's eyes open and examine the object with first a look of relief and then an apparent sense of dread.

The soldier unlocked the wagon's gate, cautiously creaking open the heavy, steel-barred wall, and waved the woeful life-mystic forward. The ring of soldiers surrounding them held their position, ready to strike. As if conceding a bitter defeat,

Tiig calmly exited the cell and was led away. Before Thayliss could contemplate action, the gate was once again slammed shut and locked.

"Come, little mystic, you've got a rough ride ahead of you," laughed the lead soldier, roughly pushing the Lii-jit from view. Thayliss was unsure what to feel. He had little capacity left for sympathy. The little life-mystic was being led to his certain demise. Once again, Thayliss could have intervened. But why? Risk his own life to save the very being responsible for the death of his family? It was, to quote the Lii-jit himself, "regrettable."

Thayliss turned back to the inside of his cell, where the other Ohlinn captives tittered nervously amongst themselves, occasionally firing a toxic glance in his direction. It took a lot to rattle an Ohlinn, Thayliss knew, but once achieved, the damage tended to linger.

Thayliss paced what little of the cage was his to roam, his mind an empty void, lacking ambition, concern, or contempt. He wandered toward a corner, resting his head against the convergence of bars and casting his vacant gaze downward.

An unsettled feeling came over him. Something had changed.

He blinked himself back to reality, trying to deduce what his mind was trying to tell him. Something was different about the cell itself. But what? He looked around, trying to solve the puzzle.

And then it came to him. The stones. The yellowed stones fastened to each corner of the cage were gone. The thin leather straps previously holding them in place were still there, but now they simply hung limp, empty.

"Tiig—" muttered Thayliss under his breath.

The Lii-jit must have somehow removed them during his supposed tantrum. If what he had said about the stones was true, then there might just be a way out. A new emotion began swelling up inside Thayliss—hope.

"Ohlinn," he addressed the spirit-mystics beside him. "I beg of you, please set aside for a moment whatever resentments you may harbor against me. There is hope for escape, but we must work together. The sacred stones that once lined this prison robbed you of your power, but the little Lii-jit saw fit to remove them so that we may live on."

The Ohlinn continued their look of disdain, barely acknowledging his plea. "Thayliss the false-Ohlinn, our fate has already been sealed, whether inside this metal box or out of it."

"We knew that our powers returned to us the moment that parasitic Lii-jit took the stones," said another bitterly. "But that changes nothing. At least in here, we are shielded from the heat."

"And kept from the ash trackers," voiced another.

"Nasty business, those ash trackers," still another agreed.

Thayliss was beside himself. "So, you're just going to let yourselves be enslaved? Or murdered? Don't you want to return to the Valla Forest? To the other Ohlinn?"

"Our surviving brothers and sisters have already mourned us. When we leave this world, then and only then will we return to our families, to illuminate their dreams. Most unfortunate for you, human, that your death will mean the end of you. But that is of no concern of us."

"Besides," added the soft-eyed Ohlinn from earlier, "we are but spirit-mystics. Were we Masdazii, those immense and surly matter-mystics, we could simply melt away these metallic bars and escape. Or were we Lii-jit, we could summon a great many beasts to liberate us or at least to carry us away. But alas, we are spirit-mystics. We govern a world of shadows, of dreams. Past and future. We can speak with those no longer of this world, but neither we, nor they, can change the present." He shook his head sympathetically. "I'm sorry, Thayliss, but we cannot help you."

Livid, Thayliss walked back to the far end of the prison, slamming his fist against the bars. The entire metallic cage rattled, distorting his already skewed reflection. This time, he did not look away. Instead, he stared deeply into the bright sapphire streaks looking back at him. He had no idea whether he merely wore a mystical Ohlinn outer shell or if his transition had penetrated any deeper into his being. But he had to try.

Lowering himself to the dusty floor, Thayliss rested upon his shins, his back arched, head forward, and hands on his knees. He then shut his eyes and waited.

"Be still, Thayliss, be still," he whispered to himself.

CHAPTER FOURTEEN

Atop their fleet horses, the pack of soldiers made their way back to Lakos and Gris Hallis, where Lakos was still scrutinizing the impenetrable rock face. As the soldiers approached, Lakos looked at them, puzzled.

"The Lii-jit—you did bring him, did you not?" he asked, squinting through the cloud of ash they had kicked up.

The lead soldier dismounted his horse and calmly walked back behind one of the other soldiers' rides. As the dust settled, Lakos could see a small figure lying limp on the ground, several arrows jutting from its side. A long, frayed rope tied tightly to its ankles led up the side of the fleet horse standing before it, looping around the horse's long, muscular neck.

"What did you do to him?" he asked.

"He'll not suffice as an offering if he's already dead," chirped Gris Hallis condescendingly.

"He still lives, though by a narrow margin," replied a solider.

"We had no alternative, my lord," said another. "He was reluctant to leave his wagon, and once we began our trek back to you, he became... unruly, though we fastened the stone clasp to his wrist as you instructed. It was all we could do to keep him from escaping. We had no other choice."

Lakos's fevered glare once again turned to Gris Hallis. "Did you not assure me that the wearer of a sacred stone would be robbed of his mystic power?"

Gris Hallis was not concerned. "I did assure you of as much. And it is the unwavering truth. Wearing the stone has indeed taken from this poor creature all mystical abilities. He may summon no aid, nor alter or regenerate his own physical being. But what simple, physical traits his kind may possess, such as his speed and agility, he retains. Troubling that your men encountered such difficulty controlling a mere excitable little imp." He shot an acrid glare at Lakos's men.

"Well, have at it then." Lakos waved Gris Hallis on.

"Bring the life-mystic to me," Gris Hallis instructed the soldier, who promptly complied, untying the rope binding the Lii-jit's ankles and dragging him by the hand to the old wizard.

A touch of pity crossed Gris Hallis's face as he looked down upon the lowly, groaning figure. "Well," he said optimistically, "I suppose this does make things a little more convenient."

He reached down and grasped one of the arrows sticking out from under the little life-mystic's ribcage and pulled. The battered Lii-jit screamed in pain as the broad arrowhead reversed its course back out, tearing the bloodied wound all the wider.

"I'm afraid that this is a wound that will not be healing, my little friend," he said.

With the bloodied arrow held delicately in hand, Gris Hallis turned from the Lii-jit and faced the vast, volcanic wall. "Leave the body there. If he survives, we'll surely find a use for him once we get inside," he said, directing his words to no one in particular.

Gris Hallis then brought the arrow against the wall, its long, thin shaft an extension of the narrow, skeletal fingers holding it. He began to arc the arrowhead across the wall, its bloodied metal tip streaking tracks of burgundy along the shimmering volcanic stone. Wielding the blood-soaked instrument, he etched a giant crescent onto the rock face from the ground, up and over, and back down again, forming as wide a border as his sinewy arm could muster.

By the time his brush had grown devoid of blood-ink, he took a step back and assessed his work. A near-perfect, deep-red archway had been drawn. He squinted and leaned forward, scrutinizing several areas where the blood had been applied less liberally.

"I need more," he said, tossing the arrow to the ground and

turning back toward the injured Lii-jit, who had one arrow still protruding from his side.

Lakos intervened, pushing Gris Hallis back with his hand. "That's all the blood you'll receive. You may understand this world—" He waved toward the mountainside. "—But I understand the world of battle. And this life-mystic will be dead within one hundred breaths if left in his present state. Remove that arrow, however, and his next breath will be his last."

"So we let him die!" screamed Gris Hallis. "His life is of no consequence to us. As long as my passageway is drawn from living blood, so be it. Should he die with one more breath, I'll simply have to see the blood drawn within a half-breath."

Lakos grasped Gris Hallis by the throat. "I am in charge here. You are but a servant. I am your master now. Do not forget this." He released his grip. "If you truly are the dark and powerful mystic apprentice of legend, then you will grant me and my soldiers access to the Inner Realm without taking the life of this miserable soul. And if there is any potential use for him within these walls, then we will want to keep him alive until his utility is spent. Do not allow your bloodlust to cloud your vision."

"I am perhaps the only member of your company not blinded by a thirst for violence," fired Gris Hallis. "I strive only to see your quest completed, no matter the cost. And do not forget, I did not ask for the Lii-jit to be brought to me in this expiring state. It is the unpreparedness and over-exuberance of your men that put me in this position." With a deep breath, he continued in softer tones. "Perhaps if we remove his stone shackle, with physical restraint of course, his wound would begin to heal. The moment his wounds are no longer fatal, we re-fasten the shackles, extract the arrow, and continue forward."

Lakos wouldn't have it. "If we allow this creature access to its abilities, we'll not just lose him, we'll most assuredly be sealing our own doom. The wrath we forced this Lii-jit to bring down upon the Ohlinn last night? That will be our wrath. Our fate. I will not allow it. You've drawn your passage. Now make it real. But first, I'll have the key to the shackles."

Gris Hallis gritted his teeth and straightened his back. "Of course, my lord," he said, relinquishing the object to Lakos's open hand.

With a sigh, Gris Hallis turned back to the wall, placing his hands against the cool stone. Lowering his head and shutting his eyes, he uttered words Lakos could faintly hear but could not comprehend. As the old mystic spoke, the section of rock within the drawn archway began to lighten. A sound crackled from inside the wall, like frozen water quickly heated by flame. The section grew lighter still as the sound amplified. Gris Hallis spoke louder, his words clear but unintelligible to those around him.

Then he stopped. The wall grew silent as well, in perfect unison. The section of stone bound by the drawn archway remained several shades lighter than the surrounding rock.

Frustrated and drained, Gris Hallis sighed. "I cannot guarantee its adequacy," he said, shaking his head.

Lakos unsheathed his sword and approached the whitened wall. With the hilt of his sword, he tapped the stone, looking to Gris Hallis for affirmation. The old wizard gave none, still exhausted. Again, Lakos struck the wall, this time while pressing his ear against the cold stone. A broad smile crossed his lips.

"It's hollow!" he shouted back to his men. "Grab your swords and join me! I think we can break through!"

Several soldiers rushed over, emphatically and violently thrashing away at the stone. At first only small fragments chipped away, but within moments large, friable chunks of light, porous stone separated from the wall. The men excitedly burrowed their way through, steadily tunneling deeper and deeper, until finally they began to see light from the other side beaming through.

Lakos halted his men, the smile still on his face. He wanted to savor the moment. The chance to break through and enter into the sacred Inner Realm. His realm. Slowly raising the hilt of his sword, he brought it to the thinnest remaining section of wall and struck. The light that poured in through the tiny hole washed over Lakos's face like air to a drowning man. It bathed him and him alone.

"We've broken through! I can see it! It's indescribable!" shouted Lakos, by now having ventured many strides beyond the volcano's outer wall.

From outside, Gris Hallis stood still, seeming very much indifferent to the jubilation. Instead, he glanced down at the wounded Lii-jit, whose eyes had grown vacant and whose breath had softened and slowed.

"We've arrived," he said, smiling down at the dying mystic. "We're home."

CHAPTER FIFTEEN

The moment his eyes shut, Thayliss felt his mind slide into a darkness he'd never known. Like soaring down an icy hill in the dead of night, his consciousness steadily sank deeper, barreling toward an unknown destination. He tried opening his eyes to once again return to reality but could not. He was locked in, a helpless passenger, soaring blindly into an abyss.

Steadily, as he plummeted, light spots began appearing within the darkness surrounding him. At first they whirred by impossibly fast, but as his initial shock and disorientation diminished their speeds began to change. Some spots still surged past him as faint streaks, while others slowed considerably, yielding discrete, finite spheres of light that seemed to linger for an instant before vanishing.

The sensation of falling also dissipated, or at least grew into contradiction. While the feeling remained, Thayliss began getting the sense that it was not in fact he who was moving, but the small bursts of light around him. It was unlike any state he had ever fathomed, much less experienced.

He tried focusing on the spots of light, struggling to capture enough of a glimpse to ascertain any details. The orbs weren't tangible balls of light as much as they were discrete absences of darkness. A sense of something, surrounded by nothingness. Slowly, some of the light-spheres began suggesting something within them—shapes, colors. Still indistinguishable but verging on coherence.

Thayliss wondered if he'd gone mad. If the emotional trauma leading up to this moment had hopelessly severed him from all reason. Were that the case, he would not resist it.

As his mind drifted to the heartache of the night prior, he saw the fog permeating several of the lights begin to dissipate, like a series of veils lifting from a face. One-by-one, lights bearing increasingly clear images presented themselves, still drifting in a sea of darkness. The first one he could ascertain with any certainty was a tree—a forest. The Valla Forest. Another orb presented the unmistakable silhouette of a klacktalli bird on its descent. There were groups of beings—Ohlinn—in another. By now, he could detect motion within the spheres, which lingered much longer than before. The figures were speaking, though this strange dream-world was utterly devoid of sound. Then, he saw Leysiia—his beloved Leysiia—looking right at him, saying words he ached to hear.

He grew tense, and as he did so, the images began to dissolve, and his perceived descent accelerated once again. He had to gain control, somehow. Something inside was telling him to remain calm, remain focused. Feeling his composure steady, he poured his attention entirely to Leysiia. Was it a memory? Was she speaking to him now from the next world? He longed to hear her voice again.

Through the silence, a new sensation emerged. Words somehow delivered into his consciousness, not through sound but through knowing. A message silently intuited to him. He found himself thinking of hope. Struggle. Pain. Perseverance. Love.

Leysiia's image evaporated back into the darkness. But just beyond it, a new sphere emerged, brighter and clearer than any before. It was a barred wagon, like the one he was presently confined to. No—it was the exact wagon he was trapped within, with its arrow-riddled canopy. He saw his own likeness, kneeling in quiet repose. He saw the other Ohlinn scoffing at him, their hearts still paralyzed with fear. He saw all the other wagons stuck in the bleak desert under the shadow of a colossal volcanic ridge. In the sky, swirling above the scores of idle prisoners, flocks of vicious Bray eagles patiently waited out their prey below. That was the answer.

"Thank you, ni-Leysiia, my love," he thought.

As if bubbling up from beneath the deepest sea, Thayliss willed himself from his dream state. Opening his eyes, he felt his awareness returning to the dull, gray world around him, exactly as it had appeared in his mind's eye. However, he now had a plan.

Rising from the floor, Thayliss reached up to the wagon's canopy, pulling down each impaled arrow. The Ohlinn stood idly and watched, shaking their heads at whatever foolishness they presumed he was doing.

Having removed every arrow from the canopy, some twelve in all, Thayliss pulled a thin leather strap from the corner, snapping it easily from the wall. He then proceeded to wrap the bundle of arrows tightly with the leather, tying it securely. With a quick breath, he thrust his arm outside the bars of the wagon, lifting the bundle of arrows, point-down, toward the sky.

During his vision, he noticed that the arrows were fletched using the vibrant, red-and-purple feathers of the stout pheasant, native to the Bray grasslands a mere day's ride from the volcanic desert he now found himself in. The stout pheasant was also the main food source of the Bray eagle.

He wasn't sure if his lure would be successful, nor was he completely certain how he would define success. He just hoped that, when all was said and done, his arm was still one with his body. He may have acquired some meager semblance of Ohlinn spirit vision, but life-mystic limb regeneration was most undoubtedly beyond his abilities.

After all, Bray eagles were not an animal to be trifled with. Their curved, sneering beaks seemed at odds with the scaly, green, reptilian skin covering their foal-sized bodies. How they managed to remain airborne for vast durations was in itself a feat, as the parchment-thin webbing adjoining their long forelimbs to their sides bore very few feathers. In fact, they technically didn't fly at all. Rather, they used their powerful talons to climb to higher ground before gliding gracefully down. Within the

Bray desert, the only high ground in sight was that of the great volcanic ring.

Nonetheless, Thayliss waved the brightly colored feathers vigorously outside the wagon bars, waiting.

Apparently growing wise to his strategy, one of the Ohlinn blurted out, "Human—stop! You know not what you do!"

But it was too late. Thayliss was knocked to the ground as the first Bray eagle struck, grasping the arrows tight in its talons and gliding away, screeching its deafening cry.

Before he could pull himself up, the wagon was struck yet again. And again. A series of screams rained down from above as the wagon shook violently. The mighty raptors tore at the thick canopy, desperate to reveal its contents.

Steadily, roughly, the avian predators peeled the canopy open, a flock of ten or more perched along the wagon's now-exposed metal rim. Their heads darted forward and side-to-side, assessing where to begin.

The Ohlinn trembled in a huddle, while Thayliss scrambled against a corner and looked up, wondering what he'd done.

CHAPTER SIXTEEN

In solving one problem—how to escape the wagon—Thayliss had inadvertently created a new, decidedly more urgent one. The famished-looking Bray eagles clamped their way along the top edge of the exposed mobile prison, scanning for their next meal. The ruse of a false stout pheasant had been more impactful than he had anticipated.

Again, Thayliss searched the cell for an answer. Or a weapon. He shook his head, cursing himself for not setting at least one of the arrows aside. There was nothing. And the Ohlinn beside him seemed utterly devoid of strategy.

One of the Bray eagles, a particularly ragged-looking specimen, seemed to take special interest in Thayliss. Among Thayliss's many wounds and contusions was a rather tidy cut across the back of his left arm, which released a thin stream of blood that over the past ten hours had covered much of his left shoulder and neck in crimson. It was this that caught the raptor's eye. Wounded prey. The repulsive bird emitted a series of stifled, guttural bursts that Thayliss could not distinguish between communication to its flock or simple eagerness in anticipation of a feast.

Having shuffled laterally around the open cage to get closer, the heinous, craggy bird began craning its neck into the cell toward Thayliss, darting spastically in a motion both cautious and desperate. Thayliss backed against an adjacent wall and crouched, covering as much of his face as possible with his forearms, themselves a cut, bloodied mess. This, if anything, only spurred the animal on, as it clamored excitedly toward him, lunging its neck into the cage as far as it could—leaving scarcely a stride of air between Thayliss and its deadly, curved beak.

In a final desperate act, the eagle attempted to grasp onto

one of the wagon's vertical steel bars with a gnarled, clawed foot. Thayliss's heart stopped. He knew that if the creature lost its footing and slid into the cage with him, that would spell the end of him. But just as the vicious bird released its grip and extended a curved, razor-sharp talon toward one of the bars, the entire wagon shook harshly.

Thayliss spun around to see a second flock of Bray eagles swarming around the pack mule hitched to his wagon. The poor mule neighed and thrashed its head about as the birds stabbed and tore at its flesh in a mad frenzy. The mule took off across the desert floor, towing the wagon and its contents behind it. Thayliss and the Ohlinn were sent tumbling toward the back wall of the cage, helpless.

The tormented pack mule then collided with a stationary wagon ahead of it, knocking it onto its side and sending its own mule into a crazed fit, bucking against the toppled cage still fastened to its back and charging at every nearby wagon.

Two rogue wagons led to ten, ten led to thirty. It was chaos. The sparse smattering of soldiers who had been charged with the dull task of keeping watch over the passive, captive Ohlinn now found themselves in mortal danger. Some soldiers mounted their fleet horses and raced to safety, while a few of the more intrepid souls held their ground, firing crossbows and brandishing swords in an attempt to restore order.

It was in vain. Through his jarring view from the wagon floor, Thayliss could see ten soldiers trampled for every mule brought down. Despite the frenzy, the pack mules stayed true to their instinct, racing ahead rabidly. Where they were going, Thayliss had no clue.

CHAPTER SEVENTEEN

"I must speak with Master Lakos," an exasperated soldier begged, arriving by fleet horse to the battered archway carved into the mountainside.

"I'm sorry, my son," replied Gris Hallis, his hands held palm-up by his sides, "but I'm afraid he's unavailable at the moment. I, however, have been granted full authority on all matters outside these walls. Now speak, what concerns you?"

"The pack mules—the Ohlinn prisoners—they're all getting away," he panted, pointing back to the rising cloud of ash in the distance.

Gris Hallis looked down at the frail Lii-jit lying motionless on the ground.

"Life-mystic, it appears that we have use for you after all. But I apologize, as I seem to have misplaced the key."

The old mystic brought his boot down hard upon the Lii-jit's right hand, applying a concerted amount of pressure, and then rolling his foot forward. The Lii-jit writhed in pain and retracted his broken hand, which now slipped easily through the stone bracket.

Unveiling a small, rusted dagger from inside his boot, Gris Hallis crouched down beside the Lii-jit and held the blade to his neck.

"Now, Lii-jit vermin, bring those pack mules to me."

The Lii-jit's faint, labored breaths slowly grew deeper as he lay on the ground, clutching his fractured hand. Swiftly, his breaths deepened still, growing stronger with every beat of his revitalized heart. Moments later, his eyes grew wild as his legs jostled spastically against the stony ground.

"Now, now, life-mystic, I need co-operation, or else this will end up very badly for both of us. Most of all, for you." Gris Hallis pressed the dagger against the Lii-jit's throat, a small trickle of blood cascading over its steel edge.

"The wagons, they're heading this way!" called out one of the soldiers.

"Good, good." Gris Hallis caressed the Lii-jit's throat with the dull face of the blade. "You should feel honored to be playing such a pivotal role in the new age. There will be stories of all of this. Parents will tell their ch—"

"Gris Hallis, they're not stopping!" the soldier shouted, his voice soon drowned out by a clamor of hooves and screaming voices.

Gris Hallis glanced up to see the entire team of pack mules stampeding toward him, each still pulling a wagon, some upright and others dragged coarsely along on their sides.

With his focus shifted away from the prisoner under his blade, Gris Hallis was suddenly knocked to the side as the reinvigorated Lii-jit leapt astride a renegade mule and vanished in a cloud of ashen dust.

As they passed by the open archway, all of the remaining mules spontaneously slowed to a trot, and then finally a complete standstill. Even the bloodthirsty Bray eagles swirling above the chaotic scene seemed to instantly lose interest in their prey, each unleashing a series of shrill screams before passively gliding away.

Gris Hallis, his heart pounding in his gaunt, decrepit chest, tried to take in what had just happened. The Lii-jit was long gone, as was one of the wagons and whomever it contained. Meanwhile, the remaining lot of Ohlinn prisoners were merely brought closer to their new home in the Inner Realm. A fair trade, he surmised. He only hoped that Lakos felt likewise.

CHAPTER EIGHTEEN

"Tiig? Is that you?" a voice called out from inside the wagon.

The little life-mystic, riding atop the pack mule, spun around and smiled. "What a great fortune of fate! To be trapped together within this very wagon but a short time ago, only to be reunited once again as liberated beings. Although it could be said that I am the only being liberated at the moment, as you are clearly still encased within the wagon. However, it seems to have lost its canopy, so it is no doubt a safe assumption that an Ohlinn such as yourself could easily escape from it should you choose to do so. And even if you could not, we ride away from the ones who captured us, so even though you are still technically imprisoned, you are nonetheless free, do you not agree?"

Increasingly grateful for every stride distancing him from the sinister army at the Bray range, Thayliss felt his mood ease. He even found the image of the spastic little being chatting incessantly while seated backwards astride a charging wild animal almost endearing.

"You've got an arrow in your side," replied Thayliss, thinking of no better way to advance the conversation.

"Oh yes, indeed I do." Tiig glanced down at the arrow and, in one fluid motion, withdrew it from his flesh. While he was no doubt not immune to pain, it seemed to Thayliss that the Lii-jit had grown accustomed to the sensation. Perhaps the dramatic recoil that others felt toward pain was more a product of the dire consequences of sustaining injury—a way to send a clear message to the brain that such behavior should not be repeated. As a being capable of regeneration despite, seemingly, any trauma, Thayliss speculated that this feedback mechanism may have devolved out of the Lii-jit. After all, if one healed from any abuse, then why stress over its recurrence in the future?

"What about the other Ohlinn?" asked Thayliss, suddenly

recalling the final moments before his escape from the caravan. "Should we go back for them?"

Tiig shook his head, a pained look on his face. "I tried to take them with me," he said solemnly. "But something about that mountain wouldn't let me. I could feel an energy building within it—a dark energy. We were lucky to escape at all. But I am truly sorry for your kin—they, too, deserve freedom. And had those humans and that corrupt mystic of theirs not abused my gifts, they would still be free."

Thayliss could hear the pain in the little Lii-jit's voice. "So, where is it you're taking us?" asked Thayliss, trying to change the subject.

"That depends entirely upon where you wish to go," answered Tiig cheerfully, his sorrow seeming to vanish in the blink of an eye. "Seeing as how I am outnumbered eight-to-one, the notion of riding back to the Sani-jai rainforest to visit my own kin seems a tad selfish. However, despite being outnumbered eight Ohlinn to one Lii-jit, it is the one Lii-jit who is directing this fine animal's course." He laughed, a rich, guttural laugh, and spun back to face forward. "I'm only aiming to kid you, to play with you. I would not deprive my fellow travelers their journey home. I will take you to your home. The Valla Forest. Really, a very lovely place. It is not far, relatively speaking. Which really is the only way to speak, I would think."

"Stop this vehicle," one of the other Ohlinn called out.

The Lii-jit complied, seeming to command the galloping pack mule to a full stop without so much as an overt gesture or spoken word. He looked back into the wagon, not saying a word, and awaited further instruction. But there was none.

With typical grace and agility, the seven Ohlinn leaped through the open canopy and onto the dusty, barren ground.

"The Valla Forest is not your home, Thayliss," voiced another Ohlinn, peering at Thayliss through the bars as if speaking to a caged animal.

"It was never your home," said another. "This matter is settled. You will never again set foot within the Valla Forest, lest you be spirit-stricken. So it is said, that all must abide."

The words pierced through Thayliss far deeper than any mortal blade ever could. The Ohlinn were, by nature, a peaceful, serene race, with no innate sense of violence nor traditional weaponry. But what they lacked in corporeal artillery, they more than made up for in the ethereal. To be spirit-stricken was, in Ohlinn mysticism, to be disconnected from one's very soul. Not to be killed, or even physically wounded, but to be lost from the next world.

On death, all Ohlinn transitioned to the next world, an energetic continuation of the present one. Whether all life followed this path was a matter of great philosophical debate, with many claiming the entire concept of the next world as simply an Ohlinn fabrication, aimed at enhancing their stature within this world.

But Thayliss knew better. He knew that the Ohlinn were in possession of a most sacred gift, the ability to serve as a link, a conduit, between the two worlds, thereby gleaning insights into the future and communicating with those already passed.

In contrast, when the spirit-stricken died, they simply ceased to be. Gone from this world, and never to see the next. Never to rejoin lost loved ones. It was as though they never existed at all. It would almost be more merciful if, at the time of enacting the curse, the Ohlinn would also kill the poor being. Were that the case, it would at least spare them however many bleak, empty seasons they had left, knowing that it was all they would ever have. This was a damnation rarely incited and gravely abided by. In all the history of time, the ancient texts read, never had one of the spirit-stricken had his curse lifted. It was not done.

Thayliss had little choice but to comply. "I will do as you ask of me. But please," he pleaded, his hands tightly gripping the steel bars, "tell my—tell the Ohlinn—that I did the best of my ability to serve them with honor. And that I gravely apologize for my failures."

"We shall do no such thing," an Ohlinn replied. "For we, too, shall not be returning home. This will be our final resting place. It is our future. We shall remain here in these forsaken lands and meditate until we leave this world for the next. But know that word of your banishment has already reached the Valla Forest. For the true Ohlinn are granted insights that an imposter shall never receive."

With that, the seven Ohlinn wandered off into the flat, unchanging dune, no longer under the vast shadow of the Bray Mountain, though never beyond its view. Clouds of ash swirled around the old mystics until they appeared to be consumed by the desert.

Looking around, Thayliss decided that he had had enough of being trapped in a cage. Hoping that his new appearance also meant that he now possessed the lithe athleticism of an Ohlinn, he leapt up to grab hold of the top railing. However, his attempt still fell several hands short. By the time Thayliss managed to grip the top of the cage and rather inelegantly hoist himself over, he found the little Lii-jit sitting atop the pack mule staring at him, somewhat amused and somewhat perplexed.

"Have you sustained injury, Thayliss the banished Ohlinn?" he asked, a look of genuine concern across his spritely, golden-brown face.

Thayliss hadn't the energy nor the inclination to discuss what had just transpired. "Yes, Tiig. Injuries everywhere."

"Then I know where to take you. If you've nowhere to go, you've now somewhere to go!" He paused, thinking. "Though I figure you'll not care to climb back into the cage, especially in light of the great challenge it presented you just trying to climb out of it. No, no. I would not ask that of you. However, I can sense that this pack horse has only the energy to carry myself upon his back. She, too, has sustained injuries, much like yourself. But alas, also like yourself, she is bravely forging on. Such a wonderful trait that some creatures possess. The forging on despite injury and impediment. I'm not certain what exactly one would call that trait, but it's certainly a better thing to have than not to have, wouldn't you agree?"

"So I'll just walk, then?" asked Thayliss, suddenly finding himself on the verge of collapse.

"Oh my, my, no." Tiig gently lowered his head and mumbled something. A brief moment later, he raised his head back up and smiled at Thayliss. "The closest specimen to our present location who meets our needs for strength, stamina, carriage, and overall wellbeing. Should do nicely."

Thayliss looked around but saw nothing at first. But then came the sound. A deep hum that joined the chorus of the whispering wind. The hum grew louder, finally coinciding with a dark gray spot jostling over the horizon. That shape, that movement—Thayliss had seen it before.

"Oh no," he muttered under his breath. "Not that."

Slowly but steadily, a lone bastik wolf made its way toward the two travelers. By the time it arrived, its mouth was agape, panting, exposing a row of nightmarishly wicked, angular fangs. Tiig remained on his pack mule, appearing rather pleased with himself.

"Shall we?" he asked, gesturing toward the murderous beast.

"I think I'll walk," Thayliss replied.

"Nonsense," said Tiig. "Completely within my control. It seems quite often that the more savage the beast, the easier to persuade. I suppose it's only natural—less evolved intellects are almost always more readily manipulated. Take humans, for example." He laughed, clearly pleased with himself. "Come now, it's perfectly safe."

Reluctantly, but sensing no alternative apart from perishing in the desert heat alongside his former Ohlinn brethren, Thayliss approached the beast. As he drew nearer, the bastik wolf lowered itself down to the ground, beckoning its rider.

"This is not normal," said Thayliss, slowly putting a leg over the filthy, gray animal until he had it sufficiently mounted.

"He likes his neck rubbed, you know," added Tiig. "They don't all like that, but some of them do. This one surely does."

"Well, that's not going to happen." It took all of Thayliss's strength just to remain calm as the animal extended its long, narrow legs and began trotting alongside Tiig and his pack mule. "Let's just get where we're going, preferably as quickly as possible."

"Very well," replied Tiig. "To Sani-jai. My kin will take care of you."

The two entranced animals burst into a full gallop through the desert. Thayliss, forced to grasp the scruff on the beast's thick neck just to stay atop it, shut his eyes and prayed for the ride to be over. Tiig, meanwhile, let his arms hang free, a smile across his lips as he felt the dry, hot breeze against his face.

CHAPTER NINETEEN

The moment had arrived. Lakos took his first steps into the Inner Realm, bathed in the light of a deity. *He* was a deity. Now encircled by the immense curved face of the great crater, he felt at once safe and invincible.

The ridge's massive gray outer fringe had been specked with minute fragments of shimmering stone; an odd exterior juxtaposed against the dull desert surrounding it. Standing within the Inner Realm, however, Lakos now knew that such obscurity was but the subtlest allusion to what existed within its seemingly impenetrable walls.

The entirety of the volcanic crater's curved inner wall was immaculate. A sheer face of white, marbled stone completely encircling the vast domain within it, so perfectly smooth as to appear almost metallic.

"This must be five hundred strides across," said Lakos, eyeing the distance from where he stood to the realm's far wall.

"Six-hundred-twenty-eight," corrected a voice behind him.

Lakos turned to see Gris Hallis push past several soldiers as he crept his way through the crudely burrowed tunnel and into the Inner Realm. The soldiers, unfazed, continued busily widening the archway.

"Quite striking, is it not?" Gris Hallis asked, surveying the space before him.

Lakos's sense of awe continued as he glanced down at the ground. From where he stood, it appeared as though the realm's entire surface was covered in a homogeneous layer of fine, white powder. Only upon crouching down to inspect it further did Lakos notice the occasional yellow-white pebble mixed in, and rarer still, a stone of more substantial size. Still, nothing so large that it could not be enveloped within his clenched fist.

"The sacred tower. Is this all that remains?" asked Lakos,

grasping a handful of powder and sifting it passively between his fingers.

"Indeed, it is. Obtaining the stones required to line every corner of every prison wagon was a most arduous endeavor, I assure you." Gris Hallis knocked a small stone with his boot.

"But there were scarcely enough stones to entrap three hundred Ohlinn. What of the others? The Masdazii? The Lii-jit? In their entirety, the five realms contain a mystic population numbering easily in the tens of thousands. We lack both the resources and the manpower to control them all," questioned Lakos.

"Fear not, my lord," reassured Gris Hallis. "With these three hundred, we need not coax the remaining mystics from their hiding to bring them here. Once the sacred tower has been restored, they will come to us. And then you will have all the mystic energy you could ever require at your fingertips."

"And what of the sacred tower?" asked Lakos. "The legend spoke of its destruction at the hands of the Gray Mystic, Noryssin. If this is truly all that remains, an open field, strewn with pebbles and dust, I question how you hope to resurrect it. We cannot rebuild what no longer exists."

Gris Hallis lowered his head subserviently, the faintest smirk creaking across his face. "My lord, I respectfully remind you that within these stone walls, we are no longer bound to the world of the material. Within the border of the Bray Ridge, inside the great Inner Realm, we now stand at the gateway between all worldly existence and the beating heart that sustains it."

"Spare me your theology," said Lakos. "And do not disappoint me. You have brought us this far, and for that I am grateful, but it will all be worthless if I am to rule from a palace made of dust."

Gris Hallis paused for a moment, then continued. "This is a notion no doubt foreign to the innate human sensibility, but to govern all is truly to govern all. Your tower will rise, my lord," he stated firmly. "But it will not be built strictly from forged steel, milled lumber and quarried stone. For such things comprise but one-third of your kingdom."

Lakos looked around the immense, cavernous expanse. "So where do we begin?"

"My lord," replied Gris Hallis, "we have already begun."

Looking toward the now-widened archway, Gris Hallis glanced to one of the soldiers standing guard and nodded. Within moments, an Ohlinn prisoner was led through the tunnel and into the Inner Realm. Rather, he was not led so much as he marched through under his own cognizance. Or so it seemed. The Ohlinn prisoner lacked chains or restraints, not so much as a sacred stone clasped to his wrist.

Immediately behind the Ohlinn was another. And another. Soon, a steady stream of Ohlinn captives poured through the archway and into the light of the Inner Realm. The prisoners, seemingly locked in an oblivious, trance-like state, marched past where Lakos stood, making their way toward the center of the vast crater. As the first spellbound Ohlinn approached the center of the great circular space, he stopped halfway to its origin. The spirit-mystic behind him moved to his immediate left before he, too, stopped. So the pattern continued, prisoner upon prisoner shuffling passively through the tunnel, toward the center, and settling to the immediate left of the one preceding.

Lakos looked on, mesmerized by the silent procession, until he saw the final Ohlinn captive take his place. The Ohlinn formed a perfect inner circle within the greater cylindrical wall. In unison, the mystic collective knelt down on the white, powdery ground and bowed their heads.

From beneath his feet, Lakos could feel a peculiar sensation emerge. A guttural, penetrating rumbling from far below.

CHAPTER TWENTY

As their journey to the Sani-jai rainforest progressed, Thayliss's apprehension toward the grizzled gray bastik beneath him gradually softened. Its brash, labored breaths possessed a natural rhythm with the beast's long, loping strides, and its broad, thickly padded feet touched the ground with only the slightest sound of impact. It was a rather striking animal, maintaining high speeds for long durations over widely varied terrain, the rocky desert having given way first to a gentle, hilly grassland, and now a misty, green thicket. Thayliss marveled at how the bastik's giant skull never bobbed, never wavered as it ran, maintaining a perfect balance with the blur of ground beneath its feet. This also made for a mercifully smooth ride atop its back. Its musculature was also quite remarkable. Layers of thick muscle wrapped around the bastik's oversized neck, pulsing and twitching to meet the extreme physical and gravitational demands of motion.

Thayliss found that by leaning forward and practically resting his chin upon the coarse, matted fur atop the creature's head, he could peer out and imagine the world from the wolf's perspective. Recalling the bastik's reputed lack of visual acuity only served to enhance the beast's impressiveness. A deadly weapon, perfectly suited to its needs. Occasionally, they would pass by a pack of shrews or their close relative, the striped badgett. Doing so, Thayliss could feel the bastik break stride slightly, recoiling a paw almost as if having stepped upon a thistle. This behavior would be accompanied by the faintest muscle twitch in the side of the beast's neck closest to its prey.

However, in each instance, the bastik would regain its rhythm with the next step and continue forward beside Tiig and his equally steady, if decidedly less dynamic, pack mule. Seeing

Tiig riding merrily along served as a vital reminder to Thayliss that this was indeed a rare and privileged ride, as his fateful attempt back at the Valla Forest had illustrated.

The two travelers spoke nary a word since their departure from the Bray desert, which suited Thayliss just fine. There was therapy in nature, as he had come to learn during his childhood. While reclining amongst the leaves by his treetop dwelling, Thayliss had spent countless nights observing the star formations, imagining what worlds existed in those faraway celestial realms. He had asked Leonorryn an unending stream of questions during his youth, about where he came from, where all life came from, and where it went from there. More often than not, the wise old mystic was able to placate the boy with anecdotes and comforting words. However, his paternal counsel was often flecked with caveats surrounding the limitations of human thought. An endlessly just and civil Ohlinn elder, Leonorryn always seemed to possess a slight aversion toward humans, which Thayliss had found rather peculiar, especially in light of Leonorryn having willfully elected to raise one alongside his very own Ohlinn daughter.

Leonorryn taught him that while humans theorized that the stars were where spirits traveled upon departing this world, this notion was false. He told the boy that humans had an inborn blindness to worlds existing beyond their own senses. They longed to know where they went when they left this world, he would say. And since their limited intellects necessitated a tangible answer to even the most ethereal of questions, they looked to the sky.

Even some of the more enlightened humans, he continued, were still incapable of appreciating the true magnitude and majesty of the world. The so-called truth seekers and other wise men likened the next world to a continuation of this world, just beyond human comprehension. An ability, a sense, to which different beings were afforded varying degrees of perception.

A bastik wolf sensed ground tremors to a degree greater than human or mystic capability. It was still a sense possessed by all parties, it was simply the magnitude of the ability that separated them. But the next world, reasoned Leonorryn to the young Thayliss, as with all mystic powers, existed on a plane so foreign to humans that it could not be justly described or understood. Unfortunately for humans, this seemed to violate the one, most powerful innate drive they did possess—the need for answers.

"Infernal humans," were the first words to break the silence and pull Thayliss from his musing.

Thayliss looked over to Tiig, who rode beside him, having slowed both animals to a trot.

"I'm sorry?" asked Thayliss, uncertain how to take the comment.

"Infernal humans," Tiig reiterated, a look of disgust on his tawny, cherubic face.

Through the sparse outcropping of tall, green shoots, Tiig pointed toward a lone figure in the distance, pacing back and forth, appearing to stand watch.

"A sentinel," Tiig whispered. "A human soldier, stationed here to survey and assess the environment. We are nearing the Sani-jai. I do not know why he has come here, but humans never cease to foreshadow death and tyranny. And once he reports back to his lord news of our meager numbers, we will perish, all of us. The humans do not send their kind to regions they do not aspire to conquer."

"But you are Lii-jit, a life-mystic. How can you harbor such resentment toward another life? Another manner of being entirely?" Thayliss asked.

"Because true human life ceased with the demise of the Gray Mystic, when the world fell into chaos. My kind have spoken of it since before my birth. That which breeds only death cannot in itself be deemed a life. The human order is a plague, worse than any drought, famine, or flood. It has disconnected completely from all rational notion of need, with a hunger that never abates. It grows, competes, and burns, scorching all in its wake. My kind protects all worldly life—all but that which exists only to harm it."

Thayliss did not know how to respond. He apparently still bore the outward appearance of the Ohlinn. But there were more pressing concerns to be addressed.

"The sentinel—can you not just summon some nearby beast to dispatch him?" he asked.

Tiig shook his head, leaving the back of the pack mule and hunching down amidst the reeds. "Do you not think I already tried that the moment I first set eyes upon the loathsome being? I could not. There's a block, preventing me from exerting any influence within a twenty-stride radius of where he stands. Perhaps the same force that robbed me of my abilities back in the wagon. The stones. And they'll undoubtedly use the very same to entrap my kin, as they did yours."

The little Lii-jit motioned for Thayliss to dismount his ride. "We must walk the rest of the way to Sani-jai. If the wretched human sees us, his cunning may somehow deny me my power. Were that the case, I would not envy the soul within range of a bastik wolf's footsteps."

Thayliss slipped from the back of his bastik, pausing to caress its side as he walked past it and into the mist. Tiig nodded silently to both the bastik and the pack mule, sending them swiftly off in the direction they had come from, though at an ever-widening angle respective to each other.

"The bastik yearns for sustenance," said Tiig, "but my pack mule deserves a day of mercy." He returned to the task at hand. "Now come. We must return to my home deep in the rainforest and warn the others. A war will soon be upon us." He crept further into the damp, steamy thicket, away from the distant soldier.

Taking one last look at the pacing sentinel, Thayliss followed his companion into the mist, his sapphire eyes dimming slightly.

CHAPTER TWENTY-ONE

Feeling the ground beneath him rumble with steadily increasing fortitude, Lakos stood firm. He turned to Gris Hallis. "What is this?" he asked, his voice wrought with concern.

Several of the soldiers who had ventured with him into the Inner Realm anxiously pushed past each other to seek shelter under the carved stone archway.

"There is nothing to fear, my lord," laughed Gris Hallis, a trace of condescension in his voice. "It is merely the next step in fulfilling your destiny."

The vibrations aggressively resonated through the ground, shaking the very foundation upon which they stood. Like dust on a tightened drum, the vast, circular ground grew obscured as the fine white powder hovered in a diffuse cloud around their feet. The ring of Ohlinn still knelt, transfixed by whatever divine end they had been assigned to.

Then, contributing no sound to the guttural din, a tall, narrow entity of translucent white began to rise from the very center of the circle. Like a silent specter, the pointed veil of light rose higher and higher, growing taller and wider from a foggy, ever-expanding base. From the other side of the entity, the faces of Ohlinn still deep in meditation remained, obscured by the mist before them but still visible. Up rose the form until, mere moments after its emergence, it reached the very threshold of the volcanic ring's upper rim. Without slowing, it ventured further, seeming to extend endlessly into the sky.

Lakos watched in awe as the mighty form continued upward for some time before finally freezing in place. A precise, conical dream. A colossus of hazy white, seeming to dwarf the otherwise imposing Bray Ridge surrounding it. Lakos was speechless.

"Your tower, my lord," said Gris Hallis.

Lakos approached the tower with sheer infatuation, but as he drew nearer, he could see that the mystical structure before him was, in fact, no structure at all. It retained its vaporous texture, devoid of brick or stone or any tangible material at all. By the time he stood at its base, having walked between two oblivious Ohlinn, he grew angered.

"This is no tower," he cried back to Gris Hallis. "This is but mystic trickery. The mere illusion of power, nothing more." He extended his arm directly into the mist, swatting furiously as the vapor swirled in the wake of his hand before dissolving back into the sea of luminous white air.

Gris Hallis walked toward him. "This is the work of three hundred Ohlinn. Spirit-mystics whose energy resides within the ethereal. The transparent. Once we have harnessed the power of the other two mystic orders, those rooted within the material and the living, your sacred tower will become as real as the ground you stand upon. And with it, your kingdom. The Inner Realm, the tower, and I, shall be the instruments through which you will exert influence over your domain."

The sentiment caught Lakos off-guard. "When I assume the throne of the Voduss Grei, will I not have direct control over the world beyond?" he asked, perplexed.

"My lord," said Gris Hallis apologetically, "the power will be yours and yours alone. However, as a human, you will need a mystic life through which to truly blend with the energy of this world. To channel your desires and see them realized. And I will loyally serve you to that end."

Lakos's eyes narrowed as he glared over at the old mystic. "So, I'm to be forever dependent upon you, am I?" he asked, pacing restlessly. "Trusting my life, my kingdom, to your supposed loyalty?"

"I spoke repeatedly of my relevance to your ultimate objective, how it could not be done without my assistance," replied Gris Hallis defensively. "There are limitations to human authority. There are rules to nature."

"I grow weary of you, Gris Hallis," threatened Lakos. "You have led my army far from the mystic lands we seek to conquer, and taken me to this useless, empty ruin. You speak solely to inflate my ego, while your actions serve only your own, dark motives. I know a trap when I see one. Guards!" Lakos shouted, walking further from the tall column of light, toward the old mystic.

Several guards intercepted Gris Hallis as Lakos approached. With his arms hastily pulled behind his back, the gaunt, weathered Ohlinn passively stood and waited.

"I was a fool not to have seen it sooner. A fool!" Lakos unsheathed his sword and slashed at the hard ground beneath him, not breaking stride. "Ever since I was a child, I strove to one day exact my revenge against mystics like you. To extinguish from the world mystic treachery and begin the human age. But then, on the very eve of executing my plan — my life's ambition — you appeared. Through whatever foul magic you used to pollute my mind, I actually believed that I could assume the throne of the Voduss Grei. But the illusion is over. I shall lead my army back to the Valla Forest, and unleash the wrath that I had originally intended. That I spent the past thirty years dreaming about. But not before doing the same to you and the other Ohlinn within our camp."

"I have only spoken the truth," said Gris Hallis, his head hanging down. "And strike me down if you wish but do so with the knowledge that you are sealing your own fate."

Lakos, now within several strides of Gris Hallis, stopped, his chest throbbing with rage. "Finally, your true identity revealed. Lashing out threats the instant you realize that your mystic deceptions no longer cloud my mind."

"My Lord, it is mere statement of fact," replied Gris Hallis calmly. "And I assure you, your kingdom is far closer than you can imagine, closer than it will ever be should you end my life and execute your original plan. Without me, your kingdom and your prophecy will never be more than the vacant mist you see before you, and even that will fade in time. You dreamed of slashing through the hearts of all mystics, burning their homes to the ground, not because that is your path, but because you knew no other way."

"Do not speak of my dreams," spat Lakos. "You may have used your foul abilities to spy on me and my men, but do not profess to read my mind."

A solemn expression cast down upon Gris Hallis's face. "But I have seen the dreams that compel you. And the nightmares that torment you. During my meditations, I was apprised to more than merely your actions and your ambitions. From within my mind's eye, I saw the haunting images that continue to plague you every time you shut your eyes—the horrific scene that flashes by, over and over. Awoken by your mother's screams from within your humble, one-room cabin. The giant Masdazii warrior standing at your doorstep, wielding the long, metallic chains with which they thrash their prey. And the sound of yet another cry from your mother as you raced as quickly as you could toward the safety of the forest."

"That's enough!" screamed Lakos, bringing his longsword to Gris Hallis's throat.

"You were just a boy," said Gris Hallis, pain in his soft, blue eyes. "Alone in the world, thrust into adulthood in the span of a night."

"I survived because it was my destiny," gritted Lakos through clenched teeth, his own eyes glistening. "To one day take back the freedom and innocence that was taken from me. Or at the very least, to take those very things from those who wronged me." He slowly lowered his sword.

"Then take it from them," said Gris Hallis. "It is the future you desire, I can see it. Ever since my arrival at your camp, it was clear that you knew in your heart that this was your destiny. You are meant to be more than a mere warrior, or a killer. You are meant to rule this world." The old spirit-mystic waved his hands across the Inner Realm surrounding them. "And my Lord, I am but a loyal servant."

"Away with you, wizard," growled Lakos, examining the vaporous monolith behind him.

With that, the guards dragged Gris Hallis back toward the carved archway, his bright, sapphire eyes wild with fear and desperation as he looked back at Lakos. Just as the shadows of the tunnel cast over him, he saw his window of opportunity rapidly narrow.

"There is another way!" cried Gris Hallis, just before disappearing into the tunnel. The guards stopped their procession to await Lakos's response, but there was only silence.

Again, Gris Hallis spoke. "There is a way to breathe mystic power into you. To grant you direct authority over all realms."

Still hearing no reply, Gris Hallis shouted his one, final plea, "I can make you a god among men!"

"Bring him back," ordered Lakos to his guards. He turned back to examine the hundreds of Ohlinn, still kneeling around the great hazy structure in deep, numb meditation.

"So, you would instill mystic powers in me," he said, slowly walking to the center of the great realm. "After which, there would be no use for you. So why do it?"

"If you are to kill me regardless, then at least I would die with the knowledge that the lineage of the Voduss Grei has been restored," Gris Hallis shouted through the echoes of the vast, empty space.

As he walked, Lakos had abundant time for contemplation. He loathed the mystics with every trace of his being. The whole of his adolescence and adult life had been devoted to the sole purpose of either ruling them or eliminating them from this world. But as much as he despised the fact, Gris Hallis was right. Ever since the notion of wielding the all-encompassing power of the Gray Mystic had entered his mind, it consumed him. He no longer saw vengeance in the form of invasion and simple warfare. He needed more. And now, on the precipice of accomplishing that very objective, he found himself burdened with a decision. If he was to see this quest through, he need either instill his power and trust in a mystic who emanated deceit and cunning or dare become one himself. He was at a loss. Previously, in times of uncertainty, Lakos sought guidance from his tactical training. He realized that this was no different. It was, however, a scenario without victory. There was no right answer.

But then, from the deep recesses of his mind, an ancient parable from his childhood in Merrin Ells rose to his consciousness. It alluded to an earlier time, when the greatest fishing vessel in the realm was in the midst of yet another prosperous venture.

The brave captain and his crew had been pursuing the dangerous, though exceedingly valuable, razorback—a thick bodied, silver fish five strides long, with a sharp dorsal ridge running down its back. The razorback used this weapon by approaching its prey and then, just prior to impact, quickly tilting its head down and lunging forward, completing a revolution in the water that exposed its prey to the entire length of the razor spine, severing even the thickest prey in two. Then, as the revolution completed, the fish's head rotated forward again in time to devour what remained.

Chumming the water with bait, the men anxiously waited. They did not need to wait long. One after the other, the fish were speared and brought upon the deck. It was an expedition for the ages.

But then, without warning, the sky grew ominous, and the winds howled bitterly. A storm was upon them, the massive, frothing waves relentlessly battering the ship to pieces. The craft and the men upon it fell to the raging sea.

As if having accomplished its diabolical purpose, the storm abated, and the seas once again grew tranquil. However, one-by-one, the men were taken, sheared in half and consumed by the throngs of razorbacks still drawn to the area. Soon, there was only the captain, fighting to stay afloat within the eye of a hurricane of silver swirling all around him.

Sensing a strike to be imminent, the brave captain struggled to loosen his knife from his belt, which he knew would be of no use against the great fish. Instead, he spotted the razorback closest to him and, keeping his knife held close to his chest, jutted his free arm in the direct path of the approaching fish. The pain was excruciating as the razorback began its forward loop, its spine shearing completely through the captain's hand. He fought to maintain composure as the sea around him turned crimson. Then, as the fish's open jaws surged toward him, the captain brought forth his knife, piercing the razorback through the upper palate and into the brain. The fish died instantly.

But there were others. The captain valiantly continued this way, attack after attack, each time his amputated arm growing shorter, the water redder. And each time, successfully killing the fish as it completed its revolution, jaws agape and eyes rolled back.

By the time the fish had all been killed, the captain, now missing the entirety of his arm, was brought ashore by the tide. The bodies of two dozen lifeless razorbacks awaited him, having already washed up on the sandy beach. The weary captain returned home alive and forever a legend.

Lakos was not entirely sure why this old tale had entered into his mind, but nonetheless, he now knew what he had to do.

CHAPTER TWENTY-TWO

"Just relax—relax, please, sir. You're making this far more difficult than it need be," said the young female Lii-jit, attempting to clean Thayliss's wounded knee.

"I keep telling you, I'm fine. I don't need any attention," said Thayliss, rising from the wooden bed and walking somewhat gingerly toward an opening in the wall and peering outside.

Deep inside the lush Sani-jai rainforest, the Lii-jit colony had thrived for countless seasons, relying exclusively on the land and its fellow inhabitants. As they typically kept to themselves, little else was known about the life-mystics apart from their exuberant nature and their propensity to live in trees. Not above them, as with the Ohlinn dwellings, but actually inside them.

The traditional Lii-jit dwelling, the folliad, consisted of a hollowed-out tree with a wide trunk, preferably fifteen-to-twenty strides tall, expertly chosen and carved to ensure the continued health of the tree itself. At its center, a long, vertical, wooden beam rose through the entire structure, with only the narrowest rungs etched into it along the way. Impractical for most any other being, it nonetheless allowed the small, agile Lii-jit residing there to freely make their way to one of the folliad's three-or-more floors. Each floor was appointed with as many rooms as was deemed necessary, separated into wedged sections by uncarved sheets of wood, or simply left as open space. Privacy, it seemed, was not a fundamental Lii-jit condition.

The inside of each room was as densely and vibrantly furnished as the rainforest itself, with beautiful flowers and vines wrapping around the inner wall, all still very much alive. Small sections leading into the open forest air were cored from the walls on each level, serving as both windows and entryways for any nearby birds, snakes, or rodents who saw fit to pay a visit.

While Thayliss had long imagined what it must feel like to be inside a genuine folliad, he presently had other things on his mind. Brushing a bright orange-and-blue bird from the ledge, he peered out the narrow, makeshift window and sighed.

A handful of Lii-jit warriors patrolled the area, some crouching amidst the layer of fog, while others scrambled expertly up to the thick green canopy to secure a better vantage point. On arriving at the colony, Tiig had assured him that they would be well protected for the night and assigned one of his many siblings, his youngest sister, Mawi-naa, to tend to Thayliss's wounds while Tiig foraged for food.

"I assure you, Ohlinn, if those wounds are not tended to appropriately, a vicious infection will set in," Mawi-naa warned, breaking Thayliss from his daydream as she sat on the soft, moss-covered bed, waving a cloth.

"It's fine. Don't concern yourself with it," repeated Thayliss, still peering outside, an unsettled feeling in his gut.

"The concern is not mine to hold," she replied candidly. "My elder sibling instructed me to tend to your wounds. But apparently he seems to have befriended an Ohlinn who knows more of nature than the Lii-jit." With a slight, self-satisfied smile, she pushed herself up from the bed and walked toward the opening in the floor. "I only ask that you do not curse my name when you awaken seven nights from now unable to walk. For that is what lies ahead should you forego attention." She paused. "But, of course, you already knew that, didn't you?"

Before she could leave, Thayliss turned. "Stop—Mawi-naa—please." He walked to the other end of the small room and sat down on the bed. "You're only trying to help. I apologize."

Mawi-naa returned to the bed, gently unfolding the cloth before tamping it down against his knee.

"Wicked nightshade!" he bellowed, wincing from the pain. "What are you doing to me?"

The pretty young Lii-jit lifted the cloth. "The sap of the colominus tree. Wonderful ability to heal stubborn wounds. But yes, a tad painful at times." Avoiding eye contact, she smiled gently before resuming her work.

Thayliss feigned interest in the explanation, still blinded by the absurd discomfort shooting up from his knee.

Her smile widened as she paused once again. "Wicked nightshade? That's a rather funny thing to say."

"What?" Thayliss collected himself. "Oh—yeah. I guess it is. It's an Ohlinn expression. Well, more of a profanity, really."

Mawi-naa shrugged. "The nightshade is one of my favorite plants. Did you know that consuming the ripe fruit of the spider nightshade temporarily grants one the ability to move faster than the sound they make? It's true. You think my brother moves quickly now. If you gave him a bite of spider nightshade, he'd run to the Sani-jai waterfall and back before you could even say goodbye." She smiled, still focused on her task. "Sadly, its use is discouraged in our culture, as consuming the unripe fruit is fatal." She retrieved a thin fabric from her pocket and wrapped it around his knee before surveying his other leg. "But that's hardly the fault of the plant."

Thayliss was uncertain whether she was serious or not. He assumed the former. "You're not like your brother," he said, allowing her access to the wound on his shoulder. "You're a lot less…" He was at a loss for a word.

"Animated?" she offered, smiling as she tended to his shoulder. "Quite typical of the male Lii-jit. Full of spontaneity and vigor. Not that we females are lacking. It's just that we tend to… think a little more before we act."

"And talk a lot less," he said, instantly hoping he hadn't offended her or her brother.

"Indeed," she acknowledged. "Now, this is a rather deep one." She looked around the room. "If only I had a drop of hornet's venom."

"Why don't you just summon one?" Thayliss pointed toward the open window.

Mawi-naa shook her head solemnly. "The manipulation of any living thing for personal gain is a violation of our mystic bond. We Lii-jit are tasked with protecting, guarding, and guiding the living world, not controlling it." She sighed. "I know that my eldest brother has been reckless with his gift, as have many of my kind in the years following the Three Betrayals. But it is nonetheless a tenet that I take most seriously."

"Ohlinn!" a voice bellowed from a lower level.

Thayliss rose from the bed, rushing past Mawi-naa and peering down the open core, wondering if he should attempt descending the narrow rungs or just leap down. "Tiig? What is it? Are you all right?"

Straining to look down to the room below, he suddenly saw Tiig's beaming face staring back up at him. Held tight in his fists were thick bushels of carrots, robust turnips, mustard greens, and several other brightly colored items.

"Tonight, Ohlinn, we feast!" he boldly declared, before scurrying away to prepare a meal the likes of which Thayliss had never before encountered.

CHAPTER TWENTY-THREE

"Where do we begin?" asked Lakos, taking a deep breath.

"First I must caution you," said Gris Hallis. "This is merely speculative. I recall Noryssin once postulating how such a thing could theoretically occur, but this is by no means an assurance of its safety. The make-up of a human and a mystic of any order is more dissimilar than one might think."

"Do what you must, wizard," Lakos replied. He was ready for whatever awaited him.

The old spirit-mystic was about to continue but stopped. "My Lord, before we proceed, I graciously request from you one thing. You see, as it is truly my life's mission to serve you, I will adhere to your bidding regardless of your answer."

"Speak, Hallis. What is it?" barked Lakos.

"Well, you see..." Gris Hallis fidgeted. "As you, yourself, noted, by endowing you with the ability to directly govern the mystic realms, I fear that in your estimation, I will have exhausted my own... utility. I merely ask that I am permitted to humbly remain in your service once this task is complete."

"Of course, Gris Hallis," replied Lakos. "There is no greatness without benevolence. You have my assurance; we will find purpose for you regardless. Now get on with it."

"As you wish," said Gris Hallis, lowering his head.

After softly muttering something Lakos could not decipher, Gris Hallis removed a pair of necklaces from his pocket—each consisting of a worn, leather strap tied around a solitary stone. The stone itself was beautiful, shimmering with the very same bold, sapphire blue as his eyes. The old mystic placed one of the necklaces around his own neck and then handed the other to Lakos, gesturing for him to do the same. Ever cautious, Lakos slowly complied.

"And now," said Gris Hallis, "You must walk into the mist.

Completely into it, so as to be fully enveloped by it." He pointed toward the sea of white mist at the virtual tower's immense base.

Lakos once again stepped between the kneeling Ohlinn and, taking a deep breath, strode into the dense, white fog.

He was awestruck by what he saw around him. The ethereal tower looked strikingly different from within. What had appeared from the outside as an expanse of translucent white was now utter darkness. It felt as though he had entered the night sky itself. The only similarities from before were the tiny, persisting swirls of light undulating everywhere, coursing in little rivulets in all directions, up toward the tower's distant peak dizzyingly high above before returning back down, and in ribbons that cascaded gently before his face and all around.

As he ventured further into the space, the tiny lights seemed affected by his motion, spreading before his extended arm and coalescing silently behind in a turbulent wake that soon settled back into its own organic flow.

From beyond the black space, Lakos could hear Gris Hallis speaking to him, his voice muffled but clear. "This is your first step into the true Inner Realm," he said.

Gris Hallis continued speaking, though to Lakos, his words had grown unintelligible. The sound of his voice grew intense, and though he could not understand what was being said, the words themselves seemed to be floating all around him. Like a faint mist turning swiftly to a downpour, the echoes from Gris Hallis's indecipherable speech soon radiated from every minute particle around him. Lakos covered his ears and shut his eyes. The sound was excruciating. He struggled to remain upright. To remain conscious.

Beneath his closed eyes, he could see a glow of bright blue. He gazed downward to see his necklace beaming like its own star.

And then all was silent. Lakos wondered if the transformation was complete. He looked over to where Gris Hallis and his soldiers had been standing but saw nothing. Nor could he see the three hundred Ohlinn that encircled him. He began to panic, his breath growing labored.

Then he noticed that with each breath, the miniscule flecks of light all around him seemed to enter into his lungs as he inhaled, like dust drawn into an opened bellows. Dumbfounded, he instinctively drew in a single, deep inhalation. Instantly, his chest burned and seized, dropping him to his knees in agony. He tried gasping for air, but each breath only drew more of the little lights inside of him.

The darkness around him, the waves of light, he could handle no more. He collapsed to his side, tears in his eyes, as he stared blankly into the dark.

And then he felt nothing.

CHAPTER TWENTY-FOUR

As Thayliss soon discovered, a Lii-jit banquet is an experience unto itself. After preparing his harvest for what felt like an eternity, Tiig carried plate upon plate out to the largest, widest folliad in the colony, burrowed into the trunk of a massive sana-meissa gum tree. Thayliss followed closely behind, balancing plates of his own while Tiig's eleven siblings—five male, six female—did the same. Ducking his head to fit through the miniature entrance, Thayliss was shocked to see the spaciousness of the room, the large number of attendees, and the wide variety of foods upon the room's round central table.

Curiously, the seating inside the room consisted of one continuous bench, again carved resourcefully from the tree as it rose up from the floor. The bench wrapped around the entire inner circumference of the tree, gapping only at the entryway. Patrons seated at the bench could either face the tree's inner wall, where a corresponding table surface also made its way around the room, or the open center space. Not surprisingly, the sociable little beings almost entirely chose the latter.

Realizing that he had considerably greater headroom than inside Tiig's humble home, Thayliss stood just inside the entrance, plate-in-hand, and glanced up. Rather than containing several floors, the interior of this giant tree possessed only a main, ground floor, with a high ceiling that glowed as one, uniform sheet. Squinting harder at the curiously illuminated ceiling, Thayliss noticed that the entire glowing surface appeared to ripple, like waves atop a small, electric sea.

"Sollus bats," said Mawi-naa, following his gaze upward as she stood beside him. "They possess a pigment that lets them illuminate at night."

"Convenient for us," smirked Thayliss, "but what's in it for them?"

Mawi-naa returned a gentle smile. "They feed only on trigger berries, these equally wonderful little plants that wrap their leaves around their fruit when the sun goes down. But when the plant detects the light emitted by the sollus bat, it thinks it's daytime again and opens right back up, exposing its fruit. And the bat gets what it wants."

"Ingenious," said Thayliss.

"And since we Lii-jit can't very well be mounting torches on our walls, we simply coat our ceilings with trigger berries, and the rest takes care of itself." She sat down at a free section of bench, facing the center of the room. Thayliss did likewise.

Tiig sat on his other side, a half-eaten sweet potato in his hand. "And this poor Ohlinn fellow, he had to go along for the ride!" he laughed, apparently in the midst of regaling several other captivated Lii-jit with his recent adventure.

"So how did you escape?" asked one of the life-mystics, her eyes wide.

"By the skin of my teeth, I tell you! Arrows jutting out from here and here!" He chortled, small pieces of potato spraying from his mouth as he pointed to his sides.

Thayliss couldn't believe that the little Lii-jit, captured, tortured, and forced to commit heinous deeds not one day ago could now be laughing and joking so callously.

Mawi-naa, seeming to sense his discomfort, leaned toward Thayliss and whispered, "This is how we Lii-jit deal with fear and pain. As our bodies heal more quickly than most, so, too, do our hearts. Please do not think us insensitive or uncaring. Tomorrow we will face the day however is required of us. But tonight, we celebrate this life, this moment."

Popping the last morsel of sweet potato into his mouth, Tiig loped over to Thayliss, wrapping a powerful little arm around his neck. "Eh, Ohlinn? Lucky to get out of there in one piece, we were. Actually, truth be told, I didn't!" He flexed his left hand in front of his face. "This is a right new one!"

Laughter filled the little room, as the great feast continued.

Thayliss couldn't help but admire these zealous little beings. Their behavior proved a sharp contrast to the plodding, lingering Ohlinn sensibilities he had been raised with. To the spirit-mystics, all experiences of magnitude, be they joyous or anguished, required long periods of quiet reflection. And after coming to peace with whatever event may have transpired, its memory was to always remain. Another layer, added to the texture of the spirit.

While Thayliss had only heard stories from the night of the Three Betrayals, he knew that what transpired that fateful night had changed Leonorryn forever. A layer was wrapped around his spirit so thick that it bound him for the rest of his days. Thayliss only hoped that now, in the next world, the great spirit-mystic found peace.

Thayliss smiled at his exuberant little friend and looked around the room. His heart still heavy with grief, he couldn't bring himself to eat. But he allowed himself to experience the moment to the best of his ability.

CHAPTER TWENTY-FIVE

When Lakos regained consciousness, he found himself lying on a cot within his tent outside the Bray Mountain, bathed in the soft flicker of a lantern. Having heard him rustle, a guard pushed his way through the cloth entryway.

"Feeling better, my Lord?" The soldier wore a look of genuine concern.

"Yes. I believe so." Lakos's tormented final moments inside the tower flashed in his mind. The pain. The darkness. The light.

"The old mystic had to drag you out of there, and then I carried you all the way back here," said the soldier with more than a trace of pride.

"Thank you, you may return to your post," replied Lakos. "Wait—any other news?"

"No, my Lord. That's the extent of it. All else is much as it was when you... as it was before." The guard bowed his head and exited the tent.

Lakos slowly rose to his feet, assessing his condition. He did not feel any more powerful or connected to the world. He had no new or heightened awareness. Apart from mild dizziness, he felt no different than before. Perhaps the Gray Mystic's theory was flawed, or more likely still, perhaps Gris Hallis simply lacked the skill after all to carry out the transformation on a human. There was also still the possibility that everything had, in fact, gone according to plan and that this was simply how he was meant to feel. Or, most probable of all, that this was all the product of still more mystic deception at the hands of Gris Hallis.

Lakos exited his tent and breathed in the warm, dry, night air. Still collecting his thoughts, he soon approached the archway leading to the Inner Realm, not noticing that the sapphire stone placed around his neck was now buried entirely within the flesh above his heart, casting a halo of faint blue underneath his garments.

Guard upon guard lowered his head in reverence as Lakos strode past, promptly resuming watch as he went by. Arriving at the entrance, Lakos waved the guards to part and was on the verge of entering the passageway when he heard a commotion behind him.

"My Lord, something approaches," a guard declared, lowering his glass magnifier and pointing out into the darkness.

The eerie, starless sky spread as far as he could see, with the glow emanating over the rim of the volcanic ring serving as the desert's only source of light.

Before even attempting to peer out into the dim night sky, Lakos called out, "The Masdazii approach." This sudden burst of intuition surprised even himself, but as the dark shapes drew nearer, his suspicions were quickly confirmed.

In his travels, Lakos had come to know a great many beings, both ally and foe. By far, the most technologically advanced civilization he had ever encountered was that of the Masdazii. The matter-mystics. The Masdazii were savant masters of innovation, construction, and the overall manipulation of materials. One such example was in their chosen weaponry — the sazaa. Comprising the sazaa was a series of ceremonial metallic bands, shiny metal rings that clasped like a bracelet, one after the other, down the length of each matter-mystic's thick, bloated arm. Among some of the larger Masdazii warriors, it was not uncommon to wear up to thirty such bands along each arm, extending from the base of the arm down to the wrist.

The solid metal bands themselves offered protection to the Masdazii's soft, friable flesh, but the true merit of the sazaa lay in its tendrils — the long, flexible, metallic strands descending from the underside of each ring. The tendrils trailed well behind the Masdazii and terminated in a small, teardrop-shaped silver cup with a sharp tip at the end. With one swat of his massive, pale arm, a Masdazii warrior wearing a full set of sazaa could hurl several dozen metal cups at his enemy at blinding speed. Like the crack of a whip, the razor-sharp tip could slice cleanly through virtually any substance. If an attack from a greater distance was required, a sufficiently advanced Masdazii warrior could combine this whip-attack with a spray of white-hot flame ignited from within each metal tendril's central column and ejected through the silver cup at the base. A terrifying sight from an otherwise oafish figure.

In as clear an example of irony as one may ever witness, the matter-mystics were also cave dwellers. However, this is, not surprisingly, an oversimplification. The Masdazii cave network was a dizzyingly complex interweaving of subterranean arteries, swift, hydraulic means of transportation, and even a plumbed community water system. But as far as Lakos was concerned, they were still no more than cave dwellers. Savages endowed with immense knowledge, but not a trace of intellect among them.

Of course, a lesson he had learned early on was that it was a far greater mistake to underestimate an enemy than it was to overestimate him. An enemy must be studied and learned. Not just his weaknesses but his strengths. For once you deprived an enemy of his strengths, all that remained were weaknesses. And in some cases, the strength of desperation alone may prove sufficient to turn the tide. Lakos had learned a great deal from his time secretly observing the obscure matter-mystics, often wondering how he could ever hope to defeat them when their technology enabled them to adapt to nearly any challenge and still thrive.

As he stared out into the near-darkness, Lakos could just make out the rows of Masdazii windchargers coasting along the Bray desert toward him, and smiled at the sight. With the same sense of heightened intuition that informed him of his visitors' identity, Lakos was also afforded knowledge of their intent. They were not coming to confront him, or to liberate their captured Ohlinn brethren. Lakos knew that they were merely the next step in his ascent. He no longer needed to concern himself with besting their divine technology, for that very technology now operated under his authority.

The approaching Masdazii windchargers were yet another example of matter-mystic ingenuity at work. Not impressive to look upon but laden with brilliance, much like the Masdazii themselves. The single-rider vehicles were comprised of a deep, padded seat mounted atop a flat, triangular base; its pointed end directed forward. The triangle's flat back edge ballooned up into a large white sail that billowed up ten strides into the air directly behind the rider. The true genius of the windcharger was in fact the material comprising the sail itself. Despite appearing like an accessory functioning only to slow the vehicle down, the sail provided both the means of propelling the vehicle as well as altering its course. As Masdazii cave dwellings were typically located beneath seaside cliff faces, the windcharger proved a useful means of traversing not only rocky, uneven terrain but, for short distances, the very surface of the sea itself.

The origin of the fabric had never been divulged outside of the Masdazii order, but what little information leaked outside their walls asserted that the fabric consisted of impossibly tiny particles arranged into some sort of minute lattice. The particles, so the claim went, could selectively radiate energy or absorb it, all on the unspoken request of the rider. Radiated energy propelled the vehicle, whereas absorbed energy slowed it. The percentage of the sail radiating at one moment in time dictated the windcharger's speed. Somehow electing to radiate those particles on one half of the sail would force the vehicle to turn in the opposite direction. Pure genius.

Lakos surmised that the name "windcharger" may well have been propagated by the Masdazii themselves to oversimplify their creation to a curious outer world, as it did not seem that wind had anything to do with it. Especially on this eerily still, windless night, the sheer velocity of the windchargers betrayed any credibility their name may have retained.

The hiss of the vehicles as they sliced through the fine layer of ash covering the ground roused a fair number of resting soldiers. One-by-one, the soldiers tasked with night duty assumed their posts by Lakos at the entrance to the Inner Realm while the others slept. Despite assurances from Gris Hallis that all mystic arrivals would be docile and in the same hypnotic state as the three hundred Ohlinn inside, as well as what Lakos's own newfound intuition was telling him, he would not deviate from protocol.

At Lakos's instruction, the soldiers formed a line of one hundred, matching the breadth of the incoming Masdazii. The soldiers stood in front of the Bray Mountain, hands on hilts, ready to draw.

"Twenty-five riders per row... appears to be twenty-five rows," called out a scout, peering through a magnifier. "Six-hundred-twenty-five Masdazii."

Lakos laughed to himself. The Masdazii were also notoriously particular when it came to organization and symmetry. Apparently, trances did not relieve them of this proclivity.

The first row slowed to a complete stop mere strides from where Lakos and his men stood. Seconds later, the second row stopped right behind them. Then the third, the fourth, and so on, until the perfect grid of vehicles lay idly on the dim, desert ground.

As if rehearsed to excess, the Masdazii situated to Lakos's far right exited his vehicle first and lumbered toward him, walking right past the soldiers in the direction of the chiseled archway leading to the Inner Realm. Lakos held his breath as the giant matter-mystic ventured toward the narrow tunnel, but the corpulent being made it through without issue. The Masdazii to his right subsequently exited next, following closely behind the first. And so it went.

Since his time observing the Masdazii in their native territory, Lakos had largely forgotten just how repugnant the matter-mystics truly were. Even in the dim, starless night, spared of their invariably offensive disposition, Lakos found them difficult to look at. With a height averaging a head taller than himself, but with thrice the girth, they were difficult to miss. But what Lakos found still more unsavory was their skin—parchment-thin and utterly hairless, flaking and spotted, with thin streaks of dark blue vessels coursing just beneath. It was almost the look of an undercooked berry pie that had been left in the sun for too long, with an odor to match. Perhaps the

Masdaziis' vile aesthetic was the consequence of decreased activity owing to an over-reliance on technology, coupled with a series of lifetimes spent shielded from the sun. Regardless, Lakos peered back out into the dark desert, eagerly awaiting the next arrivals.

He did not have to wait for long. Up in the sky, a series of dark figures approached. They were smaller than the klacktalli birds of the night before and seemed to lack entirely the fluid motion of wings. Lakos was perplexed. Who was approaching? What was approaching? This time, his intuition divulged nothing. He squinted at the vague mass, but it was no use. He gestured briskly to the nearby scout, who handed him his magnifier. Again, it was futile. It was simply too dark to see.

But then, just as he lowered the magnifier, Lakos saw the sky suddenly brighten, the white glow from the volcanic rim now twice as intense as before.

"My Lord, look!" shouted a soldier, pointing up behind him.

Lakos turned to see a beam of pure white light rising up from the apex of the volcanic wall. Though impossible to assess from his current vantage point, it seemed as though the sacred tower was growing taller still.

With the night sky now alight with the stark white glow of

the expanding tower behind him, Lakos once again faced the approaching mass and peered through the lens. This time, he was afforded a much clearer view of his impending visitors.

"The Lii-jit," he muttered, his voice thick with anticipation.

CHAPTER TWENTY-SIX

The Lii-jit banquet roared on well into the evening, but as late night slowly transitioned to early morning, the vast majority of revelers retreated back to their respective folliads for rest, including Tiig's many siblings. In fact, everyone but Tiig and an utterly spent Thayliss had concluded the evening.

While Tiig seemed content to continue the festivities through to the new day, Thayliss was desperate for rest. During the party, he had tried his best to share Tiig's enthusiasm, even partaking of a mug of sweet, aged spice water that left his head spinning. But eventually even the luminous sollus bats rejoined their natural domain, leaving the final two merrymakers sitting in near total darkness for the better part of the last hour.

Thayliss sat in silence, fighting to stay awake. Ohlinn custom dictated that an invitee never leave a social engagement before the one who invited him. Thayliss had spent much of the past hour trying to convince himself that Ohlinn customs should apply only to Ohlinn participants. However, his conscience would not allow it.

For Tiig's part, he hadn't said a word since the room grew dark. Perhaps he had gotten comfortable atop an expanse of bench and was now dreaming of whatever it was a Lii-jit found in his dreams. Thayliss had seen him consume an exorbitant volume of spice water.

"Ohlinn, can you see the future?" a small voice asked from the darkness.

Thayliss paused, recalling a time when he had asked Leonorryn the very question. "An Ohlinn cannot see the future as a glance down an unknown road," Thayliss said, as he himself had been told so many years ago. "Or a page in a book, to be referenced as needed. To the Ohlinn, spirit visions are merely the product of a meditative sense of receptivity. Less a look through a window than the opening of a window. What flies into the room once the window is open is beyond Ohlinn control. But the very presence of the window, that is what makes the Ohlinn special."

There was again silence. Thayliss wondered if he had over-answered the question.

"Have you seen what happens by the coming of the new day? What becomes of my kin?" asked Tiig, a fragility in his voice that Thayliss had not yet encountered.

Thayliss wanted to tell the poor life-mystic that he foresaw a great victory with Tiig at the forefront of an epic battle, heroically emerging victorious before his adoring family, and with all order once again restored to the world. He wanted to lie.

"No," he replied finally. "I have seen nothing."

"So be it," sighed Tiig. "I reckon we should get back to—"

An anguished scream cut through the rainforest, triggering an outburst of cries, caws, howls, and hollers from every creature within a hundred-stride radius.

"My family!" said Tiig, grabbing Thayliss by the shoulder. "We must move."

They raced out into the jungle, tearing through the tangle of vines, rocks, and muddy creeks leading to Tiig's folliad. Dozens of startled Lii-jit scrambled through the trees and across the misty ground all around them. Another scream echoed from off to one side. The jungle was alight with frantic activity, everyone seemingly racing to a different place.

Finally, they arrived at Tiig's folliad. He stormed into the base floor and looked around. "Is anyone here?" he called out, but there was no reply.

Thayliss was on the verge of stooping to enter the folliad when Tiig ran out past him and began climbing the outside of the tree, a blur of activity darting upwards, leaving only a trail of shaking branches and jostled vines in his wake. Thayliss contemplated following suit, having spent his entire life in the trees, but the Lii-jit's blinding speed convinced him otherwise.

Another Lii-jit ran past Thayliss, disappearing back into the dark, steamy flora as quickly as it had appeared. The little beings zipped in all directions. It was chaos.

Thayliss suddenly felt a small hand on his shoulder, grasping it tightly.

"Thayliss, thank the spirits. Something horrible has happened. I think it's the humans." The utter terror in Mawi-naa's voice cut through Thayliss.

He turned around, but before he could offer words of comfort, he saw her eyes suddenly grow wide. She released her grip from his shoulder, her hand dropping loosely to her side. Slowly, breathlessly, she stumbled backwards, her lip trembling, eyes fixed on Thayliss.

Tiig appeared from overhead, dropping to his feet from an obscene height. "Mawi-naa, my dear sister. The humans are taking us away. They've already taken the others. We must flee," he pleaded, reaching his hand out to her. "Thayliss," he added, "see if you can find any—"

Tiig stopped in his tracks, turning his head back just enough to see the scant early morning light shine through the canopy onto the face of Thayliss. The human.

CHAPTER TWENTY-SEVEN

Lakos watched with pleasure as the stream of Lii-jit filling the sky ahead drew near.

When required to travel great distances or in large numbers, the Lii-jit occasionally utilized the services of the desiccadi moth, a giant, winged creature with a robust abdomen and set of fur-covered antennae. The antennae possessed the ability to gauge subtle changes in wind currents, as the slightest unexpected gust could bat the great behemoth from the sky. However, as they could also remain airborne while burdened with a great weight, the Lii-jit would suspend large woven baskets beneath them, sufficiently sturdy to accommodate up to twenty passengers.

To Lakos's delight, that capacity appeared to be exceeded in almost every instance as the swarm continued its circuitous path toward him. He had imagined the life-mystics would prove the most difficult acquisition. Not that the Masdazii or the Ohlinn were themselves without a degree of elusiveness, but for some reason, Lakos had always viewed the Lii-jit through a slightly different lens. In some ways, they were the most human. Their temperament, their social and family structure—fiercely protective of their own kind—were traits more easily relatable. There was no baseless abstraction or mystery, like the Ohlinn. No obsessive Masdazii industriousness. They were simply a being, fighting for their place in the world.

As the swarm reached the mountainside, they did not slow. Nor did they descend to the desert ground. Rather, they continued over the top of the volcanic upper rim, toward the monstrous, glowing white spire within it.

"Moths to a flame," Lakos muttered to himself, recalling Gris Hallis's words.

He watched the travelers soaring high overhead, before

disappearing into the light beyond the ridge. As he did so, any lingering trace of the reverence he once harbored toward the Lii-jit degraded back to contempt. In spite of whatever mystic witchcraft he had subjected himself to back in the Inner Realm, he was human to the very core. The mystics were his sworn enemy. When his mission was complete, he would rule the mystic orders without mercy. He did not want their respect. He wanted their fear. Their lives.

Like grease to a fire, Lakos felt his rage build and glow hot. He felt a power course through his body that he had never before encountered. Looking up at the horde of mammoth insects above, Lakos smiled a sinister grin.

Without conscious awareness of what he was doing, Lakos found a specimen to his liking and studied the undercarriage of the woven basket packed with mystified Lii-jit.

Compelled by a strange, new awareness, Lakos willed mayhem upon his chosen target. At that precise instant, five-hundred strides above where he stood, a brief flash of white light illuminated the dim, early morning sky.

As the sky regained its subdued, purple hues, Lakos could see the intricately woven basket soaring high above mysteriously come apart. The group of Lii-jit clustered within it fell through the opened flooring. As the eighteen tiny figures descended, Lakos savored every second of their journey, eagerly anticipating their impact on the unforgiving desert ground. He watched in ecstasy. It appeared as though his experience within the mist of the budding sacred tower had indeed been a success. He was becoming a weapon. A god.

Lakos watched as the Lii-jit descended closer and closer to the ground. None of the other captives seemed to take any notice, with the line of Masdazii still marching dutifully through the passageway, and the remaining Lii-jit continuing their trek across the sky and over the volcanic ring. Only Lakos and a number of his enthralled soldiers watched the event unfold.

Then, just at the moment of impact, the eighteen plummeting Lii-jit vanished. In their place, eighteen clouds of ash burst upon the ground, gradually assimilating into the surrounding desert debris.

"What?" screamed Lakos, enraged.

Near the archway, edging his way upstream against the incoming goliath Masdazii, was Gris Hallis.

Lakos glared at the old Ohlinn.

"I gave their spirits to the Inner Realm. As was their purpose," said Gris Hallis, sternly. "We must be prudent. There will be ample time for exerting authority, but this is a time for gathering power, not dispensing it. I know what you must be feeling, my lord. The intoxicating, boundless energy surging through you. You wield within your being a power greater than any previously experienced by mankind. But be cautious, for your tower is not yet made of stone. That moment will swiftly be upon us, but until that time, your kingdom is still but a haze. An illusion."

Lakos was livid. "Hear this, Ohlinn, it is I who wield the power of the Inner Realm now. You may have facilitated my transformation, but you are no more than a servant. A servant who has an unfortunate tendency toward overstepping his boundaries."

"But you wield a power you have yet to fully comprehend," Gris Hallis persisted. "The mystics no longer require crude prisons lined with stones to join your army. As the energy within the sacred tower grows, so too does its thirst for it. And just as the rose embedded within the outer wall drew one of your soldiers near, the power flowing from the Inner Realm now encompasses the whole of our world."

"You are mistaken," fired Lakos. "The tower obeys my command. For as you can see, only mystics are brought to me. All humans beyond our realm remain free, for I have willed it to be so."

Gris Hallis would not relent. "All sentient beings are drawn to the Inner Realm, including humans. However, the force of attraction is relative to the inherent power within the being itself. Humans do not venture to the Inner Realm because the realm itself has no use for them at this time. Likewise, the mystics who do come are but the most powerful of their kind. But fear not—once the sacred tower is complete, all beings shall be under your control."

A cold calm washed over Lakos. "Mystic, how you have managed to elude my blade for this long, I shall never know. All the same, I promised to spare your life—a promise I had fully intended to keep. But I now see with a wisdom and clarity that even an ancient Ohlinn like yourself could not hope to comprehend. And do you know what I see? Jealousy, spite, desperation, and deception. The truth is, the age of the human has arrived. And I now wield a power greater than any mystic order. Or any tower." Lakos stepped toward the old mystic, slowly unsheathing his sword. "Unfortunately, what is equally clear to me is that your allegiance lies not with me, but with your kind. And I can't very well have that now, can I?"

Still, Gris Hallis stood his ground. "My lord, as I have said since our first meeting, my support of your ambition is unwavering. I will follow you to the end. But your threats of violence against me must cease," he said bluntly. "I request that you re-sheath your sword before you do something you'll regret."

"Old wizard, I'm afraid that this will be an action I will never regret," laughed Lakos, raising his sword in front of the old mystic.

"The—the stone—the necklace that you wore, during the ceremony at the Inner Realm..." Gris Hallis blurted, squinting, and turning his head away from the imposing figure before him.

"What of it? If you wish it returned to you and buried with your headless body, I'm afraid I will do no such thing. Perhaps

CHAPTER TWENTY-SEVEN

I'll pawn it for a mug of cider. Now return to your spirit world, demon!"

"Without the necklace, you will die!" cried Gris Hallis.

Enraged still further, Lakos pressed the blade of his longsword against Gris Hallis's neck. "Speak wizard, or your time will end."

"The—the necklace—it binds us. Our spirits were linked when you entered into the tower." Gris Hallis turned his face away from Lakos.

"Wizard, what have you done?" The edge of Lakos's sword wavered before the old Ohlinn's throat.

"It is the Tierren bond," continued Gris Hallis, "an ancient Ohlinn mark of brotherhood. A way our forbearers prevented warfare within the order. The leader of every worldly Ohlinn realm would become bound, as you and I have become, with a substance derived from pure mystic energy. The moment this energy penetrates the flesh, it envelops the very heart of its owner, and the bond is established. Should one king ever attempt to take the life of another, and the sacred bond become broken, the energy absorbs that of its owners, and all in that brotherhood would perish. If you kill me, you, too, will die."

Lakos eased his grip on his sword, letting his arm fall to his side. Instinctively, he touched his chest and glanced down, for the first time noticing the faint blue glow permeating through his flesh.

"Trickery!" he screamed, outraged but helpless.

"I granted you the powers you requested," replied Gris Hallis. "I merely afforded myself the assurance of a role within your kingdom."

Lakos peered at one of the guards who stood by, watching in disbelief. "And if I simply have one of my guards dispatch you?" he asked.

"A death by your order is a death by your hand, my Lord," replied the crafty Ohlinn. "Starve me, poison me, unleash a pack of bastik wolves upon me. The intent is such that your blade, held in your hand, may as well have cut my throat."

"So, my life is forever dependent upon yours..." muttered Lakos, feeling his knees weaken beneath him.

"In a sense. Now, were I to perish from natural causes, or even through the sword of an unrelated party, you would suffer no ill effects. But any degree of relation, any process whereby you stand to gain through my loss, and your demise would swiftly follow. So, to that end, yes, our lives are forever linked."

Lakos returned his sword to its sheath. In the span of a heartbeat, his elation twisted to blind rage, before finally descending into acrid despondency.

"My Lord," chirped Gris Hallis. "Think not of me in ill terms, I implore you. I wish only to serve and to survive to see the prophecy realized. These are not woeful times. Your sacred kingdom blooms before you." He ventured back into the Inner Realm.

Lakos, his mind scattershot with thoughts and emotions disturbingly foreign to him, followed closely behind.

CHAPTER TWENTY-EIGHT

Tiig glared at Thayliss. "You betrayed me! You deceitful, villainous creature. I brought you to my home. My family tended to your wounds," he said, the very words causing him pain. "I could end your life, wretched human, and you would never see it coming."

Mawi-naa anxiously tugged on Tiig's arm. "Tiig, please, we must do something. Our family is gone. Hundreds from our colony have boarded the desiccadi and taken to the sky. Their sense has abandoned them. They are in some manner of trance and cannot be revived. So many have already been taken, and still more prepare to leave."

"Yet another plague wrought by black human hearts," said Tiig bitterly. "The Ohlinn were wise to expel you. And I a fool to trust you. This is not forgotten," he said, following Mawi-naa farther into the jungle. "This shall never be forgotten."

Thayliss stood on the dim rainforest floor, helplessly watching as all manner of creatures scurried madly about. The world was slipping away from him. He had lost his home and his family—his love—in the span of a day. He had been imprisoned and battered. Banished and accused of involvement in the very atrocities that destroyed his own life. Was it even his world to lose?

Thayliss had begged for death while held captive in that rolling cell. But the spirits showed him no mercy, just like the human behind his anguish, the one they called Lakos. Thayliss was an innocent victim. Even if all around him marked him a villain, he knew the truth. Leysiia and Leonorryn, his two most cherished spirits, undoubtedly waiting for him in the next world, knew the truth as well.

Thayliss recalled the meditation he had experienced while inside the cell. The vision of Leysiia showing him the way out.

She did not simply comfort him in a time of distress, as spirit visions were often said to do. Nor had she nodded peacefully in acknowledgement that his pain and suffering would soon end, thus reuniting them within the next world. She wanted him to escape from that prison. To be free. To fight.

Thayliss would be a victim no longer. He had not asked for this to happen, and he did not deserve the wretched fate brought down upon him. He knew he was innocent, but innocence did not prevent pain. The Ohlinn passivity toward injustice would not stand. While he was raised Ohlinn, he was born a human. He had been wearing a mask, just as the Ohlinn captives had accused him of. He longed to be a spirit-mystic, like the kind and wise Leonorryn, like Leysiia, but he was human and that could not be changed.

He would be passive no longer. He would fight back.

Thayliss gathered his senses enough to notice the telltale blur of a Lii-jit, darting across the mossy floor before leaping to the vines nearby. After watching it scramble up the tree beside him, Thayliss leapt to the lowest branch and pulled himself up, climbing in fast pursuit. Wherever they were headed, he would go too.

Despite lacking the typical balance and proportions of an Ohlinn, Thayliss fancied himself an excellent tree climber, able to ascend one of the great Valla oaks back home with near the same speed, if none of the finesse, of a true Ohlinn. His abilities, however, proved sorely inadequate in the realm of the Lii-jit, as the little sprite he sought to follow climbed up and out of sight by the time Thayliss was little more than ten strides up.

Up above the thick rainforest canopy, Thayliss could see a broad, whirring motion, as if two small ships' sails were being shaken by some demented sailor. The motion was so great, in fact, that Thayliss could feel the breeze reaching down through the tangle of leaves and vines and brushing his face.

Then another Lii-jit raced past him on its way up to the

canopy. Then another. He reached futilely for the next branch, but it was too late. The whirring intensified, so much that the branches of the densely packed rainforest trees pushed apart, their flexible trunks bending away from each other, affording Thayliss a clear view of what was transpiring above the canopy. A number of Lii-jit, he counted at least fifteen, had boarded a type of woven carriage. Above them, attached to them somehow, was a monstrous, frightful-looking winged insect. The insect beat its wings faster still, raising both itself and its many passengers just above the tree line before flying away.

Thayliss's heart sank as he slid back down to the ground. All around him, occasional streaks of color darted to and fro as Lii-jit bustled to whatever destination beckoned, their numbers greatly reduced from the masses that had brought the jungle to life just a few moments prior. The once deafening clamor inside the jungle had also quieted considerably, and Thayliss felt the moment passing him by.

He refused to give up. He scanned the treetops, desperately searching for another carriage. It was difficult to see through the lush bloom of flora but he saw one, off to the side. However, before he could reach it, it, too, raised to the sky and vanished. At the far end of the jungle, perhaps one hundred strides across uneven, shrub-laden terrain, Thayliss could see what appeared to be the last of the treetop baskets, the broad, whirring wings above it slowly beating faster.

Thayliss wouldn't accept defeat. He paced the rocky, shrub-laden ground, anxiously searching for a solution. Then it came to him.

"The spider nightshade!" he shouted.

Thayliss scanned the layers of lush, abundant plant life all around him, desperate to find the miraculous fruit Mawi-naa had spoken of. Unfortunately, he had no idea what to look for. He saw countless exotic organisms, all of which were completely foreign to him, but nothing that seemed to suit the name.

"Spider... eight legs... eight stems? Eight leaves? A web? Grows in a web? Forms a web?" He searched and searched but to no avail.

Off in the distance, he could hear the small cluster of trees begin shaking more vigorously, each of them starting to bend away from the others from the force of the giant wings beating above them.

Thayliss persevered, leaping over decaying logs, ducking under vines, and sifting through piles of fallen leaves, but nothing suitable emerged. Finally, exhausted, he collapsed upon a boulder and rested his face in his hands.

Defeated, he glanced down at the base of the large rock beneath him. Then he saw it. Right where the boulder met the ground was a bulbous, fist-sized, purple shell, sitting inconspicuously atop some leaves and broken branches. Radiating from all sides of the round, shiny object were what appeared to be long, furry roots, eight in all. Thayliss was sure that within the hard outer shell he would find the fruit of the spider nightshade. He had to.

Hearing the trees in the distance bend back still farther, Thayliss knew there was no time to waste. He grabbed the object and pulled, separating it, along with all eight of its roots, from the rock. He struck it hard against the rock, but it did not split. Again, he brought it down against the massive boulder, harder than before, but still without success. Sweat poured down his forehead, stinging his eyes as he looked helplessly at the encased fruit resting defiantly atop the rock.

Beside the fruit, a tiny insect crawled along the surface of the boulder. Thayliss watched in amazement as one of the nightshade's long, pendulous roots began snaking along the side of the rock, heading toward the insect. He noticed that along the underside of the fruit was a base that appeared hollow, as if a very narrow core had been drilled into it. He picked up the fruit and brought it down onto the insect, core-side down, and held his breath. Within moments, the fruit's outer shell simply peeled back, revealing a brown, gummy inner substance.

Thayliss's surge of relief quickly vanished as he recalled the second part of Mawi-naa's story—that consuming the spider nightshade's unripe fruit was fatal. The bilious brown mass inside did not strike Thayliss as meeting his definition of "ripe", but he had to take the chance.

Delving several fingers into the goop, Thayliss scooped out as much as he could, shut his eyes, and forced it down his throat.

When his eyes opened, the chaotic world around him seemed to be operating at a fraction of its previous pace. He could see every insect and animal swirling in space. Gravity itself had slowed, though he seemed to not just be immune to its effects but to be experiencing the reverse. A toad leapt toward the rock he sat upon, and he watched every tense muscle, nearly frozen in time, as the small animal soared through the open air. Thayliss also saw a small handful of Lii-jit slowly pass by, waving their hands toward the final departing treetop carriage.

He needed to act. Thayliss rose to his feet and started off in the direction of the bent trees. Mid-way into his first stride, he found himself so far beyond the running Lii-jit that he could barely see them racing behind. He arrived at base of one of the trees before his next breath.

Glancing up, he saw that the basket had already detached from the canopy and started its departure. Taking another breath, he began climbing the tree as fast as he could. He ascended fluidly up the tree, pushing off from the thinnest of branches as if they had been made of the sturdiest oak. He surged upward, breaking through the canopy to see the basket still several strides above him. Planting a foot on the uppermost branch, Thayliss readied himself to jump, his hand stretching out toward the basket full of Lii-jit who merely stared blankly forward, oblivious.

As he leapt, he suddenly felt the effects of the nightshade

wear off. The thin, spindly branch he lifted off from snapped as the world around him resumed its normal pace. He lunged weakly into the air toward the carriage, far above the unforgiving ground below.

His body stretched to its limit, Thayliss felt his fingers barely curl over the top of the basket. Bringing his other hand over the edge, Thayliss pulled himself into the basket as the giant insect directly above him fluttered, taking them far from the rainforest.

Thayliss collapsed in a heap and hung his head, utterly exhausted. Looking around him, he could see the cluster of Lii-jit still lost in their collective daze, unaware of their current predicament, let alone his presence among them. Suddenly, the bitter, overpowering taste of the nightshade fruit overtook his senses. He felt his abdomen seize and he gagged, coughing and sputtering until the pangs of nausea gradually subsided.

It was going to be a long trip.

CHAPTER TWENTY-NINE

Gris Hallis ventured eagerly through the tunnel leading to the Inner Realm, grinning back at Lakos as if nothing had transpired outside the walls of the ridge.

"A lot has changed since you retreated back to your tent for recuperation," he said. "The construction is ongoing, but we are nonetheless confident that you will be pleased."

Lakos said nothing, simply following the old mystic toward the white light beaming through at the other end.

"Your sacred tower, my Lord," proudly declared Gris Hallis, stepping through into the Inner Realm.

As Lakos emerged from the passageway, he was astonished by what he saw. While it retained its conical silhouette and striking white glow, the massive tower before him was no longer a mere ghostly haze. Giant blocks of smooth ivory stone wrapped around the column of light, each row staggered precisely above the last, raising the height of the tower. Strategically placed gaps in the stone no doubt served as windows from which to view the remainder of the Inner Realm, which, to Lakos's disbelief, had also altered itself nearly beyond recognition.

Lakos walked farther into his domain, assessing the majesty around him. On his last foray into the great, open space, the Inner Realm had consisted solely of an immense cylinder of smooth, sheer, white, volcanic rock surrounding a barren, anemic, powdery floor. But he now saw a living world unto itself, basking under the white glow of the tower. Thick strands of green ivy wrapped themselves around the cavernous inner wall, leaves unfolding and small, yellow flowers blooming before his eyes. Even the once-sterile ground beneath him had come alive, as white powder and traces of rubble were replaced with all manner of vegetation. He saw olive and other fruit trees burst from the ground, each bearing the largest, most abundant offerings Lakos had ever encountered. He was in awe.

"Your kingdom, my Lord, is now very much a reality," said Gris Hallis, directing him down an opulent white stone path that parted the copious greenery and led to the tower's surprisingly small, narrow entrance.

Lakos was still speechless, noticing more with every glance. Small creeks and rivulets forged erratic paths in the distance, weaving between large, moss-covered stones. Small, obscenely bright-colored birds fluttered from flower to flower, chirping their delight. He thought that he could even see the shape of several pygmy deer amidst the shadows of a humble congregation of willow trees.

"Everything you shall ever require can now be found within these walls. The cleanest water, the most succulent fruits and vegetables in all the realms. Animals to hunt for food or leisure. And gardens of the finest spice trees you are likely to find," declared Gris Hallis, as they made their way to the tower. "And should you require anything not to be found within these walls, at the mere suggestion of it, I will see it done."

"This realm is truly a miracle," said Lakos. "But should I have needs beyond its boundary, I will see them done myself."

Gris Hallis stopped and placed a hand gently upon Lakos's shoulder. "My Lord, you do not understand. To assume the throne of the Voduss Grei comes not without sacrifice. However, look all around you—the price of never again leaving the sacred Inner Realm is but the smallest price to pay, considering the vast power and ultimate authority it grants you."

Lakos once again felt deceived by the old mystic. However, he knew his actions needed to be muted. "Wizard," he said, attempting to contain himself, "this is to be my world, then? For the remainder of my days?"

"It is your paradise, my Lord," Gris Hallis replied. "And there is more to show. Please, come with me."

"Not quite the grand entrance one would expect for a mythic

tower," muttered Lakos, standing directly before the tower's modest entryway.

Gris Hallis again smiled. "Greatness shrouded in modesty, my Lord, much like the exterior of the Bray Ridge itself. However, this is but a temporary entrance. Come," he urged, guiding Lakos over the threshold.

Following the old Ohlinn into the tower, Lakos's ire was once again tempered by what he saw around him. In his travels, Lakos had seen innumerable castles and palatial estates, but none compared to this.

In one sense, it was no more than a straight, narrow corridor with a high ceiling, perhaps twenty strides in length. But to stand amidst the passageway's indescribable opulence was staggering. Lakos was first struck by the floor itself. Beneath his feet were a collection of porcelain tiles, each bearing colors so bold and a pattern so complex as to seem more a hallucination than an actuality. But it was all very real. He walked deeper into the corridor, awestruck by both the architecture and the quality of the materials utilized.

"Masdazii ingenuity," said Gris Hallis. "Quite striking, is it not?"

Walls of pure marble covered the narrow corridor, spanning a height of thirty strides and terminating in a ceiling of a pure white material that flowed and swirled across its entire length in a divine, almost living manner. Lakos noticed that further down the walls were intricately carved wooden sconces, adhered to the marble by some unknown force. Between the sconces were a series of inlaid sculptures, dozens in all, carved directly into the marble wall.

Lakos approached the first and inspected it closely. It portrayed a being, taller than himself but thin. Its hair was long and straight, resting just past the shoulders, and it wore a narrow, pointed beard. Its arms were clasped in front, and on its face Lakos could see a great sorrow, as if burdened with a great weight.

"That was Melleandus, the first of the Voduss Grei," said Gris Hallis solemnly. "Noryssin told me tales of his origin, of how all this first came to be." He continued down the corridor. "His was a most regrettable fate."

Lakos wanted to probe further but instead walked over to the next figure, and then the next, seeing that each marble carving bore the image of a being standing upright and solemn, with much the same melancholy expression.

"We stand in the great hall of ages," said Gris Hallis. "You will find etched into these walls the form of every Gray Mystic to have ever ruled this world."

Lakos felt the room take on a more ominous feel. As if he were being watched, judged by countless spirits, bitter that their own time had come and gone.

Gris Hallis approached the final sculpture and stared upon it, a reverent look upon his face. "Noryssin," he said, turning to Lakos. "The one who raised me."

"The one who denied you all of this," said Lakos sharply.

"Indeed," said Gris Hallis, slowly turning from the sculpture and walking away.

"So where am I?" asked Lakos, searching amongst the many figures.

Gris Hallis paused, smiling. "Such anxiety, my Lord. By the time you venture through the other end of the corridor, rest assured, you, too, will adorn these walls for all eternity. For the great hall grows ever-longer with each new age. As the virtues of wisdom and caution grow long with experience, so too must each prospective new Gray Mystic travel farther than the one who preceded him. Or her. More distance to walk, more time to contemplate the gravity of the responsibility. If this is truly to be your fate, my Lord," Gris Hallis gestured to the darkness beyond the corridor, "your kingdom awaits."

Lakos walked through the end of the corridor without

so much as a moment's hesitation. He had come too far and sacrificed too much to turn back now. He was going to see this through.

It was his destiny.

CHAPTER THIRTY

Still feeling the final waves of nausea percolating within his gut, Thayliss pulled himself to his feet and turned toward the mass of Lii-jit.

"Please," he pleaded. "You must all listen to me. Whatever spell they've pulled you under, you must fight it. This dark power—it destroyed my home. They enslaved the Ohlinn, and they'll do the same to the Lii-jit if you don't stop them. Listen to me—We must fight!

Thayliss watched as his impassioned plea fell on deaf ears. The crowd of Lii-jit merely stared blankly ahead, silent.

He had to do something before it was too late. He grabbed the shoulders of the life-mystic nearest him and shook. "Please, I beg of you, summon the strength to break free from this curse. You can control these creatures—you can turn them around, all of them, and send your kind back to the rainforest. If you do not do this, the freedom of your kind may be lost forever!"

The wiry little mystic looked up at him, saying nothing. Thayliss felt a sharp pain in his side. He released his grip from the Lii-jit and looked down.

A tiny black bird had appeared, as if from the air itself, and pecked diligently at his ribs. Each thrust of its tiny beak brought pangs of sharp, searing pain as it repeatedly burrowed into his flesh. Thayliss cried out in pain, protecting his bloodied side while swatting at the tiny creature until finally it relented and flew safely out of range, squawking angrily at him.

Thayliss's side throbbed. He glanced down and saw a dozen tiny, bloody perforations that, while superficial, stung nonetheless.

Thayliss again reached out to the Lii-jit but noticed that doing so brought the same small, black bird closer to him. Aware that such powers coursed through every fiber of the Lii-jit, Thayliss stepped back. He eyed the bird, who in turn studied him, as if assessing a threat. Eventually, seeming appeased, the tiny bird descended back down to wherever it had come.

It was futile. Any attempted intervention while still airborne would be akin to suicide. He would have to wait.

Massaging his aching side, Thayliss grasped the wall of the basket and peered out into the space around him. By this time, the morning sun was bisected evenly along the horizon, casting its soft, yellow rays across the varied lands below. Glancing down, Thayliss could see that they were traversing a flat, open grassland.

In the distance, he could see many realms all around him. Left in their wake, he saw the edge of the Sani-jai rainforest and the mist from its great waterfall, small in the distance. Not far from there, he saw the rocky coastal outcropping where the Masdazii had reportedly retreated to long ago. He wondered if they, too, had been recruited to serve Lakos's evil purposes. Thayliss scanned the many distant lands, spotting numerous miniature congregations of buildings, smoke pouring from their faraway chimneys — the unmistakable mark of human settlement.

From the other side of the carriage, away from the sun, he could only faintly visualize the gentler, more hospitable seaside clearing at Merrin Ells, its smokeless chimneys not yet stoked for the morning's fires. Nearby, he could also see the greenery of the Valla Forest, still shrouded in early morning darkness.

The sight brought to mind memories of the countless mornings he'd woken to the sounds of Leonorryn fussing to replace or repair any and all aspects of their modest little cabin. One morning, Thayliss had woken to a bright strip of early sunlight cast upon his face, squinting his bleary eyes to see the old Ohlinn in the midst of replacing one of the planks of his bedroom's outer wall. Despite possessing by a wide margin the most intricately carved abode in the community, the great elder never seemed satisfied with the state of their living arrangements. The notions of valuing possessions or of elevated status were unheard of in the Ohlinn culture, and Thayliss never could determine why Leonorryn was perpetually restless, tweaking, adjusting, and improving their humble home. And he had never thought to ask.

Turning his gaze from the Valla Forest, Thayliss shifted his attention to the direction they were now headed. Specifically, the one feature conspicuously dominating the landscape. The Bray Ridge, no less imposing while looking down upon it, rising defiantly within the void of gray desert surrounding it.

However, the most striking sight was not the great volcano itself, but what shone within it. A brilliant white spire rose high above the volcanic outer rim, surpassing the mountain's height by half and appearing to pierce the sky itself. The light emanating from the mystical structure seemed in competition with the rising sun, casting much of the desert around it in full, stark daylight.

Thayliss knew full well where this ride was taking him. He need but trace the unending stream of giant insects coursing ahead of him, each bearing a multitude of passengers, for that to be made abundantly clear. But he felt a new sense of dread on actually seeing his destination boldly displayed before him.

CHAPTER THIRTY-ONE

Having traversed the corridor, Lakos strode into the cavernous, circular room beyond. The grand courtyard was endowed with all the opulence of the hallway preceding it. Long reels of rich, vibrant tapestries cascaded down the walls, the bold colors vividly portraying a collection of noble figures wearing all manner of regalia. Yet another effigy of the lineage of the Voduss Grei, surmised Lakos. Alternating between the portraits were wall-mounted torches that burned brightly from within their tarnished brass sconces. The courtyard's staggered stone flooring was interrupted by a series of tall marble columns that rose stoically to suspend the vast, high ceiling above. It was truly the threshold of a kingdom.

Along the perimeter of the room stood a series of tall archways, ten in all, spaced evenly along the curved wall around him, with each leading down a separate dark, stone passage. Deviating from the pattern was the one archway immediately in front of him. The darkness beneath its threshold was not the simple black of unlit space. Rather, it possessed the same ethereal quality that Lakos had experienced during his earlier transformation. The darkness beyond the archway ahead was speckled with the same swirling lights coalescing and dissolving of their own celestial accord, clearly visible from across the room.

Gris Hallis approached the first passageway to his left. "The prison catacombs begin here," he said with a chortle. "Masdazii nature, obsessed with digging bewildering networks of tunnels and arteries. Brilliant in its own way, mind you, and a startlingly effective dungeon, but a challenge on first acquaintance. Fear not, I know every stone, every shadow in this tower. And soon you, too, will grow accustomed to it." He pointed to the next door. "This door leads to the food storage chambers. You'll find that—"

"What of this passage?" Lakos interrupted, pointing toward the emptiness beyond the archway ahead of him.

"Of course," replied Gris Hallis, starting off in the direction of the mysterious archway. "There will be plenty of time to explore the other passages. Within this archway lies the black gate, which leads to your throne room. Come, follow me."

Lakos trailed behind Gris Hallis as they crossed the shimmering floor, within moments crossing the threshold of the open archway. As he stepped out of the brightly lit main room and through the arch, Lakos was once again enveloped by the sensation that he was amongst the stars. The sound of their footsteps echoed almost metallically in the void, and Lakos made sure not to lose sight of Gris Hallis as the old mystic navigated through the black.

"Set your fears aside. You'll not experience a repeat of the discomfort you last felt while walking in this domain. Traversing through the black gate is merely a physical journey. A mystic staircase if you will. And surely better than the alternative." Gris Hallis smiled, his words muffled almost as though spoken underwater.

After several more strides, they approached a light. Having a target with which to orient himself, Lakos moved past Gris Hallis. With a final step, he saw the infinite tiny specks of light around him disperse, granting Lakos entry into another room.

The circular room was modest in size, but as with the great corridor, adorned with much the same opulent design and wondrous endowments. An ornate wooden railing encircled the room's outer wall, framing a broad, continuous section of wall that had been cut away, exposing the throne room on all sides to the world outside. The opening stretched five strides up the wall, with only four thin, wooden beams spaced evenly around the perimeter to support the tower's majestic spire. It was inexplicable.

Gazing through the vast, open windows, Lakos could see beyond the Bray range's upper rim and across the desert, the view extending far beyond the boundaries of the known world. He could also hear the whistling wind cresting overtop the Bray Ridge as it plunged into the Inner Realm. However, the air within the throne room, exposed as it was to the elements outside, was completely still. It seemed the throne room, as with everything within the sacred tower, was laden with secrets.

Lakos's eyes continued up the solid wall above to the top of the tower, where the conical peak converged into a single point from which a glorious, golden-white chandelier descended. Lacking the traditional space for candles, the metallic patina of the entire piece brilliantly illuminated the room. At the very center of the room, directly beneath the chandelier, stood a throne bearing the same majestic yellow sheen. The seat was draped in lush red fabric, its arms and back wrapped in vines bearing crystalline purple and white flowers.

With Gris Hallis by his side, Lakos approached the throne, running his hand along one of the vines, and took his place at the helm of his kingdom. He peered out the vast, open panorama before him and sighed.

"What is your first order of business, my Lord?" asked Gris Hallis, like a lost child overjoyed to be returned to his father's side.

"Just enjoying the view," said Lakos, absorbing the sensation.

As Lakos gazed through the open span of window, something peculiar caught his attention. The tiny sparks of organic light darted across the window's surface, though in drastically lower numbers than within the black gate. Rather, they comprised the window's surface. The tiny lights were somehow responsible for the energy required to keep the tower's narrow spire hovering in place. Watching the sparks dart and swirl, blaze bright and then fade, Lakos was enchanted.

"My Lord," said Gris Hallis with urgency in his voice,

directing Lakos to the other side of the room.

Lakos turned to see the tiny light fragments grow cloudy within one section of window. As they gathered, the lights formed an opacity that obscured his view. However, the rippling white canvas soon projected an image upon itself. It was of a desiccadi moth, one of the many currently delivering its cargo across the Bray desert. Inside the woven vessel it carried, one passenger appeared starkly incongruous to the rest.

"He aims to rob you of your power," said Gris Hallis. "He comes here to stop you."

Lakos stared at the figure—a human, but with an odd familiarity about him.

"My Lord? What is your plan?" asked Gris Hallis.

Lakos's glare grew deathly cold. "To take him from the sky," he replied, his hand tightly gripping the arm of his throne. "And this time, you shall not deprive me of watching this one perish."

CHAPTER THIRTY-TWO

Thayliss saw the terrain below transition from flat grassland to the dull, ashen desert he had escaped from just the previous day. The Bray Ridge, with its massive, blazing, white central peak, drew nearer.

After his attempts at reasoning with the Lii-jit on board the craft proved futile, Thayliss had spent the duration of the flight devising a new strategy. With limited options, he figured he stood as good a chance of success as any by simply trying to disappear within the crowd of Lii-jit upon landing.

While close inspection, or even marginally close inspection, would show otherwise, he had, over the past day, come to the conclusion that he was not so different from them. Morphologically-speaking, at least. He was a head taller, with paler skin and longer, fuller features than the muscular little beings, but he seemed a more reasonable Lii-jit doppelganger than he ever did an Ohlinn. He also thanked the spirits that he was not being forced to blend in with a group of Masdazii. He lacked both the physique and the rancor for that.

As he had carefully laid out in his mind, Thayliss would wait until they landed inside the massive crater. He did not know what immediate fate awaited the captives upon their arrival, but he had noticed that one-by-one, each giant moth soared over the volcanic ridge and slowly descended with its cargo. He also noted that shortly thereafter, the giant insects would leave the ridge again, this time unencumbered by either passengers or their woven vessel.

Once on the ground in the crater, Thayliss would attempt to disappear into the mass of congregated Lii-jit, slipping away into the shadows at first chance. Once free, that was where his plan grew more muddled. He had yet to fully settle on the next course of action, but he figured that it would come to him once he got acclimated to his surroundings.

It was far from a perfect plan, or even a complete one, but with alternative options a troublingly scarce commodity, it would have to do.

They drew ever closer to the great range. Thayliss could see less than ten groups of Lii-jit hovering in the queue ahead of them. In a moment, they would make their descent over the daunting and mysterious Bray mountainside.

Suddenly, a bright flash of white lit up the sky, blinding Thayliss for an instant, before dissolving back into the subdued morning light. He then heard a troubling sound from immediately overhead.

Rather, what was troubling was the absence of sound.

Since departing the Sani-jai rainforest, their flight had been accompanied by a dull, resonant hum created by the impossibly rapid fluttering of the desiccadi's wings. But now that sound had ceased.

Thayliss looked up to see that while the wings still shook, their amplitude and rate had both slowed considerably.

The Lii-jit all around him, oblivious to this tragic turn, still stared blankly toward the Bray Ridge.

Thayliss watched in horror as the wings, still oscillating, began to disintegrate into the turbulent wake behind them. The entire creature, twice as large as the wagon that first brought him to these cursed lands, was slowly brought to dust, taken apart against the very winds it forged into.

Thayliss then felt his left foot grow suddenly immobile. Glancing down, he saw a strand of thick, splintered bark rise from the woven flooring and wrap itself tightly around his lower leg, locking him in place. He watched in panic as the same thing happened to every Lii-jit captive around him.

They were held in place by some heinous, malicious force, free-falling one hundred strides above the hard, desert ground.

CHAPTER THIRTY-THREE

As they plummeted, Thayliss grasped the woven railing beside him, his foot still hopelessly restrained. The Lii-jit around him all seemed content to simply shut their eyes and allow the warm desert air to envelop them until their sudden, final moment.

Thayliss's life played through his mind like a streak of color. He missed Leysiia more than life itself, and part of him embraced the surging ground, for it would deliver him swiftly to her. But as he pictured her, pictured holding her again in the next world, he felt her love burning within him. Not a vision as he had seen during his Ohlinn meditation, but a notion. A simple feeling. Telling him to fight until the very end.

With nothing more at his disposal and a scant few moments left, Thayliss examined the design of the tightly wound basket. While the Lii-jit possessed skills far beyond any seen among the Ohlinn, he was not a stranger to such things. And once again, in a time of great calamity, Thayliss felt his consciousness fill with the soft memory of the life he so cherished.

Of the many aspects of Ohlinn culture that Leysiia had shared with him, one of the most captivating was the art of wind whistling. Using sturdy, sun-dried leaves from the top-most forest canopy, she would weave a collection of lovely, simple structures, from boxes to purses to long, narrow cylinders that she would affix to a long section of twine. Then, finding a suitable breeze, she would release the leaf structure into the air, holding tight to the end of the twine. The shapes, sometimes as many as twelve at a time, would catch the wind and get pulled up into the current.

Each little structure was constructed in such a manner as to allow air to strategically pass through it to make a whistling sound. Different shapes and sizes created sounds of varied pitch, amplitude and quality. Together, a glorious, sublime chorus would ring out into the open air.

To Leysiia, it was merely a hobby. A way to pass time on an otherwise uneventful day. But for Thayliss, it was perfection. She had tried on many occasions to teach him the craft, but he was never able to create anything remotely airborne, let alone capable of creating such enchanting music as hers. Soon he resigned himself to simply watching her work and basking in the wonders of her talent.

As he looked down upon the basket now tethered to his foot, Thayliss attempted to decipher its construction. He followed the lead band of bark around all four walls of the basket and across the floor until he saw where it attached. If he could only get to it, he might be able to slow its course.

But the bark wrapped tightly around his foot would not relent. He struggled and fought, but that only seemed to lock him firmer in place. The point of attachment was merely three strides from where he stood — he was so close; he could almost reach it. He lunged with his one unencumbered foot, but his outstretched fingers barely grazed the threaded section of bark.

As he touched it, he noticed another small, black bird on the other side of the cross-hatched flooring, somehow clinging to the underside of the carriage and trying to attack him. The sheer velocity of the falling basket pressed the little bird against the woven fabric, but it was not deterred. The closer Thayliss's outstretched hand drew to the jutting section of bark, the more vigorously the little bird attempted to peck at his hands, occasionally breaking through the woven flooring to puncture his fingertips.

Thayliss stretched as painfully far as his body would allow, grasping desperately at the bark. The bird was soon joined by another, and another, all pecking madly in an attempt to break through and stop him. It was his only hope.

As the basket continued its free fall, Thayliss maintained his feeble grip on the section of flooring, trying his best to draw the ire of the little birds. He only hoped that it would work.

Chips of wood broke off as the tiny cluster of birds continued their assault, until the tightly coiled section of bark began to slip. Finally, with sight of the desert ground rapidly approaching through the woven lattice, the strip of bark sprang free, instantly flattening the walls of the carriage. In a fraction of a heartbeat, the carriage was pulled flat into a large, square sheet, catching just enough air beneath it to slice forward before impact.

Thayliss's awkward position during the collision snapped the wood holding his foot in place, but it also wrenched his ankle severely to the side. As the large, flat projectile glided across the unrelenting desert, friction against the dry, hard ground quickly grated away the wooden crosshatches holding it together.

The carriage began breaking apart, tossing Thayliss's liberated body to the ground, lost in a massive cloud of ashen dust. Peering up feebly, he could see the rest of the structure continuing toward the base of the range and row upon row of armed soldiers.

CHAPTER THIRTY-FOUR

Lakos vacated the throne room immediately after watching the carriage crash at the base of the mountain. If his intended target had survived the fall, he would finish the job using more direct means.

Having already grown accustomed to traversing through the darkness, he left Gris Hallis behind and entered the black gate on his own, emerging back in the central hallway. This time, however, the narrow corridor directly across from him had morphed into a wide, open entryway, affording a sizable view of the lush greenery now adorning the Inner Realm.

As he now had a clear view straight through to the tunnel that led out to the Bray desert, Lakos saw that it, too, had changed, though considerably less mystically. A number of his men had chiseled further into the mountainside, widening the original archway so that his entire caravan—wagons, tents and all—could find shelter within the Inner Realm.

While he did not recall delivering that order, he did not belabor the point, as his recollection of the last day's events was not without its blank spots. Besides, he concluded, amassing his entire army within his kingdom seemed a reasonable thing to do.

"The transition into the tower is moving ahead smoothly, my Lord," declared a soldier walking across the courtyard toward him.

"Very good," he replied. "And what of the mystic captives?"

"Imprisoned to the last, I believe." He gestured to the first heavy, wooden door.

"And the final Lii-jit carriage—the one that fell from the sky—any survivors?"

"All onboard. Liberated from the wreckage and being detained as we speak."

"Take me to them," ordered Lakos.

The soldier walked with Lakos toward the door to the prison cells, where yet another soldier stood guard.

"Please forgive me, my Lord," said the first soldier. "I'm afraid I have yet to acquaint myself with the dungeons, and it is said that they are a rather tortuous affair. My prison guard will bring you to them."

The prison guard, an older, sallow man wearing a uniform that seemed ill-sized against his depleted physique, nodded dutifully before leading Lakos into the dark, stone tunnel. The guard walked with a pronounced limp, every other step eliciting a hollow echo as his boot hit the stone. All the same, he moved swiftly through the passage.

The tower dungeons were, suitably, a stark contrast to the abundance of light and life throughout the rest of the Inner Realm. Despite having emerged from sheer nothingness hours prior, the dungeon's dark, damp path gave the impression of having existed unchanged for millennia.

The walkway continued down a gradual downward slope, seeming to follow the gradual curve of the tower. Jutting out from the walls, a series of crude wooden torches provided just enough illumination to see directly in front, but not enough to move forward quickly with any confidence.

Soon they passed a fork in the path. Then another. Within moments, Lakos could see stone walkways up above him, over to the side, and then down below. It truly was a maze, and despite feeling as though he had merely walked in a fairly straight line since entering the dungeon pathway, he was hopelessly lost.

"I pity the prisoner who attempts escape," said the old prison guard, breaking the silence. "They are more liable to perish from exhaustion or madness while seeking the exit than they are the blade of a guard's sword. Masdazii ingenuity, I suppose." With a slight wheeze, he continued shuffling ahead. "What you see around you is not merely a static maze but a living, ever-changing series of paths and turns. At times, it presents itself as an array of inclines, declines, abrupt turns, and gradual curves. At other times, it appears simply as a straight line, with no options but forward or backward. As is presently the case, the path may also be littered with detours leading to nowhere, and curves that seemingly contradict the very architecture of the tower. All with the aim of subtly inducing disorientation, confusion, and despair. A recipe for suicide if ever there was one. Brilliant. The labors of a twisted mind, perhaps, but brilliant nonetheless," he commented, shaking his head.

"Tell me, how have you come to gain these insights?" asked Lakos. "The Masdazii are not forthcoming in their ways, and even less so to a human."

"I have a long and painful history of dealing with these creatures. A history that I will not burden you with, as I know that we all have stories that led us to this point. But I assure you, the methods of the Masdazii, or of any other mystic order, are no mystery to me. Come," he said, waving Lakos further still into the dizzying network of tunnels.

Lakos found immense comfort in the confidence with which the old guard spoke but was nonetheless unsettled by the thought of venturing through the dimly lit passage alone.

"Are we nearing the cells? We've walked an eternity and seen no one," he said bluntly.

"Yes, my Lord. My apologies—at times my pride at having deciphered the code of the Masdazii prison gets the better of me. The cells are just ahead. The one you seek, the last Lii-jit cell, is past these ones."

Within several more strides, Lakos had reached the first cell, its residents a sea of forlorn faces glowing in the muted firelight. In keeping with the dungeon's outwardly traditional appearance, the prison cells were a series of small pens, each locked behind its own set of thick, heavy bars.

"The Masdazii constructed the bars using a mysterious

magnetic alloy that I had never encountered before or since. Of course, none of your other men had come across it before, either." The old guard unsheathed his dagger and clanged it against the bars. "A magnetic compound completely harmless to the soldiers outside the cage, but for anyone inside who tries to sneak in a concealed weapon—a dagger, for instance—" He tossed his dagger into the cell, unlocked the cage's door, and shuffled inside, shutting the door behind him.

The Lii-jit prisoners merely stood as before, oblivious. All the same, Lakos was appalled.

"Now, my Lord, I've been told that you possess the ability to control the minds of these creatures, is that correct?" asked the guard.

"That is correct. Though I'm not certain what the aim of this exercise is, and I don't care to find out. I demand that you take me to the prisoners of the last Lii-jit vessel," Lakos reiterated, growing restless.

"In due time, my Lord. In due time. But first, I humbly request you grant this one favor to an old soldier," said the guard, peering through the bars at Lakos. "Use your powers to relinquish every one of the Lii-jit around me. I want to show you something. If you are not suitably impressed, I will vow to remain behind these bars. Of course, as a human surrounded by a pack of angered life-mystics, I do not imagine I would last long."

"This is no time for games, guard. This dungeon is a perverse maze. If you perish, I will perish alongside you. Come, I grow tired of this foolishness."

But the guard persisted. "A great leader must know every stone in his kingdom, every secret that it holds."

Lakos had heard enough. "You have both defied my direct orders and insulted me. Why do you do this, old soldier? Do you beg for death? If so, then lead me out of this cursed dungeon, and I will gladly oblige."

"My Lord," the guard said, still within the cage, "your soldiers, your loyal men and women, will follow you to the next world if that's what you ask of us. Our belief in you, and in the realization of the prophecy, comes first, before all. My greatest sorrow for any offense I may have caused. But an audience with the great and powerful Lord Lakos is a rare and treasured thing. I must risk my life for what I hope to communicate to you, as my very life depends upon it."

Lakos nodded without a word, his mind set on placating the senseless guard until he was safely removed from the dungeon, at which point the guard would be swiftly dispatched. Lakos loathed having to take such measures with one of his own, a human who no doubt shared his dream. But all the same, incompetence and dissension had no place in his kingdom.

"I have seen the wizard who travels near you," the guard said. "He is the fallen Ohlinn, Gris Hallis."

"I am quite aware of the company I keep. Speak quickly."

"My Lord, he cannot be trusted. He feigns obedience, but his motives are very much his own. I fear for not only your life, but for the fate of our kind."

Hearing nothing he did not already know and suspect, Lakos forced a deep sigh. "So, what would you have me do, guard? The ways of a mystic are treacherous. For reasons you would not understand, his life must be spared."

"There are alternatives to murder, are there not? Look around you. Neither man nor mystic could ever hope to escape from these dark corridors. Within this dungeon, his life can be spared in perpetuity, while his snake's tongue would forever lack of venom."

It was a reasonable notion. But things still did not add up. "This dialogue could have occurred from the safety of the path and not through these bars. Why the theatrics?" asked Lakos.

"Because I, too, have a motive very much my own," replied the guard. "Despite standing before you as no more than an aged and broken-down prison guard, I wish to imprison Gris Hallis, and then I wish to take his place at your side. For my hatred for all mystics burns as bright as it does for you. But it was not always so. My home was far from these lands, a small farming community once filled with all order of beings — both mystic and human, co-existing peacefully and productively. But when the cursed Gray Mystic Noryssin saw fit to reduce Merrin Ells to ruin, all was lost. A great conflict arose in our village, as it did across the known world — a war between humans and mystics. We attempted to banish all mystics from our community, and I, once a simple farmer, led the charge. Of course, not all mystics went peacefully. There was bloodshed and death on all sides. Prisoners were taken, with my family and I among them. For one wretched year, my wife, my two daughters and I lived as captives in a mystic settlement, starved and tortured as they awaited the return of their own kind. When they learned that the humans had killed every last mystic they had captured, the mystics sought to do the same to us. I was the only one to make it back alive, and even then..." He gestured down to the remnant of his severed leg. "From that day forward, I waited patiently for the one spoken of in the prophecy to emerge and reunite the world, this time under human control."

Lakos was touched. "I appreciate your passion, old soldier. And your goal truly is my own. But these strange theatrics are pointless. You are regrettably in no shape to become second-in-command. Surely you must understand that."

But the old guard would not be deterred. "I know that I will never again feel the rush of battle on the front lines, offering my life in exchange for honor. But there is strength beyond physical power. And I assure you, my Lord, when your journey is complete and your reign commenced, you will possess more than enough power on your own. But as to where my utility lies, I can impress upon you these three facts. One: That I possess a wealth of knowledge regarding the three mystic orders from the days when we co-existed peacefully, going far beyond simply deciphering the intricacies of a Masdazii dungeon network. During my imprisonment, I studied the mystics—their manner, their customs. Their abilities and weaknesses. I understand their ways as well as any human alive. And, as a great warrior like yourself is surely well aware, one must fully understand the enemy in order to defeat them.

"Two: That despite possessing greater insights into mystic ways and tendencies than any other soldier under your command, my loathing of their blasphemous ways is also without peer. Save, of course, for yourself. And, three: The one who assumes a position by your side should be your most trusted ally, and someone who, in turn, trusts you. I would gladly give my life for you and your cause, whether on a battlefield or here in this cell. I dare say that this is not the case for the one currently lurking in your shadow. A mystic, no less, fighting the human cause? It reeks of deception, from the very one who apprenticed under Noryssin.

"But if you will see my request through and return the prisoners in this cell around me their worldly senses, you will be showing the ultimate trust that what I promised you was true. That I, even with my false leg and slow reflexes, can control every being in this cell. And if I betray that trust and mislead you, then we will both perish in this dungeon. I implore you to obey your intuition. For it is truly the greatest weapon of all. It knows who should be by your side, and who should be in this cell."

"This is madness," said Lakos, nonetheless drawn in by the guard's argument. "You have succeeded in catching my attention, guard." He took a slow, deep breath. "As I appear to have no alternative, I shall accommodate your request. However, I will not imprison myself within this cursed maze. Should it appear as though the Lii-jit have gotten the best of you, I will once again shroud them in their spell before your life can be taken, and you will promptly escort me back to the courtyard. Where your head shall promptly fall by my hand. Are we agreed?"

"As you wish, my Lord," said the guard without hesitation.

Growing more expedient in using his newly acquired gifts, Lakos lowered his head slightly and willed the prisoners to awareness.

The group of Lii-jit, numbering at least thirty within the shadows of the cell, began hollering and bounding against the walls of the cage. Noticing the old guard standing inside the door, several of the Lii-jit leapt over to him, and before Lakos could stop them, had him forcefully pinned against the bars.

Realizing what was unfolding, Lakos lowered his head once again.

"No!" shouted the guard. "Give me more time!"

Torn, Lakos lifted his head back up and watched, praying that he would not regret his hesitation.

One of the Lii-jit noticed the glint of the guard's dagger as it rested on the stony ground. He lunged down to pick it up, but as he did so, the blade soared across the room, tearing his arm from its socket and clanging loudly against the bars. The Lii-jit screamed in agony as those restraining the guard released their grip.

"All Lii-jit standing before me," shouted the guard. "We humans now possess power far greater than any mystic could ever hope to comprehend. Do not cross us. Do not antagonize us or attempt escape. You will be treated justly, but subversion will result in death at the hands of the all-powerful Lord Lakos."

The guard then turned his back to the huddled Lii-jit, opened the door to the cell, and calmly stepped out, slamming it shut behind him.

Lakos lowered his head once again, bringing the captive life-mystics back into their stupor.

Once outside the cell, the guard reached in to grasp his

dagger from the metal bars it still clung to. With but the faintest tug, the weapon released into his grip, where he re-sheathed it by his hip.

The old guard peered back into the cell and smirked. "You needn't bother with the dramatics, Lii-jit. You know full well that the arm will soon grow back."

"What is your name, guard?" asked Lakos, his face expressionless.

"Belwellin, my Lord," replied the guard.

"Belwellin, the passengers from the wreckage—where are they?" asked Lakos, still focused on his primary objective.

"In this one." Belwellin opened the final Lii-jit cage and swung the door open.

Lakos entered the cage freely, inspecting each of the little mystics inside. "Do you recall a human among them?"

The guard seemed taken aback by the question. "A human? No, my Lord. To my knowledge, there are only Lii-jit, Ohlinn, and Masdazii residing in this dungeon."

After inspecting every vacant face in the cell, Lakos stormed back into the walkway. "Belwellin, if you truly wish to demonstrate your worth to me, you will see to it that the traitorous human who accompanied our most recent Lii-jit captives rejoins his associates behind these bars."

"My Lord," replied Belwellin, "I seek not to evade your charge, but I suspect that this human you speak of may soon be taken to the next world without our intervention."

"What do you mean?" asked Lakos, once again intrigued by the unimposing prison guard.

Belwellin spoke confidently. "The imprisoned Masdazii grow restless, as they do when sensing an impending disaster. Even in their current dreamlike state they are aware—connected to the matter around them. I have seen this prescience from their kind before, and it never fails to come to pass. In the moments before you joined me in my dungeon, I overheard a growing number of Masdazii captives murmuring through their trance. They spoke of a coming storm, violent and brutal, with torrents of metallic pellets raining down from the sky, destroying all in its path."

"Metallic rain? Nonsense." Lakos snorted.

But Belwellin continued in sincerity. "My Lord, I speak the truth. The notion of iron or steel falling from the sky does indeed sound preposterous, but I assure you, the Masdazii have never been wrong. And if this is no exception, then I would wager that once the storm hits, no one left outside the Inner Realm will survive."

Lakos was unconvinced. "I will take note of all that has transpired here. But do not mistake tolerance for reverence. It will take a fair deal more than ambition and a fool's bravery to raise you from the prisons to the throne room. Now, see me from this wicked dungeon," he ordered.

The two men walked in silence back along the eerie, shadowy, stone path, until they emerged from the dark tunnel and out into the bright, lively courtyard.

"Assume your post, prison guard," said Lakos.

"Of course, my Lord," replied Belwellin, nodding anxiously as though a crucial opportunity were slipping through his fingers. "You must beware the fallen mystic who follows you, for he lives in deceit," he blurted. "His subservience is a lie. When your distrust of him mounts to its breaking point, he will manipulate you into trusting him all the more. And he will not rest until your power is his."

Without a word, Lakos walked away from the guard, who remained dutifully at his post. However, after several strides, he paused, and turned back to the old guard.

"Belwellin, I offer you no guarantee of any fate but the one you currently serve. But should I call upon you to discuss matters further, see to it that you bring one of your captives with you," he said, nodding in the direction of the dungeon door.

Appearing slightly perplexed, Belwellin quickly bowed. "I shall do as you request, my Lord."

With that, Lakos strode across the courtyard toward the black gate.

CHAPTER THIRTY-FIVE

Thayliss had little time to make a decision. The rapidly settling cloud of ash around him would at any moment cease to provide cover from the legion of armed guards patrolling the base of the mountainside. Once exposed, unarmed, and wounded, his fate would be sealed.

Twenty strides to his right, he saw the remnants of Lakos's caravan, the vast majority of which had vanished. What few of the tents and other transient structures remained were being industriously dismantled by crews of soldiers and transported into a large entryway carved into the side of the Bray Ridge.

A soldier had just vacated the tent nearest to where Thayliss lay, leaving it, to the best of his estimation, empty. It was a chance worth taking.

Thayliss pushed himself up off the dusty ground, realizing that he was now plainly visible to all around him. His first step toward the tent brought electric flashes of pain up from his ankle. Shuffling awkwardly, he moved across the desert floor as quickly as he could, expecting any moment to hear a guard sounding the alert to his presence or, worse still, feel an arrow tearing through him. But on he limped, across the longest twenty strides of his life.

Finally, mercifully, Thayliss arrived at the tent. He quickly lifted the main flap and stepped inside. Once there, he realized that he had no idea what to do next. The structure he had chosen as his temporary reprieve was part of a caravan clearly in the midst of relocation.

At any moment, a soldier would most certainly burst in on him, his presence unexpected but hardly a threat to an armed guard. All the same, the one advantage Thayliss did have was the element of surprise.

He scanned the contents of the little tent, disappointed by

what he saw, or didn't see. He had expected to come across a rack of arrows, a sword, a knife, a spear. Something. To his chagrin, he did not see a single object within the tent that could be used as a weapon. All he saw was a row of six wash basins, each filled with murky water, a collapsible wooden table upon which a stack of woolen trousers was neatly folded, and a pair of leather boots resting on the floor. The laundering tent. Thayliss cursed under his breath.

He saw the silhouette of a soldier, outlined along the wall of the tent. The soldier appeared to be wielding a long, sharp object. After turning to shout something at another soldier, he laughed and then neared the tent's flap.

Thayliss searched madly for some form of weapon. There was nothing. So, almost instinctively, he reached for a pair of trousers and slipped them overtop his own torn, blood-stained garments. He slipped off his tattered old shoes and buried his feet into the leather boots. The boots were too large for his feet, which thankfully made them easy to pull on in his haste. Then, just as the soldier placed a hand upon the tent flap and moved it aside, Thayliss quickly pulled his torn, yellowed shirt over his head, tearing the leather draw string around his collar in the process, and collapsed to his knees, plunging the shirt into a wash basin.

"My pardon," said the soldier, stepping into the tent, a long, metal tent spike in hand.

Thayliss, feigning a battle with a difficult stain, thrashed his hands about in the basin. "Oh, no trouble at all. Just trying to keep respectable."

"Indeed," the guard replied. He looked closer at Thayliss. "I do not recognize you, soldier."

"Likewise, you do not look familiar to me," replied Thayliss quickly, feigning a quick upwards glance. "But we are a large camp. It is only natural for some of us to be less well-acquainted than others."

"I suppose," said the guard, seemingly unsatisfied. "From which land do you originate?"

Thayliss wiped the filthy water across his perspiring brow. "A great distant land, near the Valla Forest. Teeming with those wretched Ohlinn. I joined the fight alongside the great Lakos to bring an end to mystic tyranny." He waited to see if the tactic worked.

After an uncomfortably long pause, the guard responded, "Personally, I find the Masdazii far more loathsome. Huge, repellant creatures. Of course, all mystic orders are but different shades of the same rotten fruit. Regardless, you'll need to quickly wring out your shirt and put it on. Orders from the sacred tower are to move every tent into the Inner Realm with haste. Fear not, the desert heat will dry your shirt as you wear it." The guard grabbed hold of one of the basins and dragged it laboriously out of the tent, pouring it on the ground outside.

Thayliss knew that emerging from the tent with anything but a standard issue military uniform was not an option. His hands searched desperately in the frothy black water, but he felt only his own, foul shirt. He dove his hands into the basin beside it, but it was empty. As was the one beside it, and the one beside that.

"This is not the time for obsessing, soldier," the guard said, suddenly re-appearing at the tent flap. "Each basin is as filthy as the next. Now take your shirt and go. The weather is taking a swift turn, and there is a rumor that a great storm approaches. We are under strict orders to retreat within the Inner Realm immediately. I shall drag you if I must, for your own safety." The guard's expression had grown humorless.

Finally, Thayliss reached into the last basin, his hands immediately coming upon a soldier's shirt. Attempting to conceal his immense relief, he nonchalantly lifted it from the water, wrung it out once, and then pulled it over his head. The cold, wet garment sent a chill down his spine which quickly subsided within the warm, stifling tent.

Now looking the part, Thayliss headed toward the tent's entrance, suppressing with all his might the agony his ankle elicited with each step. As grateful as he had initially been by his oversized footwear, he now realized that they offered little of the ankle support he direly needed.

Reaching for the flap, he heard another soldier approach.

"News from the sacred tower is that a human traitor lurks among us," Thayliss heard the voice say. "Our orders are to inspect every remaining tent, wagon, and storage cart before the storm strikes to ensure that the wretch is not in hiding among us."

"And if we find the traitor?" asked the guard, his hand tightly grasping the tent flap as he stood just outside.

"If co-operative, bring him directly to Lord Lakos. Otherwise, kill him."

A sound resonated from the roof of the small, white cotton tent. Some small object had struck it. And then another.

As the sound of precipitate continued its gradual escalation, Thayliss maintained his focus on the two silhouettes beyond his tent. It was hopeless. Even if he could somehow elude a quick death at the hands of the two soldiers, whatever weather anomaly was on the verge of erupting would surely do the job.

"Well, I'll be certain to keep you posted should I come across any suspicious activity. A fellow soldier was tending to his laundering, and we'll be returning to the Inner Realm momentarily."

"Make haste, for the storm is imminent."

Thayliss heard the other guard leave, after which the first soldier returned inside the tent. Thayliss could tell from the sinister glint in his eyes that he had been caught.

"You're going to come with me, traitor," said the soldier, removing a gleaming, snub-nosed blade from a sling across his chest. "Lord Lakos will reward me handsomely for bringing him your head. Or your entire body. Alive, or dead. I have yet to decide. Now walk."

The guard waved the blade at Thayliss, prompting him to exit the tent. As he limped toward the entrance, another small object struck the roof, this time tearing cleanly through the fabric and splashing into one of the thin, metal wash basins. The loud, resonant clang startled the guard.

As the guard turned toward the sound, Thayliss lunged at him, grabbing the hand wielding the knife and trying to pry his fingers apart. They wrestled back and forth, with the guard slowly gaining the upper hand, driving Thayliss farther into the tent. Thayliss's ankle screamed with every step.

The guard brought his other hand behind the one gripping the weapon, slowly lowering the blade's arc closer and closer to Thayliss's face. All Thayliss could do was slow his attacker down, buying small fractions of time before the inevitable. But the soldier kept increasing pressure, moving Thayliss farther backward and the blade closer to him.

In his blind retreat, Thayliss tripped over the edge of a full water basin, falling backward into it and taking the soldier down with him. As he fell, his momentum as well as the weight of the soldier atop him submerged his head and upper body completely under the murky water. The moment his head plunged under, he heard a deafeningly loud clang.

Feeling the air knocked from his lungs, Thayliss fought to push his attacker off of him, but the soldier's body had gone completely limp upon hitting the water. Thayliss thrashed urgently, trying to remove the oppressive weight, finally grasping the rim of the basin and pulling his head up above water level. He pushed the soldier to the side and scrambled back to his feet.

Wiping his face with the equally drenched shirt he had found moments earlier, Thayliss peered into the basin and saw the filthy water now clouded red and the soldier's lifeless body sprawled within it, his legs dangling over the rim.

Thayliss was in shock. In shock from being attacked and, even more so, for having taken a life. He told himself that he was merely trying to defend himself and that it was an accident, but it was of little consolation.

In Ohlinn culture, there existed no crime more heinous than the murder of another being, be they mystic or human. As such, no penalty exceeded the severity of that which followed.

It was called the torment. The offending party was not expelled from society, nor were they subjected to the fate of the spirit-stricken. For the Ohlinn, the price for murder was eternal agony at the hands of those already in the next world, often including the very victim of their evil deed. Whereas the spirit-stricken simply ceased to exist upon departing this world, the tormented received a long lifetime of anguish.

Often, they grew violently ill from inexplicable disease without ever expiring from it. They were subjected to any form of disaster, emerging alive but always the worse for it. Abandoned by loved ones and without fortune, caring, or support in any form, the tormented invariably chose to disappear from society, often going mad long before their days in this world were spent. It was truly the plague of plagues.

Since childhood, Thayliss had feared this wrath more greatly than any other. And now he feared that he had just brought this most nightmarish of fates upon himself.

Another small projectile tore through the tent, striking the ground by his feet. Glancing down, Thayliss saw that it appeared to be metallic. A perfectly round, silver sphere. He could hear the impacts of numerous such pellets upon the desert ground surrounding his tent.

He pushed aside the flap and looked outside, where waves of silver rained down around him. An increasing number of the spheres struck the tent, perforating the roof until a corner of it hung limply. The entire structure was on the verge of collapsing around him.

The torment had begun.

CHAPTER THIRTY-SIX

"Did you see the human?" asked Lakos, stepping through the black gate's veil of darkness and into the throne room.

"I lost sight shortly after the landing. The projections dissolved once the storm hit," replied Gris Hallis, staring out at the glimmering silver torrents battering the desert ground.

Lakos peered out the vast window before him, silently observing the tiny silver fragments descending beyond the ridge. Finally, he spoke. "The storms that ravage these lands are an aberration. Through the seasons, they grow in frequency, strength, and obscurity. From simple droughts and treacherous winds to this. Never in my time has metal fallen from the sky. It is as though the very world itself strives to keep me from my goal." He stood beside Gris Hallis, facing the vast openness beyond the tower. "May you and all so-called spirits gazing down upon us witness my charge. For I shall not abate. And I shall not fail. This world, as all worlds, will soon be held tight in my grasp."

Gris Hallis turned solemnly from him, pacing the throne room, his silence speaking volumes.

Lakos glared at him, his eyes alight. "Do you doubt my power, wizard? I have already taken what you have given me and far exceeded its scope. I feel the strength of all mystics right at my fingertips."

"You speak of a power that you have yet to possess, my Lord," said Gris Hallis. "Respectfully, you wield a power generated by the few mystics weak enough to become entrapped by your luring. Your strength is transient, your power still developing. Immature."

Lakos laughed. "The power I yield is already greater than you could ever imagine. Your jealousy toward your former master re-emerges with me and will surely get you in trouble."

He glared at the old mystic—through him.

"My lord," said Gris Hallis calmly, "I respectfully speak the truth. I question not your authority, I merely stress that your power has yet to reach its zenith."

"And when do you suppose that will happen?" Lakos asked dismissively.

"To truly fulfill your destiny, you require the power of not just the handful of mystics sequestered within the tower dungeons, but of all mystics, through every worldly realm. However, to gain the power necessary to draw their energy to the sacred tower, you must launch your attack when your power is at its greatest. Each day, the energy channeling through the sacred tower to the world outside cycles, reaching its nadir under the midday sun, and its peak during the darkest hour of night. On the first night of every new Gray Mystic's reign, this midnight power grows more potent still. By the end of this day, as the sun fades and darkness emerges, not a star will appear overhead. Only the moon will cast its light downward. The moment the night grows darkest and the sun's rays furthest from our sky, the moon itself will briefly disappear. Then, and only then, will you see your reign truly commence and the power you wield far exceed the brief, insignificant flashes you have thus far exhibited."

Lakos scoffed. "During my early childhood, living by the sea, I grew to appreciate the magnitude of the celestial powers. Regulating tides, guiding ships, even seeming to direct the flow of aquatic life. The bodies in the sky can give us much and teach us even more. All the same, I'm afraid the coming of this moonless night will signal the end of your time by my side. For whether you aim to deceive me or not, your utility will have run its course. And since I am regrettably unable to dispatch you to the next world, I will see to it that you spend whatever remains of your time in this world safely within the tower dungeon."

"My Lord," pleaded Gris Hallis, "This is just the beginning.

I can offer far more to you once you officially commence your reign as successor to the Gray Mystic tradition and ruler of all realms."

Lakos was doubtful. "Your words reek of desperation, wizard. I am no fool. I encourage you to savor what remains of your time here, Gris Hallis. Look out at the world, for it will be the last you see of it."

"My Lord, there is much more to assuming the throne of the Voduss Grei than mere power. There is also a great burden. Did you not see the faces etched into the Gray Mystics lining the tower corridor?"

"Their pain is of no concern to me," smirked Lakos. "They were weak, and that is why they failed. Only a human is capable of truly ruling over others. For that is woven into our very nature."

"You do not understand," Gris Hallis muttered, exasperated. He took a deep breath, continuing with great reluctance. "It was not my design to laden you with this troublesome information, but I feel that you leave me little choice. The legend of Melleandus, the first Gray Mystic, is one of great tragedy. It is a tale shared only within the Gray Mystic lineage, as no other beings, neither mystic nor human, possess the immeasurable strength required to carry its burden. Noryssin, the one who trained me, shared this with me only once his own strength began to crack under the weight of it, and it is a burden I have struggled with mightily in the years since."

"The story, then. Have at it," urged Lakos plainly, with no trepidation toward what was to come.

Gris Hallis composed himself and then spoke. "I begin by discussing the time after Melleandus's rule. Every Gray Mystic to follow Melleandus lived in the known, documented history of our world. We have records, indisputable proof, that they once roamed these lands. Artifacts from their time can be readily seen, touched, and experienced. We know that the great bridge, linking the north coast to the lush, fertile soil of Siel Tantas Island was devised by and constructed under the rule of the eighth Voduss Grei. The scepter forged by Masdazii artisans to honor the incoming twelfth Gray Mystic supposedly exists to this day in a special room within their vast network of caves. Shrines abound in the many realms of this world, each erected in its time by the Gray Mystic seated at the very throne of my former master, Noryssin. However, the one Gray Mystic to never have looked out upon his world through these wondrous shimmering walls was Melleandus himself."

Uncertain whether or not his audience was even listening, Gris Hallis continued. "Melleandus never ruled these lands, for you see, he never existed in this world."

Lakos was unimpressed. "Very well. He was a myth. That holds no bearing on anything. Fully half of what you mystics build your faith upon is mere conjecture anyhow, if not more so. Your stalling with pointless tales merely delays the inevitable and reinforces my decision. Accept your fate with dignity, wizard, should that be a trait capable of your possession."

"I implore you to hear this. For I possess answers for why you are here, what you are to do, and what will become of you. My fate is intertwined with yours, Lord Lakos, and I have much to share."

"Very well then. Speak, but do so with haste." With the confidence that his sacred tower was nearing completion, and that any potential insurgent would no doubt meet his end amidst the shimmering tempest outside, Lakos was willing to grant the old mystic one final tale.

Gris Hallis nodded in reverence. "Think what you will of our mystic orders, but saying that Melleandus did not exist in this world is not saying that he did not exist at all. He was not merely a false ruler created to initiate and justify the worldly design you see before you. Rather, memory of his existence took shape gradually, in the visions of all Voduss Grei to follow him. You see, each successive ruler, up to Noryssin, experienced visions of those who came before them, often arising during adolescence and young adulthood. Through these visions, one could see the triumphs, the failings. Lessons to be learned, warnings to heed, and simple images of life during the reign of another. The presence of such visions, in fact, comprises one of the requisite steps to one day joining the lineage of the Voduss Grei. Or, rather, it used to." He paused, glancing to the floor.

"A thinly-veiled insult to a non-mystic ruler? Your insolence knows no bounds," scoffed Lakos.

"Far from it," replied Gris Hallis. "When Noryssin first accepted me as his apprentice, it was I who was meant to break from that particular tradition. And much to my point, through the visions of generations of Voduss Grei, it gradually became known that Melleandus was from no known order, mystic or human. In fact, it appeared that the first Gray Mystic belonged to not just a long-forgotten era, but an entirely separate, living world, predating our own. And, while I realize that the history of Melleandus does not interest you, I am obliged to inform you of his fate."

"Neither his history nor his fate is of interest to me," countered Lakos. "All that matters is that the power from his world remained, somehow transferring to this world. To me."

"With respect, my Lord, you fail to recognize the issue. Melleandus wasn't the first Gray Mystic of this world, he was the last Gray Mystic of that world. And he disappeared when his world did, amidst an intensifying chain of seemingly unnatural events not unlike those unfolding before us."

Lakos stood silent and listened.

"The torrents of rain, the crushing gales of wind, the metallic shards falling from the sky, these very scourges were all envisioned by the Gray Mystics before us as plagues from the last world. It is not known from whom they were sent or why. But once they began, it was not long before that world, and all living upon it, were destroyed." Gris Hallis took a slow, anguished breath. "Well into his rule, my former master, Noryssin, envisioned that these events would once again come to pass within this world. Though these new, unrefined visions were vastly more vague and ambiguous than the others, he nonetheless saw how this would happen and sought to take measures to prevent it."

"His measures involved the destruction of my village." Lakos seethed.

"An ultimately futile attempt to prevent the fulfillment of the prophecy," replied Gris Hallis, turning to look directly at Lakos. "A prophecy that goes far beyond the legends the rest of the world has come to know. But all of which has been divulged to me, and me alone."

CHAPTER THIRTY-SEVEN

Thayliss had a choice to make. Either seek shelter from the storm before it was too late, or simply stand where he was, do nothing, and allow the wrath of the torment to take him.

With each passing ordeal, with each seemingly insurmountable obstacle placed in his path, Thayliss had grown both confident and defiant. Once again, he would not stop trying, so long as he had the choice.

The frequency of small, silver projectiles falling from the sky onto the dry, cracked desert intensified. Thayliss had to act.

He tilted one of the basins, spilling its contents across the tent floor. Lifting the thin metal receptacle and holding it over his head, he ran outside the tent and into the harsh open air, his injured ankle screaming in protest.

The pellets hit the ground with such volume that the sound of the impacts blended together into a continuous, deep murmur, rippling across the desert floor. As a wave of metal shards struck the basin, the resonant sound was deafening. Thayliss had to move. Before long, the silver precipitate would tear through the basin, and soon thereafter through him.

Out in the open, Thayliss looked toward the archway carved into the side of the volcanic rock face. It was manned by several armed guards standing just inside the tunnel, who scanned the surrounding area. Entry into the refuge of the tunnel and whatever lay beyond it was no longer an option. Those soldiers would identify an imposter as readily as the now-deceased guard in the laundering tent had. And once the guard's body was found, Thayliss's punishment would be all the more severe.

A large number of Masdazii windchargers rested on the desert ground by the entrance, but using one to escape was also not a viable option. Even if he could somehow get close enough to one without being spotted by the guards—an even more challenging task while wearing a large metal basin that echoed a deafening pattern of sound—the metallic precipitation appeared to be taking its toll on the vehicles as well, battering the frames and punching holes in the crucial trailing sails. Besides, he had no idea if a human was even physiologically capable of operating such exotic modes of transport.

With no means of escape or any other means of sheltering himself from the storm, Thayliss needed to find another way to the center of the Bray Mountain.

The mammoth white tower beyond the Bray Ridge appeared immune to the waves of silver precipitation, and Thayliss wondered what great and ultimate power surged within it. It seemed as though the human Lakos was still in control, but such powers vastly exceeded mortal capabilities. The Lii-jit mind control and the grim fate befalling the giant desiccadi moth that brought him here involved forces acting on a scale that Thayliss had only heard about as a child—the Voduss Grei. The long-extinct sacred order of the Gray Mystic.

Was the prophecy truly coming to light? In spite of all that he had witnessed, Thayliss still oscillated between fearing that it was all true and telling himself that there must be some other explanation. Perhaps it was of little consequence. All Thayliss knew was that an immensely powerful energy was carrying out the ambitions of a black heart, and he strove somehow to stop it.

Ignoring the pain in his ankle as best he could, Thayliss ran in the direction opposite the guarded archway. He reasoned that an ancient structure as obscenely expansive as the Bray Ridge must have been equipped with more than one entrance in its countless generations of existence. However, this reasoning was driven more by desperation than logic, as he currently had little alternative.

Limping along the great ridge, Thayliss peered inside every deep vertical crack in the sheer rock face in the hope of finding an alternate way in. But in each instance, the fissures merely extended a handful of strides inward before once again terminating into solid rock.

The first hole tore through the basin held over Thayliss's head as a small streak of silver flashed before his face, burying itself deep in the ground by his feet. He had to seek shelter. Immediately.

Thayliss pushed on, desperate, exhausted, and in pain. Finally, he saw a path of clean, white stones originating right where he stood and leading directly into one of the larger vertical cracks before disappearing into darkness.

As he squinted into the shadows beyond the path, another metallic pellet ripped through the basin, this time tearing through his ill-fitting military issue boot. The sight of a hole burrowing through his boot took his breath from him. However, Thayliss soon realized that the silver projectile had punched through the ample open space afforded by the oversized boot.

Without another moment to spare, Thayliss veered from the open desert ground and limped down the white stone path. A feeling of immense relief washed over him once he saw that the geology of the large crack blocked the falling pellets just a few strides inside the path. Tossing the battered basin to the side, he staggered deeper into the mountainside.

Before long, the path seemed less like a crack in a stone wall and more like an artificially chiseled tunnel, much like the heavily guarded one just past the fleet of Masdazii windchargers. Strangely, despite the tunnel's lack of sunlight or torches, Thayliss's visibility remained excellent. He suspected that it had something to do with the rich mineral deposits embedded in the tunnel walls around him. The compounds appeared to not just reflect light, but to generate it. It was striking.

Thayliss moved on. He only hoped that he'd be able to locate the captives once inside the Bray Ridge, and that Tiig and Mawinaa would be somewhere among them.

The look of hurt, anger, and betrayal on Tiig's face back at

Sani-jai still haunted Thayliss. He wanted to tell Tiig that he wasn't behind any of this destruction, that he was a victim just as Tiig was. That he'd lost everyone he'd ever cared about. That he was alone.

The kindness Tiig and his family had shown to him in such a short time, without knowing anything about him, brought Thayliss a new sense of family. Part of him questioned if it was wise to continue investing emotions into the lives of others when the fates seemed so intent on cruelly taking such things from him. To make matters worse, the whole of his bond with the energetic little Lii-jit had been built upon Tiig's misguided belief that Thayliss was, in fact, an Ohlinn. Perhaps a friendship built upon a lie, whether deliberate or otherwise, was always destined to end in pain.

As Thayliss negotiated the narrow, white stone path that snaked its way progressively deeper into the mountainside, the sound of his footsteps was joined by another, fainter sound. The path had not branched, so he knew that the sound originated either in front of him or behind him. He stopped and looked in both directions for the source of the noise, but all was again quiet.

He resumed his walk, but two steps ahead that same noise echoed through the stone around him, this time slightly louder. It sounded almost like... his name.

Convinced that the stress and trauma were making him delirious, Thayliss continued walking. Suddenly, a loud thud emanated from the left, a mere half-stride from where he stood. Startled, Thayliss spun around. To his horror, he saw Tiig inside the rock, banging against the tunnel wall and shouting Thayliss's name. Around him, the stone appeared so thin as to have become almost transparent, with only the same bright flecks of light to suggest any matter at all between them.

"Thayliss!" Tiig shouted, his voice muffled. "You must get me out of here! They put me under some kind of spell and took me from my home. Oh, Thayliss—they've killed them all. They've killed Mawi-naa, the rest of my family. My entire colony is gone." Tears streamed down his face. "I'm alone now, Thayliss. Just like you."

Thayliss staggered back, leaning against the tunnel wall behind him to remain upright.

"You've got to help me, Thayliss. Please," Tiig begged. "You've got to break through the wall before it's too late."

Thayliss searched for something to use to break through the thin sheet of rock, but he found nothing.

"I'm so sorry," he said, helpless. "I don't know what to do!"

"Strike it," said Tiig. "You must strike the wall with all of your might. Please, Thayliss, quickly. You must help me."

Thayliss got an idea. He slipped the boot off his injured ankle and held it by the shaft. The military boots possessed a thick, heavy leather heel. It just might work.

Thayliss took a step toward the wall, boot in hand, and tilted his arm back, cocked for impact. But before striking the shimmering stone wall, he paused. The imprisoned life-mystic said that he was taken from his home while under a spell, but Thayliss had watched him leave with Mawi-naa of his own free will in an attempt to rescue the others.

The more he thought, the more it didn't feel right. That the very being he had been thinking about had appeared in the rock he ventured through.

"Thayliss," cried Tiig desperately, "please, you must save me! If I die, you will have no one. Not a being in all of the five realms will care about you!"

Thayliss slowly placed his boot back upon the white stone path and slipped his foot back into it. "I'm sorry," he said, "but I can't."

"No!" The figure behind the stone wall screamed, banging its fists against the solid wall of the tunnel. Then a rush of tiny shimmering particles swirled across the stone, and the entire section of wall flashed a brilliant white before subsiding back to its more natural mineral-encrusted texture.

Now, however, Thayliss could see that the figure frozen in the solid stone was not the little Lii-jit. It was the figure of a soldier wearing a uniform much like the one Thayliss himself now wore. The soldier stood, motionless in the stone, his fists raised as if fighting to break free.

Thayliss fought to slow his erratic breathing and compose himself. It was simple. He just needed to follow his intuition, and his intuition was telling him to keep moving.

Unfortunately, it was also telling him that he was surrounded on all sides by malevolence and corruption. It hung thick in the air like a fog. And it sought to consume him.

CHAPTER THIRTY-EIGHT

"Tell me, wizard, why aid me in my quest? If your all-knowing, traitorous, murderous former master informed you that I would be responsible for the destruction of the known world, why did you come to me?" asked Lakos.

"I do not doubt the visions of Noryssin, that he indeed saw the destruction of all worlds, with a human standing at the forefront as it came to pass. But where my reservation lies is in his interpretation of what he saw, for what he saw lacked clarity. It was an abstract collection of images, shrouded in ambiguity. He merely saw the players involved and the conclusion. Regarding the manner in which each of the players interacted and the roles that they played as the scene unfolded, I do not believe he had any more a notion of that than you or I."

"Then why destroy my village? Why destroy his own sacred tower?" Lakos asked.

"Because Noryssin had grown weak in his old age. Weak and insecure. I spent the most vital, formative years of my life under his tutelage, from adolescence well into adulthood. I was his only confidante, his connection to the world. Noryssin trusted me beyond all others. But he was beginning to lose his grasp."

Gris Hallis grew somber. "I could see him unraveling before my eyes. Despite wielding more power than all beings across the five realms combined, he was still but a living being, of flesh and blood, as any other. His life was destined to be greater and longer lived than any other of his time. But all the same, his end would one day come, and the torch of the Voduss Grei passed on to the next Gray Mystic. Sensing his journey to the next world growing closer, he grew fearful. Fearful first that no competent successor had emerged — a fact which pained him even more than I. But over time, he became fearful of the exact opposite, that it was only a matter of time before someone would inevitably take his place. He so reveled in the great duty he had once inherited that I believe he grew resistant to relinquishing it. And so, he chose to interpret his vision as one of a threat to his power. Of being overthrown. By a mere human, no less. Noryssin chose to believe that his human successor would result in the world's destruction, as had befallen Melleandus, simply by equating the end of his own life with the end of all life. I, on the other hand, believed that the continuing of the Voduss Grei lineage, by human or any other being, was paramount to the world's continued existence. But alas, he could not be deterred."

"And what of Noryssin? The legend speaks of his disappearance in the immediate aftermath. The abandonment of all beings, the world left in chaos. The third betrayal. Does he still live?" A look of vengeance glowed in Lakos's eyes.

Gris Hallis smiled softly, as if to temper Lakos's mounting rage. "The once great Gray Mystic Noryssin no longer lives. He perished amidst the sacred tower's destruction. I must admit that the rumor of his escape originated with me. In the aftermath of the tragedy at Merrin Ells, the world was without a great leader for the first time in known history. The lineage of the Gray Mystic order, as I said, predates our very world itself. To declare the death of Noryssin would be akin to declaring to a world already in discord that there was no unity. That the great governing force overseeing their lives and ensuring the proper natural order since the beginning of time was gone. I simply told the lie in an effort to somehow maintain peace within the realms. I thought it better that the world feel resentment toward a vengeful governing power than to feel as though they have no one watching over them at all."

Lakos was not impressed. "Your lie did not work. In the immediate aftermath of the slaughter at Merrin Ells, and the thirty years hence, the world fell in disarray regardless."

"You forget that on that wretched day thirty years ago I, too, found myself in disarray," replied Gris Hallis. "My master and the sacred tower, the only world I had ever known, were taken from me. After the betrayals, the Ohlinn accused me of involvement, ordering me never to return to the safety of the Valla Forest, a home I have not seen since I was a child. Of course my lie did not work, but it gave me comfort nonetheless. I wanted to believe it was true. However, I also hoped that the lie would serve to bridge the gap. For I knew that one day soon a human—you, my lord—would rise to take your place and restore the lineage of the Gray Mystic, and return my home to me."

Lakos stood before the broad open window and surveyed his kingdom. "Once again, Gris Hallis, you have shared a great many insights with me. You have taken a simple warrior, blinded by vengeance, and led him to the throne of the Voduss Grei. And for that, I shall always be grateful. And I have but one, final request to ask of you."

"And what is that, my Lord?" asked Gris Hallis attentively.

"To look upon these realms beyond the ridge and burn them into your memory. For in your vast, intricate plan to earn my trust, you made one, vital mistake. You see, just as you had been observing me before our encounter, I, in turn, had been observing you."

Gris Hallis stepped back, confused.

"My sentinels saw you exiting the Valla Forest several days before you came to us. In the company of an Ohlinn. Your banishment, your very identity, is a lie." Lakos slowly encircled Gris Hallis, peering at him with a look of disgust on his face.

"My Lord, allow me to explain—" pleaded the old mystic.

Lakos merely shook his head and smiled. "I'm afraid the time for storytelling is over. It is now time to assume your rightful place in the tower dungeon."

CHAPTER THIRTY-NINE

Thayliss continued through the tunnel, fighting to shake the image of Tiig pleading for mercy through the transparent stone wall. He barely knew the rambunctious Lii-jit, and based on the last time he'd seen Tiig, Thayliss figured that he would be the last person Tiig would turn to for help. He just hoped that he'd be able to find him, along with the other captive mystics, if and when he reached the Inner Realm.

Thayliss also struggled to maintain his composure while traversing the gradually narrowing tunnel. Standing in the middle of the path with arms outstretched at his sides, he could easily run his fingers along the tunnel's entire circumference, with the walls growing ever closer with each step. He fought to suppress the claustrophobic sensation by taking comfort in the fact that the mysterious flecks embedded in the stone walls still emanated more than enough light to sufficiently light the way. For now.

As he walked, another sound echoed up ahead. It was a deep creaking, as if from the hull of a great ship forced to weather rough seas. It groaned for a moment and then stopped. Thayliss then heard the same sound from far behind. Seconds later, it emanated from directly above where he stood.

A sense of unease rose within him. Graced with but two options, retreat or proceed forward, Thayliss opted for the latter, trudging ahead, his ankle still throbbing with every other step.

As though his decision to continue onward somehow provoked the source of the sound, the groaning intensified, now coming from all directions. He shuffled ahead faster, as fast as he could semi-comfortably move.

Then the first rock fell.

It was a thick sliver of rock roughly the size of a wagon wheel, and it seemed to spontaneously chip apart from the roof of the tunnel right in front of him. Thayliss leapt backward to avoid being struck, collapsing to the ground after landing with his full weight upon his injured ankle. Lying on the tunnel floor, he saw a second stone break free directly above him. He lunged to the side as the larger stone fell, shattering on impact and spraying volcanic debris all around.

Ignoring the pain in his ankle, Thayliss labored to his feet and began to run. Once again, the increased movement merely amplified the activity as fragments fell steadily from the roof, both ahead and behind him. In each instance, Thayliss barely eluded harm while forging ahead, desperately hoping to reach the other side before becoming entombed within the fabled Bray Ridge.

The stones seemed to almost maliciously project themselves from the walls of the tunnel, with several jagged chunks knocking Thayliss hard to the opposite side of the path. Stone after stone burst forth, until much of the path behind him had become impassable.

Ignoring the pain, he continued ahead, knowing that losing his footing would be fatal. Still more vigorously the rocks fell, piling up around him until the passage seemed on the verge of total collapse. Undeterred, Thayliss pressed forward, scrambling over the growing piles of boulders and dodging the rocks propelling themselves from the walls. But the path ahead was quickly disappearing.

A few strides ahead, he could see a change in the tunnel's path—a drop-off descending into darkness. He had no choice— he had to follow it. He only hoped that he'd get there in time. The collapsing stones now poured into the narrowed tunnel, battering him from all sides.

Just as the walls of the tunnel completely gave way, Thayliss dove over a large boulder and into the drop-off. After a three-second free-fall, he plunged into a pool of cool water. Though surrounded by complete darkness as he swam, Thayliss heard the sound of several small stones following him into the water. After taking several strokes blindly forward, the sounds ceased. He swam in complete silence in the dark.

Thayliss once again fought to retain composure as he kicked his way ahead. But the moment he tried surfacing for a breath, panic set in. The channel he swam through had completely filled with water, denying him even the slightest pocket of air. Thayliss felt his heart race as he pushed ahead faster. He knew that exerting himself more intensely would only hasten his need for air, but he had no idea how far he was from an opening, and time was running out.

He kicked and thrashed as fast as he could, until finally he spotted a faint glimmer of light up ahead. His muscles burned and his lungs screamed as Thayliss felt his body's involuntary urge to inhale begin to mount. The desire was easily suppressed, but for how much longer, he did not know.

Thayliss saw the light ahead grow steadily brighter as he drew nearer. Just a few more kicks, and he would reach it. It was sunlight, beaming down from above! A feeling of hope began to ease his mind.

However, as he moved forward, scarcely a stride from liberation, the walls of the aquatic tunnel around him sharply narrowed, so much so that as his body glided forward, achingly close to the surface, his shoulders became wedged within the rock.

His arms were stretched out in front of his head, and he could feel his fingertips just barely break through the surface and into the open air, warmed by the bright sun up above. The agony was unbearable. He was so close, but there was simply no way to fit through.

It was too late. He was going to inhale. The urge could be suppressed no longer. Having been raised as an Ohlinn, living amongst the trees, Thayliss had on only the rarest occasions swum in water deeper than he could stand in. As a boy, he was always drawn to the notion of being in water, but having had little occasion to do so, he eventually grew an aversion to it. He now wondered if his aversion to drowning was, in fact, a premonition of how his life would end.

He didn't know what happened when a person drowned. Would his lungs fill completely with water? Would he gag on the first inhalation and then refuse to take another until he gradually lost consciousness? Would he thrash about violently or simply pass on? He only hoped that once whatever process awaiting him was complete, his transition to the next world would be swift.

Thayliss struggled with all his might to stifle the urge to inhale but could feel himself losing the battle. He resigned himself to his fate. It could not be stopped.

He shut his eyes, blocking sight of the sunlight heartbreakingly just out of reach, and waited for death.

The first thing he sensed was a deep and powerful tremor rumbling all around him. His body shook violently against the narrow walls that restrained him, forcing out what little air remained in his lungs. As he opened his mouth to inhale, he felt the rock around him give way. His lungs filled with air as his weak body suddenly rushed ahead like a doll.

Opening his eyes, he saw that all ahead was bright, and he surged toward the glow amidst the rushing water and newly loosened stones. The layers of rock beneath him were reduced to rubble, creating a waterfall that burst through the sheer rock face and into the vibrant oasis of the Inner Realm.

Thayliss rushed toward the waterfall like a cork, completely helpless. He could not tell how high up he was, or what awaited beneath him. He moved with such velocity that when he soared over the edge, he was propelled at least fifteen strides from the rock face behind him. He fell for what felt like an eternity, blinded by the stinging froth all around him.

Finally, he once again plunged into a pool of water. This time, he rose easily to the surface, his limp, battered body drifting with the current until he was deposited gently upon sandy shallows, surrounded by cattails and buzzing dragonflies.

Thayliss slowly sat up in the warm, foaming water and looked around. His physical suffering and the emotional strain of coming within one breath of drowning were quickly and profoundly eased by what he saw before him.

Thayliss found himself surrounded by the lushest greenery he had ever seen. Birds endowed with colors defying description soared overhead, singing songs to enchant the very spirits themselves. He glanced back up at the waterfall that had ejected him, and saw that it possessed an ethereal glow, emerging from the flat, shimmering inner wall of the Bray Ridge, rainbow-streaked and bathed in sunlight.

Scanning the landscape, he saw a rich diversity of animals milling about, living their lives—animals that had no business co-existing in the same land. But there were in fact many distinct lands, all distilled within the Inner Realm's border. Thayliss could see grassy hills, dry plains, rivers, and forests, all easily traversable within a day's trek. It seemed as though every great terrain, plant, and beast from all the known realms had been seamlessly encapsulated within this one domain.

Of course, the most striking sight of all was the monstrous white tower occupying the center of the realm. Staring at its walls of glowing white stone was utterly captivating.

Thayliss found himself enchanted by the world around him and inexplicably drawn to the glorious white tower. He was in paradise.

CHAPTER FORTY

Gris Hallis passed through the black gate and re-entered the tower courtyard, his blue eyes dull and sullen. As he stepped forward from the darkness, the metallic glint of a longsword emerged right behind him, pressed firmly to his back. The smattering of guards industriously setting up wagons and tents nearby momentarily ceased their activities to take notice. By the time Lakos appeared, sword in hand, most of the once-bustling army was transfixed by the scene before them.

"My loyal army," shouted Lakos, never shifting his gaze from the back of the old mystic, "we have a traitor among us."

"My Lord," Gris Hallis interjected. "This is a mistake, I assure you."

"You're right, Ohlinn. Entrusting my quest, my people, to a mystic was a critical mistake, and one that I shall not soon forget. For this blade does not deceive. Upon my command, it strikes down whomever I choose."

"But did I not provide you with this sacred tower? With the power now flowing through your veins? The whole of the Inner Realm?" asked Gris Hallis, his voice thick with desperation.

"Indeed, you did," Lakos replied coldly. "You thought that you could use my prophecy against me, blinding me with power, using me to rebuild what you had lost, only to overthrow me with the aid of your Ohlinn allies still dwelling within the Valla Forest. But that is where you failed. For I know how mystics view the human order—as a plague, an inferior species. Impulsive, selfish, gluttonous. But I am far more intelligent than any mystic. Although there is one thing I have yet to understand. At what point were the other Ohlinn planning to launch their attack? And how? The most powerful of your kind are safely within my dungeon, and I assure you, they are not going anywhere. But rest assured, you are but moments away from being reunited."

"My Lord, you are mistaken!" cried Gris Hallis.

"Were you not consulting with an Ohlinn within the Valla Forest in the days before our encounter?" bellowed Lakos.

"I was," admitted the old mystic, craning his neck to speak to Lakos. "But even then, I strove only to aid you in your quest, not to undermine you. As I said before, I knew that you were destined to fulfill the prophecy. I also knew that you aimed to do this solely through violence and bloodshed."

"Truly, the clairvoyance of an Ohlinn is astounding," retorted Lakos sarcastically.

"I wanted to help our world begin anew—not just the humans, but my order, and all mystics. I knew there was a better way. Knowing that your attack was imminent, I ventured into the Valla Forest for the first time since I was a child. I spoke with an Ohlinn elder, Leonorryn. I spoke of the prophecy, and that in order to both restore balance to our world and avoid countless unnecessary deaths, all mystics needed to voluntarily join with you. To embrace your destiny as I did. I told him that the original sacred tower was built using the power of free mystics, beings who supported the governance of the Voduss Grei. I pleaded with him, telling him that it was the only way that we could restore the Gray Mystic lineage without violence."

"And what did he say?" asked Lakos, his sword still pressing against the old mystic's back.

"He told me to leave," replied Gris Hallis dejectedly. "He said that he could never consent to a human Voduss Grei. That even though the prophecy was inevitable, he would resist it to the end. And that his actions in this world would govern his path into the next. So he led me out of the Valla, telling me never to speak of this to another Ohlinn, and never to return."

"And did he also tell you to capture a Lii-jit and sacrifice him to me?" asked Lakos with a sneer.

"What choice did I have? It was all I could do to see your

ambition realized while still avoiding mystic casualty. Or at least minimizing it."

"A thoughtful, amusing final tale, wizard," said Lakos, pushing Gris Hallis forward with his sword. "But we have little time for stories. You see, once you're safely imprisoned, my loyal human army and I shall partake of a great feast to celebrate what we have accomplished. And then, when the night has reached its darkest point, as you so thoughtfully informed me, the power of all realms shall be mine. You were quite right when you told that old spirit-mystic that my rise was inevitable. As is your fate."

Lakos nodded to the two soldiers nearest him. The soldiers grabbed hold of Gris Hallis and led him toward the dungeon.

"You may beat him however pleases you," shouted Lakos. "But it is imperative that you let him live."

"You would be wise to remove your men from this place, my Lord," muttered Gris Hallis as he was forced closer to the dungeon archway. "For this tower, and the whole of the Inner Realm, was intended for the Gray Mystic alone. All others will be consumed by its power, its allure. You must believe me. I have felt its pull, and I always shall. It is a curse! Send them away while you still can. I promise you, there are secrets to this realm that you still do not know!"

Lakos stood in silence, Gris Hallis's plea hanging heavily in the air, as words from a different voice commanded his attention.

When your distrust of him mounts to its breaking point, his guile will manipulate you into trusting him all the more. And he will not rest until your power is his.

"Farewell, Gris Hallis," replied Lakos, watching the frail old mystic disappear into the shadows beyond the dungeon archway.

CHAPTER FORTY-ONE

Thayliss slowly crawled out of the marsh at the base of the waterfall and looked around. He had to find a way into the sacred tower, though gaining entry was just the first of his obstacles. He had no idea where the prisoners were being kept, and once he found them, he had no idea how to safely lead them out of the Inner Realm. From where he stood, he saw no fewer than twenty of Lakos's soldiers patrolling the area, while still others darted to and fro, seemingly focused on hunting and foraging for food.

With his first step onto a dirt path bisecting a dense, wooded area, Thayliss was instantly reminded of his injured foot. That realization was soon followed by another, swiftly dissipating his already meager confidence. He was injured, unarmed, and alone, attempting to venture past legions of highly trained warriors who were more than likely already alerted to his possible presence. Thinking back to the incident in the laundering tent, Thayliss scorned himself for not having had the presence of mind to take the soldier's knife when he left.

Slowly, painfully, he crept ahead, lurking in the shadows. Only once did a soldier pass by even remotely close to where he hid, and even then, the soldier seemed more interested in tossing stones at a wide-bodied shrew as it scurried across the ground than finding a rogue human.

As he negotiated the lush array of plant life, the vibrant sights and smells of fresh vegetation began to trigger pangs of hunger. Having not had a trace of sustenance since the festivities in the Sani-jai the evening before, Thayliss began to lose focus. As if almost on cue, the greenest, most robust spring melon he had ever seen appeared before him, tantalizingly dangling from a low-lying branch. Without a second thought, Thayliss plucked the fruit and bit into it. The taste was unlike anything he had ever encountered before. Its rich satisfaction went beyond mere palatability. It simultaneously awoke and elevated every sense—the look of it, the smell, the crisp sound as he bit into it. The very feeling as he held the precious item in his hand. It changed him.

Devouring the fruit in a mad flurry, he promptly began searching for another. As he walked, he was struck by the realization that the pain in his ankle had miraculously subsided. He felt alive. He felt invincible.

Not noticing any more fruit on the tree, he looked up the path and saw another plant just through a clearing—a stout shrub with a tangle of branches jutting out in all directions. Lining each of the thin branches were numerous small, red berries. But what truly captivated Thayliss was what bloomed from its base.

It was a fungus called a rose terrafruit. The pink, multi-wedged cylinder was a true delicacy in the Valla Forest, springing from the youngest branches at the peaks of the oldest, tallest trees. Thayliss could not believe his eyes. What it was doing at ground level emerging off a petty shrub in the volcanic Inner Realm was a mystery. But all the same, he knew that it existed only for him. He had to have it.

Completely enraptured by what he saw, Thayliss failed to notice a soldier steadily approaching, scanning the area with sword in hand. Without a thought, Thayliss sprang from the safety of his wooded shelter and darted out into the exposed path. Hearing the noise, the soldier began running through the path toward the source. Thayliss, oblivious to the nearing guard, reached for the terrafruit and pulled.

Before he could dislodge the fruit from its base, something slammed into him. He soared from the path and into a small group of shrubs. A small, wiry silhouette crouched in front of him, gently placing a finger to its lips, imploring silence.

But Thayliss could only think of obtaining the rose terrafruit. He tried pushing his way past the small figure, only to find his arms and feet bound with ivy. He was immobilized.

Confused and angry, Thayliss struggled to break free but stopped when he saw the soldier standing a mere three strides from where he lay. Both Thayliss and the figure next to him hid in silence, shrouded amidst the greenery.

The soldier paused, his sword brandished. "Show yourself," he called. "I know you're here, human traitor. The others are convinced that you perished outside in the desert storm, but I know you're here."

The ensuing silence seemed only to provoke the soldier.

"In my land, I was a great hunter. You tread upon the land that Lord Lakos has entrusted upon me, so now this is my land. I shall cut down all that grows here until I find you. And then I swear to the spirits that I will take your life."

The soldier lifted his sword and slashed across a shrub right beside Thayliss and his mysterious abductor. Again, he raised his sword, directly above where they hid.

At that moment, a cluster of shrews streamed out of the shrub, spilling onto the path. The soldier lurched backwards, startled, as the little creatures scurried across his boots, disappearing again into the dark foliage on the other side of the path.

Muttering a profanity, the soldier continued on his way, vanishing as the path curved into a wooded thicket.

Sensing the crisis was averted, Thayliss brought his attention back to obtaining that rose terrafruit. His hands and feet still bound, he writhed in frustration.

"I'm sorry, Thayliss," said the figure standing in the light before him.

"Mawi-naa," he said, shocked.

"These fruit are cursed, as are all that grow here. I can feel it. All the life around us is somehow false. An illusion of giving that serves only to take from those who indulge in its bounty. To harm. To destroy." She looked at him more closely, sorrow in her eyes. "You have already been infected. Quick, we must act before the poison takes hold."

She spotted a tree up ahead. "The soldiers will return at any moment. We can seek refuge up there—its branches can support us, and its leaves will camouflage us. I will unbind you, Thayliss, but I beg of you, you must resist the call of the poison fruit."

Mawi-naa cut the vines from Thayliss's limbs, liberating him. He rose to his feet, watching the Lii-jit scamper up to the tree ahead and leap effortlessly to the lower branches.

He looked back at the shrub next to him. The rose terrafruit had been severed in two by the soldier's sword. One half remained attached to the base of the shrub, while the other lay upon the dirt path, It's succulent interior and rows of small, clear seeds visible. The temptation once again grew strong, and as it mounted, his prior feeling of bliss swiftly dissipated, devolving into desperation.

He stepped closer and reached down for it, hearing Mawi-naa calling out to him.

"Thayliss," she whispered, "you must resist it! It will consume you!"

As Thayliss's hand drew nearer to the fruit, his body grew cold from within. He dropped to his knees as a sharp pain shot across his abdomen. His vision blurred, and a high-pitched sound screamed in his ears. If only he could taste the terrafruit, all would once again grow calm. He tried feebly to grasp it, both the pain and his obscured vision causing him to miss.

Then intuition rose up through the pain, fighting to be heard. Forcing himself to obey this inner voice, Thayliss struggled to his feet, stumbling away from the infernal fruit and toward the tree across the path. His vision worsened, and the screeching in his ears tossed his balance from side-to-side. The pain spread from his abdomen up across his chest, as if his heart were held in an ever-tightening vice. His hands clawed at the bark of the tree, struggling to climb before it was too late.

And then all went black.

CHAPTER FORTY-TWO

Lakos stood alone in the narrow throne room, gazing pensively through the open window. He was of two minds regarding the imprisonment of Gris Hallis.

There had been countless moments of doubt, of questioning the old mystic's motives, from their very first encounter, when he interfered with the capture of that young soldier. The fact that he belonged to one of the orders Lakos sought to control did nothing to help the fallen Ohlinn endear himself. He had also grown increasingly obstinate, which, even if he had not held blatant designs to overthrow Lakos may, in time, have given one of the other soldiers the idea.

Lakos shook his head, confused. Everything was backward. He felt guilty about his treatment of Gris Hallis, a distrustful mystic, while beginning to doubt the loyalty of his actual human subordinates. The men and women in his charge entrusted him with their lives. Men and women who, at this very moment in the courtyard far below, were enjoying themselves with music, food, and drink. This was a human war. A human victory.

Lakos looked down at the faint tinge of blue shimmering through the flesh in his chest. The very thought of it made him ill. He fleetingly imagined cutting the mystical fluid from his chest, perhaps instilling it in another in the hopes of transferring the burden. Of course, he hadn't a clue whether such a thing could be done, and more importantly, knew that attempting such a procedure would no doubt end his own life, defeating the very purpose. The ways of the mystic never ceased to enrage him.

"You called for me, my Lord," a voice rang out behind him.

Lakos spun around to see Belwellin limp into the room. Held in his hands was a short section of coarse, braided rope that led up around the neck of a tall, thin figure.

"Ah yes, and I see you complied with my instruction," replied

Lakos, pleased.

"I selected an Ohlinn captive as they are the most docile and easily transported. I did not want to fail you." Belwellin appeared somewhat ashamed.

"This was not an exercise in strength," assured Lakos. "Rather of adherence to the orders of your superior, even when the objective is left ambiguous."

"Your motives are not for me to judge, my Lord," offered Belwellin humbly. "My role is to merely do all in my power to see them realized."

"So, is that to be your role now—the blind agreement of every foolish, irrational decision I make?" asked Lakos with a slight tilt of his head.

"I have seen too many winters come and go to waste my time with fools or my breath with flattery. The truth as I see it is that you have displayed greater composure, conviction, and rationality than I ever thought possible in a being, human or mystic. I cannot imagine the weight upon your shoulders or the scope of your experiences since first entering this realm. It is a burden greater than any man before you ever bore. In many ways, the rhythmic energies that sustained our world through the ages were a strictly mystic affair, as humans were not designed to comprehend them, let alone govern them. All of the insights that I possess were given to me secondhand by the mystics who once roamed my homeland. But you—you have witnessed them personally. Felt them deep inside. What a glorious, treacherous gift."

"It is my destiny," replied Lakos. "It is a burden that I shall proudly bear until the power of every mystic in every land is under human governance." He looked at Belwellin, speaking cautiously. "Gris Hallis spoke of my power, how it is not yet at a level where I may truly wield it with authority. And yet I feel as though I could snuff out the life of the bewildered Ohlinn standing beside you without so much as a nod. What know you of this?"

"You are both correct," said Belwellin. "Growing up, I was exposed to countless mystic traditions and legends. Stories of the Gray Mystic lineage were always those that most captivated me. According to legend, each newly appointed Gray Mystic's sacred power became whole during their first night upon assuming the throne. On that night, no stars would emerge, with the Inner Realm bathed only in the faint light of the solitary moon. As the darkness reached the midnight point, the moment precisely between the previous evening's sunset and the sunrise to come, the moon itself would grow dark. I believe they called it 'Night of the Vanishing Moon.' Supposedly, at that instant the sacred tower would emit a light so brilliant, so penetrating as to illuminate the whole of the world—of all worlds—bathing it in the power of the new Gray Mystic. On the moon's re-emergence into the early morning sky, all the world's great energies would then, and only then, flow fully through the newly reigning Voduss Grei."

"And you believe all of that?" asked Lakos.

Belwellin laughed. "I'll wager that you're the first imminent Gray Mystic to ever question the validity of his own ascendancy. But yes, to answer your question, I do."

"And once the moon has been blotted from the sky, what becomes of all remaining mystics?" asked Lakos.

"The fate of those mystics not currently imprisoned here will be just the same as those within the tower dungeons. They will be entirely and exclusively under your control. A reasonable action would be to leave them where they are—hidden in their caves, jungles, and treetops. Permit them to continue their petty existences, though ensuring that every decision they make is authored by you. Many great civilizations could be built using their powers and abilities, all to suit your whim. Imagine—all the majestic beauty you see here in the Inner Realm not just confined to these steep volcanic boundaries but everywhere, in every land. All mystics acting in your honor, subconsciously of course, and serving all humans."

"Every living mystic a slave to human thought," said Lakos with a smile.

"Now, should you choose to do so, every mystic living on this world could alternately be sent swiftly to the next world. For while murder is prohibited amongst many mystic doctrines lest they forfeit their link to the spirit realm, it is nonetheless an act afforded the ruling Gray Mystic. A manner of facilitating universal continuity in the face of danger. Sacrifice for the greater good, if you will. The freedom to destroy all who stand in your way. I'll wager your old friend Gris Hallis failed to mention that," Belwellin said with a smirk.

"Yes, it seems to have slipped his mind," Lakos replied. He looked toward the captive Ohlinn, who merely stared vacantly ahead. "So, you are telling me that, at this moment, I possess both the power to send this Ohlinn to the next world and the authority to do so without consequence?"

"From the moment you first entered the black gate, my Lord," replied Belwellin.

The world outside the throne room flashed a brilliant white as Lakos stared at the Ohlinn and smiled. The Ohlinn captive walked across the throne room, past Lakos, and toward the open expanse of wall. He climbed the wall and stood upon the ledge, facing the world outside. Then he stopped.

Lakos walked over to the Ohlinn, beckoning Belwellin to follow. "It appears as though there is a great deal that Gris Hallis did not tell me," said Lakos gleefully.

"Your power will only grow under the dark of the moonless night," said Belwellin.

Lakos unsheathed his sword, the shrill sound causing Belwellin to flinch. The Ohlinn, meanwhile, still stood upon the ledge, perilously close to falling one thousand strides to the vibrant flora of the Inner Realm below.

Lakos held the sword up to Belwellin, first as if about to strike him, but then, with a grin, offering him the hilt. Uncertain of his master's intent, Belwellin cautiously grasped the handle and took the sword.

"Now, my good soldier," said Lakos, "what if you were to take the life of this lowly Ohlinn? What would await you in the next world?"

"Despite the bloodshed I have engaged in those thirty long years ago, I was not directly responsible for the loss of a single mystic life." He paused for moment. "So my fate in the next world, should I kill the Ohlinn before me, depends entirely upon one's beliefs." Belwellin rested the sword's blade benignly upon the palm of his other hand.

"And what of your beliefs?" asked Lakos.

Belwellin spoke solemnly. "The very notion of the next world is but mystic folklore. My belief is that the only life awaiting us beyond this one is the legend we forge for ourselves. To be remembered and spoken of by the generations to follow — that, in my estimation, is the only way we live on."

"Well said, my soldier. Now strike him down and stand by me as we both live on forever." Lakos gestured toward the Ohlinn.

Belwellin slowly raised the sword toward the back of the unsuspecting Ohlinn. He then brought his arms back and began his forward thrust.

Before the strike landed, another flash of bright light beamed in from beyond the throne room, blinding him. The tip of the heavy sword clanged against the stone floor as Belwellin recoiled, shielding his eyes with his free hand.

When the light faded, Belwellin saw the Ohlinn lean over the ledge and topple silently forward, descending the height of the sacred tower onto the rocks, soil, and trees far below.

The rich sound of laughter filled the throne room.

"Give me my sword," said Lakos, a broad smile crossing

his face as he took his weapon from the old guard. "You have proved yourself most admirable. Ah, how satisfying it would be to send every cursed mystic in these lands to such a crushing demise."

"Tremendously appealing it would no doubt be, my Lord," Belwellin responded, "but it is also worth knowing that your power is fueled by these very beings, through the cycle between all worldly life and the core of the world itself. They are, regrettably, a conduit for all worldly energy. Thus, the less mystic life in the world, the less power to surge through your fingertips." Belwellin spoke softly. "Of course, the choice will be entirely yours to make, my Lord."

"Tell me, is it true that I may never again leave the sacred tower?" asked Lakos.

Belwellin looked at the floor. "The legacy of the Voduss Grei was born of mystic sensibilities," he said. "What I have been told; you are free to leave the Inner Realm at any time. However, to do so would not only forfeit your authority but also conclude your time on this world. You see, for all mystic orders, most particularly the Ohlinn, leaving this world for the next is merely the ascension of a rung on a great eternal ladder. A Gray Mystic, once assigned to the throne, cannot perish from natural causes. The only route to the next world is to abandon his post atop the sacred tower. Death in this manner is not viewed as a punishment for neglecting duty as much as a means to transition a Gray Mystic once his successor has emerged."

"Of course, this perspective only holds true if one prescribes to the mystic theory of the next world," said Lakos. "But for rational humans such as you and I, leaving the Inner Realm would equate to a swift and permanent demise."

"I'm afraid that this is true, my Lord," said Belwellin.

Lakos paused, taking a deep breath. "Now," he said, "I should say that this is enough somber introspection for one evening. There are festivities to enjoy with our fellow men, and a world to conquer immediately thereafter."

He smiled, directing the old soldier from the throne room, through the black gate, and toward the revelry in the courtyard.

CHAPTER FORTY-THREE

Thayliss woke to the most beautiful sound he could imagine. Slowly opening his eyes, he saw Mawi-naa leaning over him, looking off into the distance while singing softly in a lilting, rolling language he did not recognize. His awareness gradually returning, he realized that he was lying among the branches of a tree, a cloth draped across his brow while his head rested gently in the Lii-jit's lap.

As if sensing her companion's alertness, Mawi-naa looked down at him, removing the material from his forehead. "A compress," she said, "made from the leaves of the balamaya tree. Seemingly exempt from the poisons so rampant in this land. I imagine the powers behind these abominations neglected to value the more obscure life here enough to taint it. Which is fortunate for you, as these leaves possess compounds capable of healing the sickness."

"Sickness?" he asked, not recalling his traumatic final moments of consciousness.

"The fruit you consumed contains some manner of toxin not of the living world. It induces corruption in all who consume it, causing them to grow violently possessive of all they see." She looked across the wide, green space around them. "Never before have I seen such wicked sorcery, but these grounds are rich with it. We tread on sacred ground, not intended for unexceptional beings such as us."

Thayliss propped himself up, sitting beside Mawi-naa and sharing the expansive view as the sun's evening retreat progressed. "I—I couldn't control myself. I saw my actions unfolding but could not intervene. As if I were no more than a passive observer. I tried, but I simply couldn't stop myself."

Mawi-naa said nothing, only looking downward reflectively.

"The soldier—" recalled Thayliss. "There was a soldier

approaching along the path, searching for us. For me." He thought for a moment. "I remember we hid in the bushes as he passed. Except he knew we were there. He almost killed us..."

"Indeed," Mawi-naa said.

Thayliss paused, then looked over at her. "The shrews—you sent them running past to divert his attention."

Mawi-naa looked up, her eyes misting over. "Yes. I used my power to control another being for my own personal gain." She wiped a tear from her eye. "Something I promised that I would never do under any circumstances. My brother Tiig and others like him would do such a thing without a second thought, regardless of what our culture has taught us. But ability without integrity is gluttonous. I swore to my forefathers that I would uphold their ethics, their tradition. I was different. But now I am just as weak and selfish as the others."

"But you did it to save a life," replied Thayliss. "That soldier would have sent me to the next world. Or even worse, delivered me personally to his heinous leader, Lakos."

Something occurred to Thayliss. "But why did you do it?" he asked. "Why go to such lengths to ensure my survival, first from the soldier and now from the poisoned fruit? The last time I saw you, your brother was on the verge of sending me to the next world himself. How do you know that I'm not a part of this? I'm a human, just like the members of the army within that tower."

"I don't know anything," she said. "I don't know why Tiig and I were spared from the spell that practically half of our order fell under. I don't know why we were the only two Lii-jit out of all who were left behind to actually fight for our freedom. And I don't know who you really are, or what it is you're after. But I choose to believe in you because without you, I am alone. And I cannot do this on my own." Mawi-naa allowed a tear to roll down her cheek, her eyes staring forward.

Thayliss gently placed a hand under her chin, imploring her

to look at him. "I assure you, under the stars above, that my only involvement in any of this is first as a victim and now as one of the beings who will bring this tyranny to an end."

Mawi-naa fought to manage the faintest smile. "I appreciate your conviction," she said. "But does a promise still hold true under a starless sky?"

Thayliss followed Mawi-naa's upward glance, noticing the steadily dimming sky appear strangely absent of stars. He had gazed up at more than enough evening skies to know that something was wrong.

"What is this?" he asked incredulously. "I've never seen a sky devoid of stars."

"The elders in my colony used to speak of the starless night. The vanishing moon. The crowning of the new Gray Mystic and the beginning of a new era. It happens tonight."

"Lakos?" Thayliss could not believe it. "A human?"

"The prophecy is coming to light." She looked down again. "Your people will rule the five realms while all others shall fall."

"Then let us ensure that our world has a different fate," said Thayliss, fire in his eyes.

Mawi-naa would not be swayed. "It is impossible. I was a fool to think otherwise. We are but two beings facing an army of humans, a legion of entranced mystic captives, and a prophesied leader who strikes with the force of all the Inner Realm behind him. It cannot be done. This war has already been lost."

Thayliss's eyes burned brighter still. "You are Lii-jit, a fiercely proud order of beings. And as I saw from your brother, an order committed to existing in the only time when we are truly alive, the present. Nothing has been lost, as long as your will for it to live on remains. Of course, before we can stop an unstoppable army, our first challenge will be setting foot outside the safety of this tree without being noticed."

"Actually, before you woke, the entire patrol retreated from these grounds and entered into the tower," said Mawi-naa, a hint of optimism beginning to emerge.

"Then that's one less obstacle to surpass," said Thayliss with a smile. "But you're quite right. We've got a challenge ahead of us. Two unarmed beings against an army."

"It is a saying among the Lii-jit that the solution to any problem we may encounter lies in the natural world, and our interaction with it," offered Mawi-naa with a smirk. "The greatest beast to roam my land, the crescent bear, stands the height of three adult Lii-jit, with rows of jagged teeth and claws that could slice through the thickest trunk. It is so named because when it looms before you, the sun behind it is reduced to all but a sliver. Each season, several of my kind are killed by this great predator, too frightened by the sight of it to control its mind, even if they chose to do so. However, it can be easily taken to the ground without weapon or trap." A devious look came across Mawi-naa's face.

"And how is that?" asked Thayliss, having heard of this vicious beast before and grateful to have never personally encountered one.

"By simply diverting its attention toward one direction while approaching stealthily behind it. At that point, even the slightest nudge will send it sprawling," said Mawi-naa, rather satisfied.

Thayliss was not convinced. "But that does not kill the beast. What keeps it from simply rising and attacking again, more maliciously than before?"

Mawi-naa remained confident. "The goal is not to kill the beast. The crescent bear is not the enemy of the Lii-jit. It simply feeds as we all do. The only thing keeping it from attacking again is the fact that by the time it regains its footing, its prey has long since vanished."

Thayliss thought for a moment, peering through the trees, along the dirt path, and toward the vast, white tower in the distance. "And to do that, all one needs is someone to distract it..."

"And someone to push," said Mawi-naa, completing the thought.

CHAPTER FORTY-FOUR

By the time Lakos and Belwellin entered the tower courtyard, the festivities were well under way.

Torches jutted out from the many pillars staggered throughout the cavernous room, casting the celebration in a yellow glow. Inside the perimeter of storage carts and emptied wagons, an army of hundreds dined, sang, and drank to their glory, all in a brash cacophony of laughter and music. Bottles of wine packed prudently for the journey now lay strewn, in varied states of completion, about the array of wooden tables. At the center of the gala, a large, crudely fashioned hearth sparked and crackled as numerous pigs, goats and fowl roasted within it, the bones of those already consumed littering the interlocking stone floor.

"Look at them," said Lakos, swelling with pride. "Each of them a lifetime of struggle and pain, all in patient preparation for this very night."

Belwellin seemed equally pleased. "The courtyard may no longer look quite as opulent as it did when we first entered the tower, but it certainly looks more hospitable."

Lakos waded through the jubilant masses toward the table nearest the hearth. He then climbed atop the table, much to the delight of those seated there. Seconds later, as his presence became known, all music and conversation ceased.

"My good men and women," he shouted, "tonight is indeed a most special night. Many of the details leading us to this monumental occasion elude you—how this great and wondrous Inner Realm came to be, with trees, animals, even a waterfall emerging seemingly in the blink of an eye. Perhaps no development is more awe-inspiring than the presence of this very tower, our glorious new home. But despite the mystery of the riches surrounding us, the most vitally important question is not how we arrived here, but why. And I'll wager that the answer to this is etched upon the hearts of every last one of you. My people, tonight is the night that we create history. For before tomorrow's sun rises, we shall rule the world. This is our time!"

The crowd erupted in cheers as Lakos knelt down to pick up a bottle resting on the table. Holding it high above his head, he shouted, "To the age of the human!"

He took a swig from the bottle and leapt from the table back to the stone floor. As quickly as the courtyard had gone silent in the moments before his speech, it once again burst back to life with sounds of merriment.

Lakos walked over to Belwellin and put his arm on the old guard's shoulder. "Belwellin," he said, "go—enjoy the evening with your fellow soldiers. You've earned it."

Belwellin nodded in appreciation. "Many thanks, my Lord. I have waited a long time to savor this victory. But I assure you, I shall return to the throne room promptly before the midnight darkness falls. We are close, but we are not yet there."

"I would expect nothing less. Now go," replied Lakos, watching Belwellin reconnect with several of his fellow guards and disappear into the crowd.

Lakos surveyed the room and smiled. He could not recall the last time his loyal soldiers had enjoyed such gaiety. In fact, he could not recall the last time he, himself, had engaged in celebration.

His memory consisted of three, distinct volumes: There was his childhood, the tragedy at Merrin Ells, and then all that followed—the countless hours, days, and years of struggle coalescing into one thirty-year reminiscence. The realization that he was on the cusp of turning the page to a new chapter of his existence was overwhelming. He was going to enjoy it.

Standing before the hearth, Lakos reached in and tore a leg from a crackling, golden brown turkey, taking a bite and savoring the soft, suppleness of the meat. It was the most delicious, satisfying bite he had ever taken. The music, the very atmosphere, was unlike any he had witnessed before. Lakos felt his stomach flutter in anticipation as he waded through the crowd. He stood on the precipice of greatness, of a dream—a prophecy—realized. He weaved between soldiers and guards, healers and weapons makers, deep in thought. He had simply never felt such joy in all his life.

As he walked, he came upon a clearing in the middle of the crowd. A small section of the courtyard had been cleared, with a thick netting used for fishing wrapped around the pillars surrounding it, fencing off the space within. Beyond the perimeter were row upon row of celebrants, still singing and drinking and carrying on, but all peering into the open space before him. Lakos looked around to see what was going on.

A soldier nearby leaned over to him. "I'm sorry, my Lord," he said sheepishly. "It wasn't my idea. Some of the other men thought it amusing."

Lakos then saw two prison wagons roll toward the sectioned-off area, each of them pushed by several soldiers stumbling as they walked, semi-inebriated. Inside the first wagon, Lakos could see a young rock leopard cowering in the middle of the cage, frightened by the cheers and hollering from the sea of humans. Despite straining to see over the crowd, Lakos could not see the contents of the second cage from his vantage point.

The first image to enter Lakos's mind upon seeing the rock leopard was that of Gris Hallis, poised by the threshold to the Valla Forest, riding atop a broken-down old cat. It felt like a lifetime ago. So much had changed in so little time.

Lakos looked at the soldier and laughed. "A fine idea it is, good soldier. The battle between two savage beasts is a spectacle our forefathers enjoyed long ago. I can think of no finer way to honor them on this wondrous night."

The soldier attempted to smile but couldn't. The look of worry still drew long upon his face. "My Lord, the beast is not to fight a fellow animal—"

Before the soldier could finish his sentence, Lakos was afforded a clear view of the second wagon. Inside the cage was a mystic. A small Lii-jit. A female.

"I know that you did not consent to this, but we found this prisoner outside the dungeon, wandering along the path by the tower entrance," explained the soldier. "Perhaps she was one of the final Lii-jit to crash beyond the ridge and somehow became separated from the others after being led through to the Inner Realm."

Lakos scrutinized the Lii-jit as its wagon rolled to a stop just outside the makeshift arena.

Sensing his master's displeasure, the soldier spoke again. "She appears to be very much under the same spell as the others. In fact, when we approached her, she made no attempt to escape. She did not even acknowledge that we were there. She practically entered the wagon without prompting."

By this time, the rock leopard had been released into the pen. It prowled around cautiously, sniffing the air. The soldiers who had been pushing the wagons, like all the surrounding spectators, grew aware of Lakos's presence. Like overzealous children caught in the act of disobedience, the crowd froze, awaiting his reaction.

Lakos walked over to the wagon, the crowd parting to afford him a path to the cage. He peered through the densely woven netting at the small mystic inside. True to the soldier's tale, the Lii-jit appeared every bit as aloof and oblivious as the others.

After a long pause, he took what little remained of the turkey leg he had been carrying and tossed it into the middle of the pen, where the rock leopard quickly pounced upon it. Its long, sharp fangs effortlessly crushed the thick bone, splintering it into oblivion an instant after hitting the ground.

Lakos raised his arms high and shouted, "Send this discarded Lii-jit to the next world!"

His words were met with a roar of approval from the crowd as the soldiers unlocked the wagon's gate and guided the little female Lii-jit out of the wagon, over the netting, and into the pen.

The rock leopard, pacing at the other end the pen, immediately took notice and began stalking closer.

CHAPTER FORTY-FIVE

Thayliss watched under the cover of a nearby tree as Mawi-naa wandered by the wide, open entrance to the tower courtyard, feigning catatonia. In a heartbeat, she had caught the attention of one of the celebrating soldiers and within moments was led into a prison wagon and taken away, disappearing into the tower. Thayliss just hoped she knew what she was doing.

He had his own perilous journey to undertake.

Before she left, Mawi-naa had pointed Thayliss in the direction of the tunnel where the captive mystics were led upon her arrival. Unfortunately, while both she and Tiig had arrived together in the same crowded desiccadi transport carriage, she was the only one to elude detection and disappear into the woods of the Inner Realm. Her elder brother had been corralled back into the herd just as he was about to make his break, forced to follow the steady stream of prisoners through the dirt path, across the courtyard, and down the first tunnel on the left. She was grateful that the guard who noticed him starting to stray simply assumed that he, like the others, was entranced, but all the same, it pained her to see him taken. Leaving her to attempt a rescue all alone.

From his current vantage point, Thayliss could see into the brightly lit courtyard and hear the boisterousness and levity spilling out into the young night air. He could also see across the stone floor to the wall on the other side. Along the far wall were a series of arches, each arch cascading down to the ground only to rise up again to form the border of the one beside it.

"The first tunnel on the left," Mawi-naa had clearly instructed.

Thayliss quietly descended from the tree and crept toward the wide, open face at the base of the tower. It appeared that Mawi-naa's diversion was a success, as the sparse collection of soldiers and guards lingering along the outer edge of the courtyard had been drawn to the commotion and away from the entrance. Even the guard standing watch outside the first archway had left his post, no doubt eager to see the impending carnage.

Thayliss hoped with all his heart that such a fate would not come to pass. He was still trying to fully understand the inner workings of the Lii-jit mind, a confounding mixture of rationality, principle, and reckless spontaneity. Nonetheless, Mawi-naa was, at this point, his only ally in this world.

Leaning against the white stone wall just outside the tower entrance, Thayliss was struck by the texture of the stones themselves. From up close, it did not appear as though the tower was constructed with typical quarried stone. Instead, it seemed almost alive, shimmering with the same peculiar lights that had accompanied the vision of Tiig trapped within the volcanic stone during Thayliss's arduous journey to the Inner Realm.

As he plotted his next move, Thayliss was unsettled, feeling as though he were attempting to subvert an energy far exceeding comprehension. An energy that was always watching. Always aware.

Forcing all insecurities from his mind, Thayliss peered around the corner to see if anyone still lingered nearby. All he saw were the backs of hundreds of people, cheering and laughing in a series of raucous eruptions. Thayliss could not afford to lose focus by concerning himself with the object of their fascination. He needed to act upon the opportunity it granted him, lest Mawi-naa's great sacrifice be in vain.

Conveniently attired in the uniform of Lakos's soldiers—with the exception of the conspicuously ill-fitting pair of boots—Thayliss strode casually into the light of the courtyard. Several steps in, he glanced around to see if he had been detected, but still saw only enthralled spectators, their attention focused elsewhere.

He ventured further, trying to walk as quickly as one could

without arousing suspicion. Seeing a half-empty bottle of wine resting on the ground, he picked it up and took a sip, both to complete the image of a hearty reveler as well as to help calm his rattled nerves. The bitterness of the wine made him cough, which he did his best to stifle. The vile concoction sorely lacked the mild sweetness of Ohlinn wines.

Nearing the first archway, Thayliss saw that it opened into a long tunnel dimly lit by flickering, wall-mounted torches that seemed to fade into an abyss. Feeling the eyes of paranoia upon him, Thayliss forced down another gulp from the bottle and forged ahead.

From his first step onto the dungeon path, Thayliss felt everything change. In stark contrast to the opulence and rigid perfection of the courtyard, this tunnel was different, assaulting every sense and instilling in Thayliss a vague dread. The way his footsteps echoed on the uneven, asymmetrical stone floor, the musty smell, the sinister manner in which the torchlight danced off the jagged walls.

Venturing farther down the path, Thayliss felt his very sense of equilibrium oddly strained. But on he walked, deeper into the ominous tunnel, searching for the prisoners.

As he walked, passing by torch upon torch, he began feeling as though each subsequent torch was identical to the one preceding it. In fact, even the exact manner in which the flickering light cast its shadows upon the walls and flooring seemed eerily similar. Had he been traveling in circles? It was impossible, he assured himself. He had been walking in a straight line the entire time.

But as he thought further, he realized that the angle at which he first entered the tunnel would have taken him into the curved wall of the tower by now, forcing him, at the very least, to turn slightly to the right. But he was certain that he had not turned.

Feeling panic well up inside him, he began walking faster, spilling the wine over his hand and onto the dusty ground. As he passed by the torches with increased speed their striking similarities grew all the more disturbing, down to the streaks of ash surrounding the carved wall mounts. It was impossible!

He ran down the tunnel, smashing the bottle on the ground. But still the same light passed by, over and over. His lungs burned from exertion within the thick, suffocating tunnel, but still he ran.

Eventually, he could see a change in the scenery up ahead— finally! As he approached, he noticed that the variation he had seen was a splash of dark burgundy staining the uneven, stony ground.

His heart sank as he reached down and swiped a finger across it, coloring his fingertips red with wine.

CHAPTER FORTY-SIX

Mawi-naa descended calmly into the pen, fighting every impulse within her to do otherwise. She now had two options — to relent and once again use her mystic abilities to control the rock leopard staring hungrily across at her, or leap from the pen and hope that she could return to the safety of the trees.

Unfortunately, neither option was without extreme risk. Should she render the savage beast docile, she would expose herself as not being under the same spell as the rest of her imprisoned kind. Similarly, simply relying on her speed and agility to evade both the beast and the wall of netting surrounding her would yield an identical predicament: being surrounded by hundreds of soldiers, each with a sword strapped to his waist and bent on seeing mystic death.

Perhaps, just perhaps, the rock leopard would somehow grow perceptive to her natural Lii-jit gifts without her having to use them and yield at her feet without issue. Such behavior, though rare, was not unprecedented. Unfortunately, such phenomena were typically associated with Lii-jit much stronger and energetically inclined than herself.

Tiig once claimed to have found himself in such a situation while exploring the caves behind the Sani-jai waterfall. Accidentally stepping into a den containing several young bear cubs, Tiig turned to leave but saw a large, female crescent bear blocking his path. Paralyzed with fear, Tiig shut his eyes, awaiting his demise. Instead, however, he heard the sound of the giant bear shuffling past him. Opening his eyes to see only the cascading waterfall outside the cave, he ran to safety.

As exhilarating as the story was to hear, Mawi-naa had concluded that in all likelihood, Tiig had used his abilities, as he often did, to force the bear into timidity. She also thought it equally likely that there never even was a bear.

Now, however, she hoped with all her being that the story was true.

Mawi-naa stood with her back against one of the marble columns around which the mesh netting wrapped. Still forcing herself to appear calm and oblivious to her surroundings, she watched with utter immersion as the narrow, pointed head of the rock leopard swayed from side-to-side between its massive, angular shoulders, jaws open, panting loudly. She knew that the animal was stalking her.

While she had always sought to resist using her abilities to control another life, she often found herself keenly aware of what they thought and how they felt. The sense was as much a part of her as seeing the animal or hearing its call. Whether it was hungry, tired, content or in pain, Mawi-naa could sense all of these. In fact, the only beings for which she lacked this ability were mystics and humans, though in her limited interaction with humans, she felt that such extra-sensory gifts were rarely necessary.

The throngs of screaming, laughing human soldiers surrounding her served as abundant evidence of this fact. The humans crowding closest to her forced their arms through the netting to grab hold of her, attempting to push her farther out into the pen. Though she knew it may betray the stupor of compliance she feigned, she simply could not bring herself to move from her spot in front of the column.

However, the commotion drew the attention of the great predator, and it skulked steadily toward her. As it neared, like a distant form coming into focus, Mawi-naa found herself growing aware of its intent. The rock leopard was frightened and confused by the mad frenzy around him. He was in good health, but he was hungry, having traveled with the humans in a cramped cage for many days. He needed desperately to feed.

Mawi-naa stood perfectly still amidst the furious commotion resonating within the courtyard. She stared directly into the mottled yellow eyes of the rock leopard as it looked back at her, assessing its prey. Slowly it drew nearer, its jaw lowered as its panting deepened. It was going to strike, she knew it. But she refused to change its course, not out of fear of being exposed to the vile army around her, but out of respect. And love.

As she stood, awaiting her brutal demise, she knew, for the first time, why she resisted succumbing to the temptation of abusing her gifts. Though she respected her forefathers greatly and sought to honor them and the great Lii-jit culture they envisioned, it was not in their honor that she followed their decree. It was because she felt as strong a bond toward the animal and plant life she lived amongst as she did with any so-called intelligent being. The natural world was so beautifully crafted, so perfect, that to be but a small part of it was a privilege. And to alter that world to suit her own needs and ambitions could only render it less perfect.

Mawi-naa stood, feeling her body relax and grow calm. The boisterous sounds around her evaporated as she stared ever deeper into the eyes of the approaching beast. She did not wish for death, but suffering such a fate through an act of nature would appease her soul infinitely more than simply falling upon the sword of some crude mercenary.

With the rock leopard a mere three strides from her, Mawi-naa saw the beast lower its head just above the stone ground and raise its haunches, preparing to strike. She bowed her head and stretched out her arms by her side, awaiting the end.

The rock leopard leapt. Feeling no impact, Mawi-naa looked up to see the great beast soaring over her and over the mesh barrier.

As it descended upon the shocked onlookers, panic erupted. The crowd frantically fought to disperse, at once and in all directions, as the rock leopard took its first victim.

Seeing that all attention had shifted from her, Mawi-naa ran. She ran as fast as she could, darting to the far end of the pen and leaping over the netting. She hit the ground silently and continued running toward the courtyard entrance and the dark, wooded sanctuary beyond it. In her wake, she could hear anguished screams as the starved beast sought to nourish itself. The sound pleased her, though she felt a mild guilt at feeling so.

She approached the threshold to the tower courtyard, the cool outdoor breeze brushing against her face. Taking one final leap toward the dirt path ahead, she was suddenly blinded by a brilliant white light filling the entire space beyond the tower. Disoriented, she fell in a heap upon the ground.

As the darkness of night once again returned to the air around her, Mawi-naa struggled to rise but was unable. Below the waist, her body had grown numb. Hearing the sound of footsteps behind her, she craned her neck to see who approached.

"An interesting ploy, my dear," said the voice behind her, silhouetted by the glowing torchlight inside the courtyard. When her eyes adjusted, Mawi-naa saw the figure of a man with long waves of dirty blonde hair, clad in faded, leather garments.

The figure turned to face the interior of the courtyard and waved his hand. Another, more brief flash of light erupted around her. When it, too, faded, Mawi-naa looked on in horror as the rock leopard ceased its attack and grew rigid, like a fallen leaf in the heat of the sun—frozen in form, back arched and jaws bared. Within moments, it seemed as though all hydration left its body, and it slowly crumbled to dust in the cool breeze drifting in from outside.

"Nature without control is chaos, Lii-jit," said the figure, turning back to her. "I am Lakos, and I am your king."

CHAPTER FORTY-SEVEN

Thayliss was at a loss. He had begun his journey into the dungeon tunnel with designs of rescue, and now he, himself, was in need.

It didn't make any sense—none of it. What appeared as merely walking in a straight line was in fact a convoluted series of bends and turns, no doubt designed by a mind no less twisted. He felt as though he had been walking for ages but had yet to come upon any semblance of an actual prison cell. Which underscored yet another element of the dungeon's vexation, the fact that he had lost all sense of time since entering the cursed tunnel.

Somewhere outside in the courtyard, Mawi-naa was subjecting herself to the whim of a crazed and bloodthirsty mob. Sacrificing herself to grant him the opportunity to make a difference. But he was failing her. He was failing them all.

Thayliss slumped to the ground, lost and alone.

Sitting on the cold stone floor, he pondered why he was fighting so hard to save a world that seemed to lack any affinity whatsoever for him. Perhaps the intense drive pushing him forward bore no more significance than that of an insect that had lost its head. For a time, the legs still propelled the creature forward, but there was no intelligence behind it. No true direction. Its progress was no more than the product of a lag, a delay in the time it took for the body to realize that the spirit had left. But eventually, invariably, the body, too, ceased to function.

As Thayliss lay, wracked with despair, he knew that this was what had happened to him. When the villainous warlord Lakos sent his beautiful Leysiia and her father to the next world, their spirits were not the only ones to depart. After that moment on the border of the Valla Forest, Thayliss continued forward, fighting for all the things he used to believe in so passionately: justice, honor, hope. But only because his body had been trained to do so. The heart, the spirit behind it, was gone.

Thayliss felt his journey finally come to an end. Reaching into his pocket, he removed a small packet of leaves tied together with a thin strand of willow branch. Untying the strand, he carefully unfolded the bundle to reveal a gelatinous, orange substance inside.

When they were still in hiding outside the tower, devising their strategy, Mawi-naa had obtained the sap from a nearby tallacia tree and cautiously packaged it. Handing it to Thayliss, she informed him that the sap was very toxic, with merely one drop capable of killing a Lii-jit or a human. The sap was also highly corrosive, able to dissolve through even the strongest of metals. Seeing as how Thayliss sought to liberate hundreds of presumably caged prisoners without the use of a key, this seemed an innovative, if not guaranteed, alternative.

But there were no prison cells, and the prisoners within them were nowhere to be found.

Thayliss could spend what little time he had left wandering hopelessly through the tunnels, fully aware that finding and liberating the mystic prisoners would be of little consequence. With each passing moment, he grew increasingly certain that they would leave the dungeons only to step out into a world that had already been conquered.

Alternately, he could put a merciful end to his pain and suffering and depart this world a free man. It was far from ideal, as such behavior went strongly against Ohlinn beliefs, but it hardly mattered now. Besides, he was not Ohlinn. He was a human. When he left this world, there was in all likelihood no other awaiting him. The thought of reuniting with Leysiia, spending an eternity in ethereal bliss, was a fanciful notion and no more. He had lived a lie. And it was time to put that lie to rest.

Thayliss stared at the innocuous-looking orange sap in his hands and pondered its effects. If it was truly as lethal as Mawinaa had said, then this would all end soon.

About to dip his finger into the substance, he paused, distracted by what appeared to be a faint light emerging up ahead. He paused and looked up, seeing the figure of Leysiia standing before him, barely visible against the flickering torchlight.

Thayliss couldn't be sure if his eyes were deceiving him. Unlike the vibrant, detailed image he had seen during his Ohlinn meditation, what he now saw — or, at least, what he thought he saw — was little more than a vague, expressionless image. Thayliss wiped his eyes, unconvinced that what he was seeing was actually there. As he looked again, the image grew fainter still, seeming little more than the suggestion of a tall, thin silhouette cast by the play of torchlight upon clouds of dust.

"Leysiia!" shouted Thayliss, as the image disappeared completely.

He was crushed. The image offered no guidance, no support. No soft, gentle smile, urging him onward. Perhaps the sighting was no more than the product of his desperation and delirium.

Thayliss once again looked upon the orange substance held in his palm. It was time.

"Hello?" a muffled voice echoed up ahead.

Thayliss looked up, squinting into the darkness. "Hello? Is there anyone there?" he shouted.

After a long pause, the voice replied. "Yes, we are imprisoned here. You must help us!"

Thayliss gently re-tied the leaves around the orange sap, slipped the package back into his pocket, and rose to his feet. Walking ahead, he called out, "Speak again. Let me follow your voice."

"We're over here," shouted the voice. "Then again, of course we're here. Everywhere I go, I'm here. At least to me. Much as, I suppose, you are there. Wherever that is."

Thayliss heard the voice more clearly this time. It seemed to originate up ahead but slightly to the right. Despite the tunnel still lacking any perceptible branches or deviations, he now had a slight awareness that the path curved gently to the right.

"Are you here to rescue us?" asked the voice.

"I am," Thayliss replied, cautiously stepping forward. "Rather, I shall try my best to do so."

"Many blessings to you," the voice replied, louder and clearer still. "I feared that these dark walls would be my last sight on this world. If you can consider near darkness to be any manner of sight."

Thayliss turned a corner, seeing row upon row of bars before him, each containing dozens of individuals. However, within the cell directly in front of him, standing just on the other side of the bars, was the source of the voice that beckoned.

"Tiig!" Thayliss called out, feeling an immense sense of relief that the little Lii-jit was still alive. "Thank the spirits," he said, stepping close to the bars. "I feared that you—"

Thayliss felt his shoulders grasped tightly as his body was pulled against the bars, his face pressed up against the cold metal. Tiig held him in a firm grip and glared at him, seething.

"You have the utter gall to return to me, human?" he said, his jaw jutted, and lips curled. "Traitor! Scoundrel! Were I not behind these bars, the entirely of these cursed stone walls would echo with the sound of your screams as I unleashed my wrath upon you. You and your gluttonous kind are responsible for all of this."

"But, Tiig," pleaded Thayliss, "I'm not a part of this! I've come here with Mawi-naa to rescue you, all of you, and stop Lakos before it's too late."

Tiig's eyes grew more intense still as he held Thayliss so firmly against the bars that the air was forced from his lungs. "What of Mawi-naa?" he asked. "I could not elude your filthy kind, but she ran to the safety of the trees—I saw her myself. If you harmed her, I will pull you through these very bars. She was our last hope."

"I'm not one of them," whispered Thayliss, every word expelling precious air from his aching lungs.

"Then why do you dress as they do?" Tiig screamed, thrusting Thayliss away from the bars, on the verge of slamming him into them again.

Thayliss breathlessly struggled to reach into his pocket and extract the parcel. Feeling his field of vision slowly begin closing in, he dropped the package into the cell.

Tiig, peering down at the object, released Thayliss and knelt down quickly to pick it up.

"Where did you get this?" he demanded.

"I told you," replied Thayliss, leaning forward with a hand placed upon his battered chest. "I'm with Mawi-naa. She created a diversion that enabled me to enter the dungeons to rescue you. All of you. But we don't have time to argue. You have to believe me."

Tiig unfolded the package and saw the orange sap, his rage turning instantly to ebullience. "It's brilliant," he said, rushing to apply the sap judiciously to the cell's large, steel lock.

Almost immediately, the shimmering metal lost its luster, emitting an acrid gray smoke as it grew rusted and porous.

"You may wish to stand back, human," said Tiig. He kicked the gate, snapping the now-fragile lock and swinging the cell's door wide open.

"Now, I trust you know the way out of here," said Tiig, busily applying the sap to the locks upon the multitude of prison cells around them. Not hearing a reply, Tiig stopped what he was doing and turned to him. "There is only silence. Why is there only silence? Surely you did not come all this way to release us from these cells only to have us perish wandering these treacherous tunnels, did you? The sheer breadth of human ineptitude never ceases to appall me."

Thayliss had heard enough. He strode over to the angry Lii-jit and pressed him up against one of the cells. "Listen to me, Lii-jit," he snarled. "I do not know from where your bottomless contempt of my kind arose, but the acts of one hundred humans— of a thousand—do not equate to the actions of all. Your sister is quite possibly the kindest, most sincere being left on this world, but you yourself serve as living proof that one cannot generalize a race of beings on the basis of one individual. There is quite enough hatred and ignorance outside of this dungeon. We do not have use for more." With that, he released his grip on the wide-eyed little mystic.

The two beings stood in uncomfortable silence for a moment, each lost in his own whirlwind of thought.

Finally, Thayliss spoke. "I had no knowledge of this dungeon's devious design. I do not know the way out."

Tiig was about to reprimand him but stopped, appearing to formulate an idea. "The legend of the sacred tower spoke of its original construction by Masdazii builders. I cannot say for sure, but the possibility exists that this same design was adopted in its reconstruction. If that is indeed the case, then we need only liberate the Masdazii captives and follow them out. Out they go, out we go. Simple." He gestured toward several cells containing a number of the large, oafish matter-mystics.

"But what of the spell that consumes them?" asked Thayliss. "Look around—we are surrounded by hundreds of mystics, Lii-jit, Masdazii, and Ohlinn. And yet we are the only two beings in this dungeon who retain our conscious will." He pointed toward the cells whose locks were already dissolved by the sap. "These prison doors swing freely open, and yet their captives remain motionless. They still follow silent orders from the one who rules from the tower throne. Until that power is taken from him, we are the only two beings in this convoluted dungeon who aspire to leave. And as long as that is the case, it will never happen."

As much as he wished it not to be so, Tiig knew Thayliss was right. "We cannot leave without breaking the spell, and yet the spell cannot be broken while we remain here. We are in need of a miracle."

At that moment, a third voice emerged from within a darkened cell. "No, my lads. You simply need one who can light the way."

An electric rush of anger and contempt surged within Thayliss as the figure grasped the bars and leaned into the light, accentuating the deep grooves along its weathered face.

"Now why don't you see me out of this miserable cell?" Gris Hallis asked.

CHAPTER FORTY-EIGHT

"Please, my dear," said Lakos, "try to relax and enjoy the view."

Following the incident in the courtyard, Mawi-naa had been escorted up to the throne room where, forced by a power she was unable to resist, she now stood upon the ledge overlooking the Inner Realm far below. Ribbons of swirling incandescent light wrapped around her, holding her firmly in place, arms at her sides and looking straight ahead. Any attempt to struggle or break free from the mysterious force seemed to only tighten its grasp.

For some time after arriving in the room through the black gate, Lakos sat quietly on his throne, relishing in his new prisoner's struggles.

"You know, the energy that binds you can just as easily release you," he said, consuming a handful of berries he had taken from the festivities in the courtyard. "However, I doubt even a nimble Lii-jit could survive a fall of a thousand strides. Why, just earlier this evening, I attempted it with an Ohlinn, and the results were, shall I say, less than encouraging. But truthfully, it is not an outcome that I wish for you to repeat."

He rose from his seat and approached her. "There was a time, mystic, when I would have put my sword through you on first laying eyes upon you." Lakos reached out his hand, gently caressing Mawi-naa's cheek.

"Why such hatred?" she asked, slightly relaxing her tense body. "Whatever wrongdoing befell you in the past, surely the Lii-jit were not involved."

Lakos's hand grew firm as he held her jaw in place. "That was precisely the problem," he said, jerking his hand from her face and looking out wistfully upon the Inner Realm. "The Lii-jit were indeed not involved. On the night of the Three Betrayals, while the Gray Mystic was destroying my home and taking from me all that I held dear, the Masdazii joined him, causing still more havoc. But the Lii-jit, my dear, were nowhere to be seen. Your kind, the so-called life-mystics, could not have cared less for the value of human life on that night."

"And what of the Ohlinn?" she asked. "The legends spoke of Ohlinn mercy, rising up to defend and protect the humans of Merrin Ells against the siege of Noryssin. "Why do you seek to control their race as well?"

Lakos paused, as if stumbling upon a revelation. "My recollection of that night was fragmented for decades, and only now, as I stand on the brink of vengeance, do the details grow clear. On that night, when my family lay on the floor of my home, murdered through mystic savagery, I fled. I ran to seek solace in the darkness of the forest, amidst the fire and the crashing waves, the bloodshed and screams. As I ran, fearing with every step that I might feel the sting of a Masdazii sazaa tear through my back, I saw an Ohlinn standing on the threshold of the forest. I pleaded with him to take me far from the massacre around me, tears streaming from my eyes. But he merely stood, watching me, not an expression upon his wretched Ohlinn face. In my frantic haste, I tripped and fell, tearing open a gash in my leg. By the time I regained my footing and resumed my desperate race to safety, he was gone. Truth be told, I had seen numerous Ohlinn risk their own lives on that night, warding off the brutal Masdazii warriors while leading several villagers to safety, from infants to elders. But no one rescued me, a mere child. I finally made it into the sanctuary of the forest, orphaned, injured and alone. The look of shock in my parents' eyes as they were taken stayed with me for years, as did the look of malice in the eyes of the Masdazii who invaded our home. But the one look that penetrated me the most deeply, that most haunted me through these thirty long years, is the one that fully rises to my consciousness only now. It was the expression of pure ambivalence on the face of the Ohlinn standing at the threshold of the forest. The image itself may have been suppressed from my conscious mind through these many years, but the emotion behind it—the heartless lack of emotion—shone brightly every night. Every time I closed my eyes, it was there." Lakos, having immersed himself in the recollection, shifted focus back to the throne room. "There is blood on the hands of all mystics, my dear."

"That must have been a horrific experience," she offered sympathetically.

"It was a long time ago," replied Lakos, seeming strangely disconnected from the experience. "Times have changed. As, I suppose, have I." He climbed upon the ledge to stand right beside Mawi-naa.

Lakos, less than a stride from plummeting down the entire height of the tower, glanced downward and shuddered. "Oh my," he said, a smirk on his face, "that is quite the drop." He looked over at his captive, seeing the muscles twitching along her arms and legs. "Your kindness and compassion toward my experience is most appreciated. All the same, one can only imagine your frustration at this very moment, wanting nothing more than to free yourself and give me one... good... push." He hopped playfully off the ledge and back onto the safety of the throne room floor. "Well, my dear, I'm afraid you'll have to find a new set of aspirations. And I humbly offer a few suggestions."

Lakos walked behind the throne in the middle of the room and placed his hands on its back. As he did so, Mawi-naa felt herself rotate to face into the room.

"You see, whatever the misguided reason you saw fit to willfully enter into my Inner Realm and my sacred tower. As such, I would say that our two fates have now converged. I know you were not acting alone, and you can rest assured that your accomplices will soon be captured and dealt with. But I am not interested in them." He stepped around the throne, slapping the padding on one of the arm rests. "I am on the cusp of greatness.

By the time the moon above grows dark, this world, and all upon it, will be mine. Which, needless to say, includes you. So, I will present to you the options as I see them. After which you will share your opinion with me, and together, we will arrive at a decision regarding what exactly to do with you."

Grabbing another handful of fruit from beside the throne, Lakos continued pacing around the room, popping the berries into his mouth. "I am told that this is to be my home. I initially resisted the notion but have since come to embrace it. As you've no doubt encountered, we stand in a palace surrounded by natural wonders unparalleled in all the five realms. However, a kingdom without a queen is surely a vacuous place."

"This realm is without nature," fumed Mawi-naa. "All I see is blasphemy."

Lakos smiled. "I appreciate your spirit. Such strong convictions. We are, after all, both warriors. Fighting for different sides, perhaps, but there is certainly a mutual respect. Or at least I wish there to be. You see, after a lifetime spent loathing your kind, I have, in light of recent events, grown to appreciate exactly what it is you magical little creatures can offer." With a wave of his hand, Mawi-naa winced, feeling the energy field around her grow tighter. "It appears that there are rules to occupying this throne, one of which necessitates that I remain in the Inner Realm. And thus, everything that I wish to possess must also be kept within these walls. And I find that you possess a certain... allure. Your little performance in the ring with that rock leopard certainly showed a trait that I wish more of my men possessed. And so, we find ourselves at option one. Remain here with me, within the sacred tower. Perhaps more my pet than my queen, I admit, but it is nonetheless the most preferable option for all involved. Oh, and as for your co-conspirators, I will see to it that they live out their days in the dungeon. Admittedly not the most elegant of domiciles, but surely superior to a sword through the heart."

Mawi-naa, incensed, spat at his feet.

Lakos looked down at his soiled boot and smiled. "Option two is admittedly less appealing. I send you back down to the courtyard at this very moment and leave your fate within the hands of my loyal and deserving army. I cannot promise that they will be civil or in any way humane. But I do promise that when we find your accomplices, if my guards have not done so already, I will grant them the very same fate. Perhaps I will even place you together within the enclosure that my dear soldiers so ingeniously constructed. Let you fight to the death, perhaps?"

Despite Mawi-naa's contemptuous stare, Lakos continued. "Truth be told, I didn't hold out much hope for option two either. Still, I thought it civil to provide you with alternatives. Which brings us to option number three. Which, I shamefully admit, does carry a certain measure of appeal to me. I leave you just as you are, standing upon that ledge, until the night of the vanishing moon has run its course. After which, you will live to see the great prophecy realized and my kingdom come to life. Unfortunately, immediately after witnessing this momentous occasion, the secure harness now encircling you will be removed, and you will, sadly, fall to a swift demise. Your three options, my dear Lii-jit. Any thoughts?"

Mawi-naa scoffed. "Do as you please, human tyrant. The glory of the next world awaits me, which is more than I can say for a blasphemous, delusional being who actually thinks that he can rule the world." Sensing that she may have struck a nerve, she continued. "In fact, I've made my decision. I select option number three. Because nothing would give me more pleasure than to see a member of a blatantly inadequate race think that he can actually enter into the Voduss Grei. That sacred lineage belongs to the mystics, and no measure of human brutality can change that." A slight smirk etched across her lips. "The great human tragedy is not in their unending greed and desire to possess all things. It's in the misguided notion that they can ever hope to obtain them. I pity you, human," she said caustically.

Lakos remained outwardly calm, but his eyes betrayed his inner rage. "Whatever mental tricks you think you're playing, Lii-jit, they will not work. Your kind is best suited to swinging on vines and talking to animals. High intellect and subtle persuasion are simply not in your make-up. That's what's wrong with all of you mystics. Great at one thing, unbearably inadequate at all others. But when it comes to Masdazii ingenuity, Ohlinn self-reflection, and Lii-jit vigor, only one being emerges possessing traits of all three. Humans are the evolution of all beings. The grand creation arisen from your collective materials."

"You've got it backwards," interjected Mawi-naa. "You are the primitive, the flawed. The useless, directionless lump of clay which time, fortune, and the spirits molded into the heightened beings you attempt in vain to control."

"Silence!" bellowed Lakos. "You try my patience. But you shall get your wish, Lii-jit. I shall keep you alive just long enough to see the triumph of my race. At which point, supposed heightened beings such as yourself shall all become part of a stuporous collective, living only to serve my will."

Lakos once again walked toward the ledge and peered outside, his heart pounding in his chest. Beyond the jagged peaks of the Bray Ridge, in the black, starless sky above, a dark sliver slowly encroached upon the border of the brightly illuminated moon.

"It begins, my dear. The moon has already begun its inevitable journey into darkness. The reign of Lord Lakos is upon us. And you shall live just long enough to see it."

CHAPTER FORTY-NINE

Thayliss and Tiig looked at each other, incredulous.

"If you think that I'm going to let that scoundrel out of his cage, you're out of your mind," said Tiig, the small bundle of leaves cupped in his hand. "You'll have to pry this tallacia sap from my dead hands in order to get him out of there. And I highly doubt that you're capable of that."

Thayliss turned to Gris Hallis, who gripped the bars of his cell and leaned forward attentively, his sapphire eyes shining bright by the torchlight.

"The nerve of you, old Ohlinn, asking for our mercy. Did you grant my family mercy when you took them from their home and allowed your master to slaughter them?"

"There was no mercy when you kidnapped me, abused my powers, and tortured me for your sick satisfaction," chimed Tiig.

"You can never hope to repay the immense debt that you owe a great many beings. But the thought of you trapped behind these bars, forgotten, shamed, and alone, gives me at least the slightest sense of justice," said Thayliss bitterly.

Gris Hallis merely shook his head. "I am deeply saddened by the grief I have caused not only you, but all beings affected by my actions. I do not expect you to believe me and most certainly not to sympathize with me. But please hear my plea. Though my intent was just, my actions have caused more damage than a hundred lifetimes could hope to repair. But the burden of guilt and regret confines me more than these bars ever could."

He paused for a moment, before continuing. "But why I'm here has no bearing on why I should not be. The simple, undeniable truth is that I am the only one who knows how to escape from this dungeon. Unless, of course, you manage to rouse one of the captive Masdazii over there back into consciousness. But frankly, I don't see that happening. You may not like it, but either the three of us leave here together, or none of us does."

As much as he loathed the fact, Thayliss knew the old mystic was right. "Dissolve the lock," he instructed Tiig, who returned a fierce glare.

"Have you so swiftly forgotten? Look around you, human. These cells are filled with good, honest beings who were brought here against their will—robbed of their will—in order to fulfill a demon's prophecy. And none of this would have come to pass without the intervention of the one before you. The evil, pitiful wretch before you. I repeat, I will not let you release him."

A deep groan reverberated throughout the dungeon tunnel, roaring past in a wave that rattled every set of bars in its path.

"My good human," pleaded Gris Hallis, "do you hear that noise? That sound signals the coming of the vanishing moon. The reign of the new Gray Mystic will soon be upon us if we do not act now. Please, there is no time for argument. You must free me now!"

"This could all be a trap," shouted Tiig. "I will never again subject myself to being on the wrong side of a cage. You tricked me once, Ohlinn, and never again. I am not a prisoner, nor are my fellow Lii-jit. I will liberate those who have been wrongly captured. But you, spirit-mystic, are right where you belong."

"Why help us?" asked Thayliss, breaking the tension between them. "Were we to liberate you from this cage, I sincerely doubt that your gratitude would compel you to suddenly wish Lakos's plan to fail. Tiig is right—without your sinister notions, Lakos would never have had the idea, let alone the capability, to use mystic energy against the very beings that embody it. Why suddenly seek to reverse all that you have achieved when, if your story is correct, Lakos's reign grows imminent?"

"Because I was a fool," said Gris Hallis. "Because after waiting for thirty years to see the glory of the Voduss Grei restored, I became blind. Willing to cast aside the integrity and honor of the sacred lineage to peer out at the world through the lens of the Inner Realm just once more. I gravely wronged many of the very beings I so greatly cherished. I wanted to be great. To be remembered, like all of the Gray Mystics adorning the walls of the sacred corridor. I thought that even though I was never destined to rule, I could facilitate the realization of the prophecy. That by restoring order throughout the five realms, I might become a legend myself."

"Your remorse cannot erase the deeds you have done," said Tiig. "You are right where you belong."

"But you are not," said Gris Hallis. "You are correct, young Lii-jit. I do deserve to stay in this cursed prison for the rest of my days. But that would serve only to satisfy my penance. You and your kin deserve to be free, free from this prison, and free from the tyranny that beckons. And I am the one who can make that happen."

Once again, the walls rattled, kicking up clouds of dust within the narrow passageway and fracturing small pieces of stone from the ceiling. Thayliss turned to Tiig, his eyes imploring him to relent.

Finally, reluctantly, Tiig applied the sap to the lock on Gris Hallis's door. Within moments, it grew brittle, enabling the old Ohlinn to push at the gate and step out into the tunnel.

"No tricks, old mystic," warned Thayliss, realizing that he lacked any weapons with which to defend himself from such deception.

"None of the sort," Gris Hallis replied. "We must act swiftly. Lii-jit," he said, pointing to Tiig, "your kind can move at a speed far faster than either human or Ohlinn. There are numerous cages still to be unlocked. You must do this as quickly as you can, and then lead all captives out of the dungeon, through the courtyard, and toward the tunnel leading out into the Bray desert. Once through, you must get as far from this place as you can."

"But you've seen the state of the prisoners. They do not move of their own volition. I can open their doors, but they will not follow me. And as you, yourself, acknowledged, so long as the Masdazii lack the intellect to show the way from these passages, I will be going nowhere." Tiig was already regretting the old Ohlinn's liberation.

"As for the trance possessing the captive mystics, leave that to me. The moment their spell is broken, the Masdazii shall lead you from this dungeon faster than I ever could, you have my word." Gris Hallis nodded solemnly.

"The word of a traitor means nothing!" shouted Tiig.

"Tiig," interjected Thayliss, "we have no time for this. I don't like it any more than you, but it's the only chance we've got." He turned to Gris Hallis. "And what of me?"

"You will come with me," replied the old Ohlinn, heading off down the tunnel. "Oh, and Lii-jit—" he called out to Tiig, "I can never ask forgiveness for the wrongdoings I have committed both against you and through you. But by whatever mystic power still flows through my faded body, I ask the spirits to guide you safely home."

Not awaiting a reply, Gris Hallis led Thayliss hastily through the dimly lit tunnel, leaving Tiig to frantically continue his work throughout the vast expanse of prison cells.

CHAPTER FIFTY

Thayliss followed Gris Hallis through the dungeon passages, still uncertain of the fallen mystic's true motivation. However, just as he began to wonder whether or not he was actually being led out of the maze, a halo of light appeared up ahead. The faint sound of music began blending into their echoing footsteps. They were coming upon the courtyard.

Though Thayliss had no idea what to do once he stepped out into the bright, crowded area, the conviction and purpose with which Gris Hallis advanced in front of him instilled a minute sense of comfort. He just hoped that Mawi-naa was all right.

As they neared the tunnel's exit, the drifting music suddenly ceased. Almost simultaneously, Gris Hallis stopped in his tracks and shot an arm back toward Thayliss, keeping him a step behind. In the shadows at the threshold of the courtyard, they waited.

Unfortunately, they did not have to wait for long.

"You would have been wise to remain in your cell, old mystic," said a voice from inside the courtyard. "It would have been a fate preferable to the one you now seem insistent upon."

An old guard limped around the corner to block the dungeon entrance.

"Step aside, Belwellin," growled Gris Hallis. "You may have poisoned your master's already toxic mind in an attempt to take my place, but you are merely a pawn in his game. This matter goes much deeper than you could possibly imagine."

Thayliss, desperate to find Mawi-naa, stepped up beside Gris Hallis, ready for a battle.

Belwellin grinned widely upon seeing him. "I see you have brought me a gift," he said. "A matching pair with the little Lii-jit spy up in the throne room. This day grows better still."

Thayliss was incensed. "If you harmed her—" he shouted,

attempting to run toward the old guard.

Gris Hallis, however, reached out and blocked his path. "Stay where you are, Thayliss," he said calmly.

Belwellin scrutinized Gris Hallis's expression and smirked. "You know something, don't you?" he asked, a curious tone in his voice. "Something in all of this is not quite adding up, is it?"

Gris Hallis said nothing.

"Here, perhaps I can be of some assistance. Does this seem at all familiar to you?" Belwellin tapped his longsword against the wooden artificial boot. Before Gris Hallis could answer, Belwellin continued. "It should. This was the foot that you bound when you locked me in this very dungeon those thirty long years ago."

Thayliss felt his stomach drop, forcing him to lean upon the tunnel wall for support.

"Go ahead, tell him, fallen mystic—that's what they call you now, is it not? A most fitting name. Now tell him." Belwellin pointed his sword at Gris Hallis's throat.

Reluctantly, Gris Hallis spoke, his voice trembling in disbelief. "It was the morning following the massacre at Merrin Ells. The village lay in ruin, and the sacred tower crumbled all around us. I had no choice."

"You made your choice!" fired Belwellin. "I returned to the sacred tower in a weakened state, having expended much of my energy pursuing the human I saw in the prophecy. But once my grim task had proven a failure, additional measures had to be taken. What little power remained I directed inward, through the sacred tower itself, to the world's very core. In taking my sacred oath to join the Voduss Grei, I swore never to relinquish control to any being deemed unworthy of the lineage. As such, I had no choice but to sever the link between the heart of our world and all that circulated across it."

"You sought to destroy the world, Noryssin!" Gris Hallis replied.

"So you evidently thought. For once I set in motion the force to destroy the sacred tower, my last act as Gray Mystic, I lost consciousness. When I awoke, I found myself alone in the dungeon, my leg chained to the wall, as all around me crumbled to ruin."

"You had to be stopped," Gris Hallis replied, his bright eyes glossed with tears. "I knew that you would not rest until every human from that village was dead. And with no certainty that surviving villagers from Merrin Ells had not spread to other realms, to other villages, your assault would have waged on until the death of every last human. Your actions left behind a fractured world, lacking guidance or direction. I could not allow you to damage it further."

Unfazed, Noryssin continued his own tirade. "I was forced to sever my own foot. Then, I staggered from the dungeon and across the courtyard, amidst falling stones and billowing clouds of dust. And just as the sacred tower itself—my home—plummeted back into the desert soil, I dragged my weakened self into the one thing immune to physical destruction: the black gate. As no Gray Mystic is permitted entrance into the next world without the emergence of a successor, the energy within the black gate kept my spirit a part of this world. But my body was gone, absorbed back into the desert soil along with the rest of the tower."

Noryssin struck the ground with his sword. "So here I waited, year after year, for another Gray Mystic to ascend to power and mercifully grant me my release to the next world. But instead, the prophecy lived on. Promising greater harm to this, and all worlds, than my supposed betrayals ever did. Once the foolish human Lakos saw fit to restore the tower—my tower—and once again infuse it with material substance, my spirit was given a new body. I obtained a physical form from a rather obliging, now-deceased soldier from Lakos's army, and Belwellin came to be. Regrettably mortal, and still without the leg that you took from me."

"So, what happens now?" asked Gris Hallis.

"Now?" replied Noryssin. "Now I shall proceed to the throne room and take back what is rightfully mine. For two beings cannot both simultaneously wield the power of the Voduss Grei. As long as the villain Lakos sits upon my throne with his ill-gotten mystic powers, I shall remain in this pitiful human form. But I shall see to it that once the sky grows dark and the tower shines bright, the power of all worlds will once again flow through me and me alone. And the lifeless body of Lord Lakos will find itself tossed from my throne room window."

"And what of us?" Thayliss interjected, unsure whether he wanted to hear the response.

"I have a special use for you, human," replied Noryssin. "You see, I choose not to begin my second reign with the same infirmity with which I concluded my first." He gestured to his false lower leg. "I shall be granting you the great honor of serving as my corporeal form within this world, assuming your material body while your human consciousness vanishes quietly into the void."

Noryssin looked over at Gris Hallis. "And you, my old assistant. Once my most trusted ally. You were once as a son to me, but that was long ago. It pains me to say that you have no place in my new kingdom."

Noryssin raised his sword and slashed the blade across Gris Hallis's lower leg, severing his foot. Gris Hallis shrieked in agony, falling to the dusty stone floor, a pool of crimson forming around him. Thayliss, in shock, pressed his back firmly against the tunnel wall.

"Is there not an old Ohlinn adage that to step solely within the footprints of another is to have never traveled oneself?" said Noryssin. "I see that strangely apt in this instance, though you must forgive the crudeness of the literal interpretation. My poor Gris Hallis, wanting nothing more than to be remembered.

But let your final thoughts be the realization that your entire, miserable life was spent in the shadows, in darkness and obscurity. First shrouded under my greatness, and now among the shadows of a filthy dungeon floor. When you have taken your last breath, you will be lost to history."

Gris Hallis, lurching forward in pain, looked up at his former master. "How... could you..."

"This is the end of you, old friend," said Noryssin, thrusting the long, bloodied sword deep into Gris Hallis's abdomen.

Gris Hallis's head snapped back, his eyes wild in disbelief. As his body relaxed, he slumped over to his side. Noryssin leaned forward and, placing his wooden boot against Gris Hallis's shoulder, pulled his shimmering red blade from the old mystic's mortally wounded body.

Thayliss dropped to his knees beside Gris Hallis, putting his hand to the side of the old mystic's face. "Murderer!" he shouted, looking up at Noryssin.

Gris Hallis lay on the cold, stone ground, wincing in pain and sputtering blood.

"Murderer?" Noryssin replied. "I merely started him on his journey. It is true that his wound will eventually take his life, but only after hours, perhaps days, of agony. But I do not wish for that to happen. You see, I, too, entered this world as an Ohlinn, an order for whom the act of murder is strictly forbidden. When I entered into the Voduss Grei, I rose above reproach and could freely act as I saw fit without fear of consequence. But all of that was lost when my physical form perished with the ruin of my tower those many years ago. Until I retake the power of the Gray Mystic from the hands of Lakos, I am limited to this lowly, human form standing before you. So do the spirits view me as Ohlinn, as human, or as impending Voduss Grei? It is a fate I wish not to tempt. Thus, the choice is now yours, human." Noryssin unsheathed a small dagger from his hip and dropped it on the ground where Thayliss knelt. "You were undeniably born into human ways, where taking the life of another comes as naturally as taking your next breath. As the next world holds no room for your treacherous kind, you risk no persecution at the hands of the spirits. Take that dagger and send him mercifully away, as your wicked kind was meant to do. Or simply leave him be, where his final, agonizing moments, prolonged by your inaction, will forever echo in your dreams. Now make your choice."

Thayliss slowly picked up the dagger and raised it above Gris Hallis's writhing body. He saw the old spirit-mystic struggling to compose himself, slowly extending his arms toward Thayliss. Gris Hallis then wrapped his bloodied fingers weakly over Thayliss's and aligned the tip of the dagger with his own chest.

"I remember..." gasped Gris Hallis, "in the treetops of the Valla Forest... the dance of the jousting hummingbirds. I was just a boy. I see them now..." he whispered, the faintest hint of a smile curling the corner of his mouth. He then forced Thayliss's hands to drive the dagger deep into his chest. Almost immediately after, his hands slid to his sides and his eyes shut.

In shock, Thayliss withdrew the dagger from Gris Hallis's chest. The blade dripped not with blood but with a viscous, blue substance that shimmered in the light. Glancing down at the lifeless body before him, Thayliss could see shards of what appeared to be a fractured blue crystal jutting out from the center of Gris Hallis's chest.

"The mark of the Tierren bond," said Noryssin, glancing down upon the scene. "How intriguing. It appears our dear departed Gris Hallis got himself involved with an Ohlinn brotherhood. With whom, I wonder. Alas, I suppose it matters not."

Thayliss knelt upon the cold, stone floor, surveying the blue-tinged knife held tight in his trembling hand. The sacred bond of the Ohlinn brotherhood was something he knew quite well, comprising yet another chapter in the voluminous history of spirit-mystic life bestowed upon him through Leonorryn's many teachings. But, like many other chapters, Thayliss had dismissed it as mythology until seeing it right before his eyes.

Thayliss, too, couldn't help but wonder who had entered into this sacred pact with such a lowly figure. Gris Hallis had long been banished from the safety and fraternity of the Valla Forest, and it was unlikely he had encountered any Ohlinn in the decades since for long enough to forge such a bond. A bond created solely for the safety of rulers, not disgraced old mystics such as he. The question remained — Why?

"Fear not, human," assured Noryssin. "This mystic world must seem so foreign to you. But you need not concern yourself with such things. So long as the blue substance enveloping that blade does not pierce your own heart." He laughed, extending a hand towards Thayliss. "In which case, you would regrettably take Gris Hallis's place and forge an eternal bond of your own with whomever is on the other end of his pact. Of course, being but a frail human, your poor heart would probably stop beating the moment the blade pierced it, brotherhood or otherwise." He smirked, taking the knife from Thayliss's hand. "And we wouldn't want that now, would we?"

"Now on your feet," ordered Noryssin. "The moon fades ever faster. And I'm not finished with you yet."

CHAPTER FIFTY-ONE

Tiig had lost count of how many prison locks he had corroded using the orange tallacia sap. He focused only on applying the substance as sparingly as possible, in the hopes that he would have enough to liberate every mystic prisoner held within the dungeon.

It maddened Tiig to see so many from his colony behind bars, wandering passively about. They were his family, whether by blood or by culture. He despised the humans for what they had done, and he longed to see them pay.

He knew that the tower dungeons had existed long before, as much a part of the Voduss Grei folklore as the Inner Realm itself. The legends often made reference to the detainment of those attempting to overthrow the Gray Mystic, though Tiig found it hard to imagine a more justifiable reason for a rebellion than right now.

Throughout history, the ruling Gray Mystic from each age was unfailingly just, acting always in the best interests of the world he served. Until the sacred tower fell into ruin and much of the world along with it.

Though the events that unfolded that fateful night at Merrin Ells occurred before Tiig had entered this world, it always seemed to him that Noryssin's so-called betrayal was, in fact, his greatest sacrifice. Having envisioned destruction and despair at the hands of a human, he merely sought to fulfill his duty. To govern and protect all worldly life. It seemed plausible enough. Humans had certainly caused more than their share of death and mayhem toward many of the other life forms around them. It was practically inevitable for one to grow so ambitious as to attempt to overtake the sacred tower. While Tiig never delighted in the death of any being, human or otherwise, the events at that seaside village seemed appropriate within its context.

Noryssin's actions at Merrin Ells seemed all the more validated with the opening of each successive prison cell. The havoc wreaked by humans knew no bounds. Tiig only wished that the old Gray Mystic had been successful in extinguishing the life of the human Lakos on that night long ago. For the tower he sought to liberate his fellow mystics from was not the sacred tower of old.

The original sacred tower, as with the Inner Realm surrounding it, had been constructed through the desire of mystic followers to contribute to a grand temple. During the earliest known age, the most powerful mystics from each of the three orders felt obliged to share their gifts. They created an Inner Realm to both honor the Voduss Grei and illustrate to all beings the beauty and perfection that is possible when all lives are lived in unison. The living, the material, and the spiritual, circulating as one. The structure Tiig now found himself trapped within was merely an artificial, corrupted version produced through gluttonous force and human treachery.

Tiig's anger grew bolder as he progressed farther and farther down the seemingly endless rows of cells. Glancing back at the doors already opened, he saw not a soul walking out into the freedom of the dungeon passage. Looking ahead, he could see no end in sight to the sea of unharmed locks. Despite working as quickly as possible and applying the orange sap as sparingly as he could, he soon realized that the only question still unanswered was which he would run out of first—tallacia sap or time.

In stark contrast to his natural optimism, Tiig held out little hope that Thayliss and the old Ohlinn would successfully deter Lakos from carrying out his sinister mission. Entrusting his life to a human who had deceived him and a mystic who had captured and tortured him seemed a fool's errand. He loathed the very thought of it, though he had little choice. What he didn't understand was why his pragmatic, rational sister would trust Thayliss.

Thinking of Mawi-naa brought throbs of anguish to Tiig's chest. He longed to see her again, whether in this life or the next.

Smearing what little of the sap remained on the lock in front of him, he felt a wave of despair rising up inside. Within the dim, ominous dungeons, he was surrounded by hundreds of Masdazii, Ohlinn, and Lii-jit, and yet he was totally alone.

Breaking open the door before him, he looked at the mystic standing a mere three strides inside the cell. It was an adult Masdazii, a male aged somewhere along the transition from adult to elder. He stood nearly twice Tiig's own height and as wide as he, himself, was tall. A perfectly healthy, perfectly capable mystic, who by all rights should be thousands of strides from here, in a cave by the rocky shore, doing whatever it was that Masdazii adults did. Brilliant creatures, Tiig knew that much. Masters of the material world. Construction, calculation, and manipulation. And yet here he was, utterly powerless. Witless. It pained Tiig to no end seeing something so miraculous, so gifted, rendered practically inanimate. All at the hands of human greed.

Tiig let the dry, faintly sap-stained leaves fall through his fingers. He could do no more. There were still dozens if not hundreds of locked cells farther down the passage, illuminated by the ominous flicker of torchlight. The cells he had already opened contained prisoners bearing no inclination to leave. He was trapped deep within a dungeon maze from which he could never hope to escape on his own. And even if he could leave, he knew that he would in all likelihood be walking out into a world fully under tyrannical human rule.

He didn't know what to do, but he couldn't do nothing. Tiig had been called stubborn more times than he could recollect—a term that he always wore with pride. He had never before given up in his life and knew that this was not the time to start.

As he stood before the last open cage, he heard a sound echoing down the tunnel. It was the sound of footsteps — several footsteps, walking together.

Tiig approached the sound, a sense of hope igniting within him. Perhaps, just perhaps, Thayliss had done it! A vision of a liberated Mawi-naa walking down the tunnel beside the human flashed in his mind, filling him with joy.

Tiig walked faster, hearing the footsteps steadily grow louder. He heard no voices but deduced that the individuals were walking with great purpose, eager to arrive at their destination. He listened closer, with the highly acute sense of hearing possessed by all Lii-jit.

With that, his excitement vaporized. The footsteps belonged to a number of individuals wearing large, solid boots. Military boots. Each worn by individuals of considerably greater mass than himself. Based on the frequency of the steps, he deduced that at least five individuals approached, and Mawi-naa was not one of them. No — ten soldiers. Twenty. As the sound carried, it distorted, as with everything else in the infernal dungeon — no doubt deliberately designed to disorient those within it.

Realizing he had strayed from the opened cells, Tiig tried running back to them, only to find himself lost. Where he was certain the cell blocks had begun, he now found only barren stone walls, staggered by crackling torches.

All the while, the footsteps neared, maintaining their cold, unemotional cadence. An army approached.

CHAPTER FIFTY-TWO

Lakos watched with feverish anticipation as the darkness continued enveloping the moon—at present little more than a bright, white sliver cutting into the night sky.

"You see, Lii-jit, the era of human rule is but moments away," he said joyfully as Mawi-naa stood upon the ledge, still restrained by the turbulent waves of light.

"It is only the end of your life that grows imminent," replied Mawi-naa. "I only hope that the world does not perish alongside you."

Lakos merely laughed. "You see, it is exactly that sharp defiance that I find so enthralling. Especially since, in a few short moments, the whole of your kind will be under my command. A true shame to see your life come to such a tragic end."

"Perhaps she would appreciate perishing alongside her companion," a voice called out behind them.

Lakos spun around and smiled as two figures crossed from the dark gate into the throne room, one prompting the other to enter, a sword held to his back.

"Belwellin," Lakos said, "what a pleasure to have you spend this monumental moment by my side." He looked closely at the figure standing uncomfortably in front. "And I see that you've brought me a gift!"

Lakos strode across the room toward his visitors, grasping Thayliss by the jaw and moving it callously from side-to-side. "I know you. You're the human who sought to interfere with my plans while aboard one of those vile giant flying cockroaches. I would love to hear the story of how you survived passage through the Bray Ridge into the Inner Realm. It must have been thrilling. It's a pity you won't live to tell it." Lakos unsheathed his sword and swung his arm behind his head.

"Wait!" shouted Belwellin. "I do not think it is in the best interests of your kingdom to murder a fellow human, at least not yet. After all, your loyal men and women celebrating in the courtyard believe that their leader values human life above all others. It would dampen their spirits to learn that your first act during the moonless night involved the murder of one of their own."

Lakos scoffed. "And who would tell them? Besides, this traitorous human is not one of us." He paused, still poised to strike. "No, he is most certainly not one of us. The night of the raid at the Valla Forest, I took the life of an Ohlinn elder and a human female who both seemed quite protective of this one. Who at the time wore the flesh of the Ohlinn." He relaxed his stance and stepped closer to the prisoner, his nose practically touching that of Thayliss. "That's right, prisoner. You cannot hide your truth from me. For I, too, stride between mystic and human worlds. As a god, mind you, and not a petty charlatan. Still, one question eludes me. You were Ohlinn on that night, and you are human on this one. Which are you?" he asked. "An Ohlinn masking as human in an attempt to infiltrate my kingdom, or a human living among the Ohlinn, appearing as a mystic on that night through some strange illusion. And if so, then why? Why degrade oneself from human perfection to mystic abomination? You are a disgrace to your kind."

Thayliss said not a word, remaining upright, his back arched and eyes staring forward.

Lakos smirked. "Either way, you suffered great loss on that field. A family? A love?" He could see that his words penetrated deep into his captive. "It was with great satisfaction that I brought my sword through the soft flesh of the woman who held you. Just as it gives me immense pleasure to do the same to you now."

Just as Lakos raised his sword's long edge up against Thayliss's throat, he froze, his eyes suddenly wide with panic. Gasping, Lakos lurched forward into Thayliss, his full weight pressing against him.

Thayliss pushed back, forcing Lakos to stagger backwards, revealing a scarlet stream descending from the side of his chest. Thayliss glanced to his side and saw blood dripping from the tip of Belwellin's sword.

As Lakos reeled back, his arm held tight to his wounded side, a crackling array of electricity encircled Mawi-naa. Within moments, the discrete pulses of energy radiated out in all directions before vanishing into nothingness. The faint, peculiar aroma of melted steel hung in the room for an instant before that, too, disappeared.

The energy field holding Mawi-naa in place upon the ledge also dissolved, liberating her. She dropped to the floor by the window, alert and poised to act.

"Belwellin—why?" asked Lakos, incredulous, his arms soaked in blood.

"It seems that your powers of deduction are not without their limits, my Lord," sneered the old soldier, casually wiping the blood from his sword. "For the brief existence of Belwellin concludes tonight. You may now refer to me by my true name, Noryssin, the last of the Voduss Grei."

The words hit Lakos like a tidal wave, forcing him to press the tip of his sword against the floor to remain upright. "But—it can't be—you perished... I am the Gray Mystic! It was said in the prophecy—your prophecy!"

"I can already feel my powers returning. Oh, how I've missed them," said Noryssin, turning to Mawi-naa and nodding. A vacant, absent look came over her face. She slowly rose and stood, as if patiently awaiting instruction.

Noryssin glanced at Thayliss, still standing beside him, and sighed. "Ah, humans. Immune to subtle suggestion and only ever responding to force." Again, he nodded. Thayliss found his body completely immobilized, arms frozen to his sides.

Noryssin turned back to Lakos, who struggled to stay

upright, his garments saturated with blood. "I give you full credit, Lakos. You came as close as any human ever could to wielding the power of the Voduss Grei. But it was never yours to wield. This world is mine, as are all worlds."

"But... the prophecy..." muttered Lakos, edging toward Noryssin, his sword more a crutch now than a weapon.

"The prophecy ends tonight. For you have failed, and the whole of your kind will suffer because of it," said Noryssin coldly. "You are no more than another human suffering from a lethal combination of greed, prejudice, and vanity. But had you trusted Gris Hallis as deeply as he trusted you, you would be seated upon this throne as I speak, rather than bleeding to death in front of it. Such a pity you cast him aside in favor of me— one of your kind. Or so you thought. Seeing in me only what you wanted to see. What you wanted to hear. A human scarred, physically and emotionally, by supposed mystic tyranny. You were clay in my hands—the more heated, the easier to manipulate. Your weakness gave me power. Gave me life." He took several steps toward Lakos, kicking the sword from his grasp and sending him to the floor.

Noryssin stepped over Lakos's fallen body and looked out the window. Raising his arms out to his sides, he bellowed out into the Inner Realm below, "I am reborn!"

From where he stood, Thayliss could see the final, thin sliver of moonlight eclipse into darkness. As it did, the black of night beyond the throne room suddenly became a blinding, all-encompassing white as the entire outer surface of the sacred tower shone brilliantly. The stone walls of the tower emitted a deep hum that reverberated all around the circular throne room. The floor itself began to tremble, and the ornate chandelier above rattled and swung erratically. At the center of the room, the golden white throne also began to cast a yellow glow.

Noryssin turned around. He looked at Lakos, watching with pleasure as the wounded human struggled to his feet.

"A soldier to the last," said Noryssin, walking toward him, sword firmly in hand.

CHAPTER FIFTY-THREE

Tiig paced anxiously within the small section of tunnel as the army drew nearer. At any moment, they would be upon him—no doubt swords drawn and eyes alight with bloodlust. He was alone, with no weapons and no means of escape. His only options were to face the impending onslaught or run in the opposite direction in the hopes of somehow finding his way back to the prison cells.

Of course, even if he was able to retrace his steps, he would be the only one there with sense enough to defend himself. Either way, he would be fighting an army alone.

His decision was made the moment the soldiers came into view. "There he is!" shouted the human leading the charge, breaking into a sprint. Like a stream of insects surging toward a fallen fruit, Tiig could see human after human rushing in his direction. As he had envisioned, longswords were drawn and held out in front as the march proceeded.

Without further contemplation, Tiig ran the other way as fast as his feet could take him. As spritely and nimble as the Lii-jit were, they were designed more for sporadic bursts of energy than endurance. The muscles in his thighs still quivered from the haste with which he had unlocked so many of the prison cells. If well rested, he would have with certainty disappeared from sight within the blink of an eye. However, in his present state, he dashed through the dim dungeon tunnel mere strides ahead of his pursuers who appeared, if anything, to be steadily gaining on him.

Tiig fought to ignore the burning pain in his legs as he ran, seeing torch upon torch blur past his peripheral vision. He had no idea where he was going, or if he would ever find his way back to the mystic prisoners. All he knew was that he would soon collapse from utter exhaustion and, once the humans caught up with him, meet his end.

His legs fatigued, he adopted long, lunging strides in an attempt to maintain his distance from his pursuers. However, as his foot touched down upon the stone floor following one loping stride, his entire leg gave way, bringing him tumbling down. In a panic, he glanced back and saw the unrelenting humans almost upon him, shouting their profanities and clanging their swords against the stone walls as they ran.

Mustering all the strength he could, Tiig forced himself back to his feet and kept moving, this time much slower than before. He knew that in a matter of seconds, he would feel the brutal cold steel through his back. But he had to try.

He staggered farther, pushing against the sides of the tunnel to keep moving. Up ahead, he could barely make out an odd, erratic dance of light splitting the darkness. And then it came. A surging web of electric light crackled off the walls of the tunnel ahead of him. Dozens of thin streaks of intersecting light darted from wall-to-wall like a collection of sollus bats scrambling inside a giant glass jar.

Within an instant, the spastic little lights coursed harmlessly past him, continuing in the direction of the approaching army. Tiig looked back to see the lights zigzag past the soldiers as well, doing little to impede their progress.

The lead soldier, breathing heavily, slowed to a purposeful walk as he lifted his sword and approached the exasperated Lii-jit. At this point, Tiig could do little more than lean against the tunnel's carved stone wall and await his fate. Taking a series of deep breaths to calm his racing heart, he found the rather strange scent of heated metal drifting toward him from up ahead.

"There is nothing I despise more in this world than a mystic," spat the lead soldier, standing directly in front of the exhausted Lii-jit, longsword firmly in hand. "I'm going to enjoy this."

Before the soldier could thrust his sword, a thin band of

metal unfurled directly over Tiig's head, slashing across the soldier's throat. Dropping his sword, the soldier clutched his neck and collapsed to the ground, gurgling as waves of blood poured from the wound.

Shocked, Tiig spun around to see several Masdazii warriors, the arms of each adorned with sazaa weaponry. He had only read about them in stories—the long, metallic strands hanging from a series of arm bands. The razor-sharp silver cups, capable of launching fire and wreaking all manner of havoc. He could not believe his eyes.

True to their reputation, the giant Masdazii warriors said not a word, merely lumbering past Tiig, arms bent and ready for another strike of the sazaa.

The humans crowded behind the fallen soldier, recoiling in shock. However, after they regained their composure, they once again held their swords high, ready for battle.

Tiig knelt down and picked up the slain human's sword. Glancing back, he realized that he had somehow managed to return to the opened cells. However, most staggering was the fact that every mystic now seemed fully aware of where he was and what was going on. Beyond the Masdazii, Tiig could see groups of Ohlinn comforting each other and reciting prayers. Behind them was a group of Lii-jit. His heart rejoiced at watching his beloved brethren exiting the cells and looking around, eager for a fight.

In the distance, he could see other groups of Masdazii melting the locks of cells he had not gotten to, seemingly with a touch of their thick, translucent hands. Still other Masdazii warriors simply grabbed the bars of the prison cells containing them, appearing to somehow heat the metal enough to render it pliable. With ease, the matter-mystics began pulling out the molten, glowing metal bars, manipulating and reshaping them into shields and, following a deep, droning incantation, the legendary sazaa weaponry.

Several of the liberated Lii-jit raced up to Tiig, grasping his shoulder tightly, as was customary when returning from a long voyage.

"Bless the spirits," said one of them. "You came for us."

"I do not know how your spell was broken," admitted Tiig, "but I would never leave you behind. I would rather perish by your side than live a life without my brothers." He glanced up at the ensuing battle ahead. "But now we must leave this cursed place. Secure a weapon if you can and follow the Masdazii out of this dungeon."

Feeling a sudden rejuvenation within his legs, Tiig tightened the grip on his sword and raced ahead toward the leading Masdazii warriors, who thrashed their metal-laden arms at the steadily retreating human combatants. Balls of flame lit up the dim passage, soaring toward the thick crowd of soldiers. Tiig worked his way to the front line, passionately swinging the heavy, oversized sword at the soldiers blocking the way out.

A deep rumble resonated through the walls all around them, knocking debris onto the tunnel floor. Tiig lacked the luxury of concerning himself with the tunnel's potential collapse. If they couldn't get past the soldiers, they were dead anyway.

Finally, like a jet of water bursting through a crack in a ship's hull, the swarm of mystics poured out from the dungeon tunnel and into the brightly lit courtyard.

Hundreds of armed soldiers filled the room, rushing to subdue the revolt. Masdazii sazaa fire cracked in all directions, igniting tapestries and billowing smoke through the courtyard. Still other Masdazii warriors wielded the broad, metallic shields they had forged inside the dungeon, holding them up as soldiers approached. Tiig watched as, one-by-one, the advancing soldiers' swords were mysteriously torn from their grasp, hurtling through the air until they clanged against the nearest shield. Likewise, the cloud of arrows soaring through the air toward the mystic rebellion all changed course on descent, merging into several discrete groups that also clattered harmlessly against the shields. Without missing a stride, the Masdazii warriors detached the weapons from their shields and ventured forth, threatening the humans with their own artillery.

Scores of Lii-jit also furiously entered the battle, wielding broken bottles, stray swords, and anything else they could obtain, while springing off walls, tables, and each other in a graceful yet brutal attack. The highly trained human soldiers launched their own skillful series of attacks, assuming various rehearsed attack formations with swords, daggers, and crossbows in hand.

There was great bloodshed on all sides. Several Lii-jit were struck down in mid-air, their lifeless bodies crashing to the ground in a heap. The arrows that did pass beyond the metal shields and penetrate the soft Masdazii flesh only served to slow them down. However, the humans also targeted the deadly sazaa, or rather the big, thick arms within them, slashing at their limbs until finally, brutally, rendering them powerless.

The Ohlinn, meanwhile, remained motionless amidst the chaos around them, kneeling upon the stone floor in silent meditation. Far from idle, they wielded a much more insidious weapon. The spirit-mystics sought to impede their enemies by affecting the soldiers' very minds, poisoning their thoughts with distressing, tormenting images of their own death and futility. Sending voices echoing through their subconscious that there was no use. That they would fail. Many human soldiers dropped their weapons to the ground and pressed their hands against their ears, pleading for the thoughts to end. Others, however, seemed immune to the Ohlinn trickery, not slowed in the least as they rushed toward the peacefully kneeling mystics, bringing their swords down upon them.

In the middle of it all, Tiig felt more alive than ever before. He was leading his kind to victory—over the humans, no less. He bounded across the courtyard, sword in hand, slashing down soldier after soldier. He kicked over several wagons, and even picked up a burning piece of fabric, using it to set several others ablaze. He wanted no more than to see the entire wicked human empire reduced to ash.

He leapt to an ornate metal sconce mounted high on the wall and held onto it with his free hand, his feet pressed flat against the wall. From that vantage point, Tiig could see the mayhem unfolding throughout the entire courtyard. A swell of pride burst through his chest on seeing the bodies of dozens — hundreds — of human soldiers littered across the opulent stone floor.

But scanning further, he also saw a growing number of other bodies whose lights had been extinguished — those of the Masdazii, Ohlinn, and Lii-jit. His kind. His brothers. The closer he looked, the more he saw.

As the battle raged on around him, he suddenly experienced a crushing feeling of remorse. He was a life-mystic, and yet he had led so many lives to their end. The immense sadness welled up inside him, causing him to lose his grip upon the stone ledge and drop down to the courtyard floor.

Lying beside him was a human, eyes open and mouth agape, the unmistakable mark of the sazaa across his chest. For the first time, Tiig could see it. A soldier obeying his orders is no different than a beast following his instinct. A crescent bear does not kill through a conscious desire to take the life of another. It merely obeys the intangible, ultimate authority of hunger. The humans who fought to control him and his kind were perhaps much the same. Merely following the demands of their own intangible, ultimate authority. They were not the enemy. They were merely the weapon, manipulated by the one, true, villain.

"Lakos," he muttered under his breath. He then bellowed throughout the courtyard, "There is victory only through life."

Seeing many of the battling mystics turn to look at him, Tiig drove his sword into a toppled wooden table and ran across the courtyard toward the entrance. Several other mystics began to follow suit, leaving the human soldiers to swing their swords through the empty air.

As Tiig neared the lush greenery of the Inner Realm and the freedom beyond it, he saw a blinding white light beam in from beyond the courtyard entrance. The sheer force of the light knocked him and several of his companions back.

Unable to see and without a sword in his hand, he could once again hear the sound of soldiers approaching.

CHAPTER FIFTY-FOUR

As the white glow beyond the throne room wall faded back into the darkness of night, Noryssin strode toward the wounded Lakos, his eyes ablaze.

"Thirty long years have I waited to once again feel the world's energies flow through me. The feeling is indescribable. Pure, unabating intoxication." He shuddered lustfully at the thought. "Only this time, there will be no mutinous prophecy. No corrupt perversion of the sacred Voduss Grei lineage at the hands of a foolish human. But even after you depart from this world, *Lord Lakos*, I know there will be others just like you. Inspired by you. Avenging you. But once I rid myself of this frail body and feel my true power return, I shall see to it that your kind never again questions my authority. I will wipe them from this world if I must. And nothing would give me greater pleasure. Merrin Ells merely roused my appetite for human extinction."

He walked toward Thayliss, who still stood, frozen-in-place beside the throne, and put a hand on his shoulder. "As for you, my human friend, you await a different fate. I shall soon be dispatching your spirit from your body. And who knows, perhaps the next world will make an exception and grant you entrance. But regardless, you can rest assured that future generations will know your face, its stone likeness one day adorning the corridor of the sacred tower alongside all Voduss Grei who came before me. It is much as I envisioned it during my exile. When I first saw your face, it bore a certain... familiarity. I knew you were the one. That was why I could not destroy you back in the dungeon. This is your destiny. Such an honor has never before been granted to a being so inferior. Unfortunately, the spirit residing within that body of yours will be mine."

"It was... *my* destiny..." wheezed Lakos, leaning against the wall, fighting to remain on his feet.

"Ha!" replied Noryssin. "Your destiny was fulfilled the moment you restored the sacred tower and myself along with it. For there can be only one Gray Mystic. Surely even you know that? I'm afraid the moonless night arises for me and me alone."

"I will... stop you!" cried Lakos, expending what little energy he had left.

"Feeling as though you've lost something?" asked Noryssin with a smirk. "I've returned you to the meager human existence you were born with. Let the memory of your fleeting mystic abilities serve as a reminder that humans have no place within the Inner Realm. Gris Hallis should have known better, and he paid the price. I, on the other hand, grow stronger by the moment. By the light of the new dawn, the world will once again worship the Gray Mystic, Noryssin." He glanced down at the pitiful warrior before him. "How very tragic—you lived your entire, misguided life with the singular aim of seeking vengeance against me, only to serve as the very one to restore my power." He circled in front of Lakos, dragging his sword along the stone floor behind him. "You'll forgive me if I savor this moment," he said, smiling broadly. "I've dreamed it for many a night."

Thayliss stared at Mawi-naa from across the room. It pained him to see a life so bright reduced to an empty, mindless shell. The little Lii-jit had so tenderly healed him within her home at Sani-jai and believed in him when no one else did. She sacrificed her own life to give him a chance to save not just her fellow Lii-jit, but all whose freedoms were in jeopardy, whether mystic, human, or otherwise.

But now it was she who needed help, standing helpless and oblivious, unaware that her own demise was rapidly approaching. He ached to intervene but could not move. He was still frozen in place, and it tore him up inside.

Noryssin stood with his back to Thayliss, belittling Lakos as the dying soldier struggled to stay on his feet. Thayliss could see the handle of Gris Hallis's dagger emerging from Noryssin's side pocket, so closely within arm's reach. If only he could move.

Thayliss forced the entirety of his focus, of his very being, into the fingers nearest the exposed knife, trying to will them into co-operation, but it was futile. The spell the maniacal Gray Mystic had placed upon him kept him from moving even the slightest muscle. But his wits were still very much intact. Entombed within a body rendered inanimate.

The intense frustration brought with it memories of that night outside the Valla Forest. Immobilized by the final, selfless act of his dear Leysiia. Unable to stop her from sacrificing her own life to save his. Wanting nothing more than to leap in front of Lakos's cursed blade and feel its wrath so that she might have a chance at seeing one more sunrise, reflected in her beautiful, sapphire eyes.

Thayliss could hear Noryssin berating Lakos, but the verbal attack fell to white noise in his mind. Instead, Thayliss found himself remembering Leysiia and the paradise they shared within the safety of the Valla Forest. How the sun shone through the dense canopy, its shadows dancing across the rippling bark below. The forest possessed a music, a rhythm all its own, as the wind rustled its way through the wide, green leaves, punctuated by the sporadic cries of the insects and birds living among them.

In the treetops of the Valla Forest... the dance of the jousting hummingbirds... Thayliss recalled the final words of Gris Hallis back in the dungeon passageway. With his dying breath, the old Ohlinn had professed his love for the home he'd left long before. Thayliss hoped that the spirit of Gris Hallis now roamed alongside his forgotten Ohlinn brethren in the next world.

The dance of the jousting hummingbirds... I see them now...

Thayliss remembered first witnessing the peculiar little hummingbirds while still a boy. As he had spent much of his life doing, Thayliss was assisting Leonorryn with the maintenance and repair of their treetop cabin one day, which typically consisted of standing by ineffectually, holding planks of wood until Leonorryn needed them. One particular afternoon, Thayliss's attention had begun to stray. Before long, a small blur of color caught his eye, originating from under a pile of leaves at the base of a branch. His arms laden with wooden boards, young Thayliss had kicked at the leaves until they scattered down the long journey to the forest floor.

He then noticed that he had inadvertently obliterated a nest belonging to two tiny birds. The miniature, metallic blue birds were endowed with long, pointed beaks and short, wide wings that fluttered impossibly fast. With their hiding place now exposed, the little birds appeared frantic. They flew around in a circle while facing each other practically beak-to-beak, two tiny moons encircling a common orbit. Thayliss was mesmerized, watching the scene unfold from a mere stride away.

Then, to his horror, the little birds launched themselves toward each other, their long, sharp beaks piercing deep into the body of the other, killing both instantly. And as quickly as they had emerged from their destroyed nest, the two little birds disappeared, dropping silently from the sky, down through the sea of leaves and branches below.

Thayliss cried out, dropping the planks onto the branch where he stood. Leonorryn immediately stopped what he was doing and ran over to the boy who, through his tears, explained what he had accidentally done. The words that Leonorryn had said would stay with Thayliss his entire life.

"The jousting hummingbird is a delicate little creature," he said in his soothing, parental way. "Expose its nest, and its instinct will drive both it and its mate to venture into the next world. You see, my dear boy, it would rather perish while free than live as a prisoner."

Thayliss's consciousness once again returned to his surroundings as he observed the handle of the dagger, still so agonizingly close to him. Noryssin appeared to be concluding his tirade, re-establishing his grip upon his sword. By this point, Lakos had dropped to his knees, his arms limp at his sides and his face pale from blood loss.

Thayliss had to act. There was no alternative.

He fought with all of his resolve to break free from the mystic paralysis that enveloped him. He had failed Leysiia by the Valla Forest. He was not about to fail Mawi-naa. He couldn't. He was merely a human, fighting against the insurmountable power of the Voduss Grei, but he would not give up.

Noryssin retracted his elbow, pressing the tip of his sword against Lakos's chest, coiled for the final, fatal strike. Thayliss saw the dagger jostling in its sheath, its handle closer still to Thayliss's immobile fingers.

Now! Inside his mind, Thayliss screamed a furious cry that echoed through the next world.

Just as Noryssin began thrusting his arm forward, Thayliss's own arm broke free from its mystic restraint. His hand dove into Noryssin's pocket and retrieved the dagger, and in one fluid motion, hurled it toward Lakos.

With one final burst of strength, Lakos raised his hand and caught the dagger, holding it tight in front of him. Noryssin's momentum carried him forward, and his sword plunged deep into Lakos's chest, emerging out his back.

Thayliss stood, no longer immobilized but still motionless, watching the scene unfold. Lakos slumped backwards against the wall, dead. Noryssin, however, released his grip on his sword and looked down in shock. The small dagger was now lodged deep into his own chest.

With an anguished scream, Noryssin grasped the knife by its handle and withdrew it, noticing the thick, blue substance that obscured the metal blade now oozing from within his chest. He trembled as he looked over at Lakos's lifeless body, the very same shimmering, blue fluid slowly trickling down from his own fatal wound. Slowly, a bold halo of blue began to glow from deep within Noryssin's chest, growing brighter and brighter.

"The mark," he uttered in horror. "The Tierren bond... it can't be! It can't be!" Reeling backwards, he stumbled into his throne, his power—his very life—once again slipping away.

Around the throne room, the walls began to tremble. Large stone sections fell from the ceiling, as if all mortar used in its construction had suddenly turned to sand. Thayliss could feel the flooring beneath his feet growing uneven and volatile. It seemed as though the entire tower was on the verge of collapse.

Thayliss looked over at Mawi-naa, who seemed to be slowly re-gaining her awareness. He ran over to her and embraced her.

"We must leave," he said, turning to see the black gate at the opposite end of the throne room disintegrate amidst the cloud of debris. There was no way out.

Thayliss grasped Mawi-naa's hand tightly and looked to the vast, open window surrounding them. "We have to jump!" he shouted, uncertain whether or not Mawi-naa was fully aware of what was happening.

Huge chunks of flooring began giving way as the throne room proceeded to fall apart. They had no choice.

Holding his breath, Thayliss wrapped his arms around the little Lii-jit and leapt blindly out into the dark night sky. As they fell, he could see the ground below—the entirety of the once-lush Inner Realm—igniting in a series of explosions that rapidly coalesced into a vast pool of fire.

He held tighter to Mawi-naa and shut his eyes, just as she was opening hers.

CHAPTER FIFTY-FIVE

As they plummeted toward the inferno below, Thayliss thought only of how his peaceful life in the Valla Forest had so thoroughly fallen apart in the blink of an eye. What should he have done differently? What could he have done? If the spirits willed this fate upon him, for reasons he was sure to never learn, there was no stopping it.

While awaiting the inevitable, Thayliss failed to notice Mawi-naa, held tightly in his arms, muttering words in an exotic tongue.

Within an instant, Thayliss felt his descent halted, lurching his stomach down deep within his abdomen.

Opening his eyes, he saw that both he and Mawi-naa lay upon the sparsely feathered backs of several Bray eagles. The unseemly beasts flew close together, soaring as one cohesive unit toward the Bray Ridge ahead. Mawi-naa had wrapped her arms under the wings of one of the birds, and Thayliss held tighter to her, his upper body resting upon the backs of one of the reptilian-looking birds while his legs sprawled across the wings of another.

Together they glided over the swirling clouds of smoke and flame raging far below. Behind them, Thayliss could see that the once-glorious white tower had been robbed of its luster as giant chunks of stone crumbled away, sinking the sacred monument to the ground. It was as if the world's very core was reclaiming what it had never consented to resurrect.

As they neared the crest of the Bray Ridge, seeing only darkness of night beyond its jagged peaks, a great, booming rumble echoed up all around them, reverberating along the ridge's curved interior wall. The flames below grew more aggressive, spitting their embers into the night, so high that Thayliss feared that the vast, turbulent blaze would pull them from the sky and consume them. Steadily, the birds coasted nearer and nearer to the ridge, all the while surrounded by the great and ominous noise, the Inner Realm's apparent protest to their escape.

Finally, just as they soared over the ridge and into the solitude of the desert air, the entire Inner Realm exploded. A great column of fire erupted far above the volcanic ridge behind them, searing its violent light into the black night sky. Within moments, they were enveloped by an intense wave of heat, causing the birds to break their order, flailing and screeching chaotically as their descent suddenly hastened.

No longer draped across several of the giant birds, Thayliss clung desperately to Mawi-naa, his legs dangling in the open air. He knew that his weight, along with that of Mawi-naa, was too much for the one, lone eagle. Thayliss contemplated releasing his grip and free-falling to his certain end so that at least the kind Lii-jit would make it out alive. But before he could act, Thayliss caught the expression on Mawi-naa's face, as she rested her chin close to his atop the eagle's back. There he saw none of the fear that he himself felt. She appeared in total control, with even her hold on the eagle below her exuding an air of calm and composure. Her serenity calmed not only Thayliss but the other eagles as well, as they soon recovered their formation alongside the overburdened bird, softening their descent once again.

Nearing the ground, a large number of forms came into view. Thayliss could clearly make out the corpulent silhouettes of many Masdazii, as well as the tall, slender forms of the Ohlinn. A number of smaller shapes moved about energetically close by. From the smile emerging on Mawi-naa's lovely face, he knew that they were Lii-jit.

Within moments, the escort of Bray eagles brought them gently to the safety of the dry, desert ground. The moment Thayliss released his grip around Mawi-naa's waist, she leapt from the eagle's back and disappeared into the crowd. Thayliss slowly slid off the animal, relishing the sensation of having both feet securely on the ground. No sooner had he stepped away from the birds than they flapped their broad, muscular wings in unison and glided away, quickly vanishing into the darkness.

Thayliss walked toward the gathering, the joyous faces of countless mystics from all orders illuminated by the glow from the liquid stone that snaked its way down the volcano's outer face. Looking up, he saw the gradual re-emergence of the moon, slowly restoring its serene light into the early morning sky.

Apparently wasting little time putting their many gifts to use, the Masdazii had restored their weather-battered fleet of windchargers and were lumbering aboard, settling in for the ride home. To his great surprise, Thayliss also noticed that within a great many of the vehicles, riding alongside the Masdazii drivers, were numerous other mystics, both Ohlinn and Lii-jit. Thayliss was astonished. Such a sight had not been seen since long before his time.

One-by-one, the vehicles raised their billowing sails and took off across the rocky desert. As Thayliss walked by, he saw a Masdazii seated within a nearby windcharger look at him and grunt. Thayliss, caught by surprise, stopped and looked at him. In a gesture Thayliss had never before conceived from their kind, the giant matter-mystic waved toward him, inviting him to climb aboard the vessel. Thayliss smiled and waved appreciatively but shook his head, politely declining the offer. With a shrug, the Masdazii stretched out in his seat a little more, before the windcharger roared off into the distance.

"Afraid of a little windcharger ride?" Thayliss heard a voice snidely inquire.

Looking ahead through the thinning crowd, he saw Tiig, his arm wrapped tightly around Mawi-naa's shoulders. "You know, the rumors of Masdazii warriors consuming humans are grossly exaggerated." Tiig smiled. "Definitely most unlikely to occur. Though always a chance, of course."

Thayliss walked toward the two Lii-jit siblings, unsure of how Tiig would receive him. All the same, he found himself approaching them with his arms held open. Both Mawi-naa and Tiig reached out and embraced their new ally.

"Did everyone get out in time?" asked Thayliss.

Tiig shook his head, the broad smile fading slightly from his face. "But at least a whole lot more of us got out than them, I can tell you that much."

Sensing the sorrow in Thayliss's eyes as he looked out at the inferno, Mawi-naa put her hand to his cheek, gently meeting his eyes. "So where are you going now?" she asked.

Having been convinced countless times over the past few days that he would never again see his freedom, Thayliss had no idea where he would go.

"The more important question is how you plan on getting there," added Tiig, a devious smirk on his face.

Thayliss shrugged. "I really haven't a clue." The thought saddened him. For the first time in his life, he had no home. No family.

Mawi-naa feigned an overtly annoyed sigh, still smiling. "I suppose it wouldn't be the worst thing in the world were you to return with us to Sani-jai. Just until you find your way, of course."

Before he could contemplate the offer, Thayliss found himself smiling. "Of course," he replied.

"Tiig, what do you say?" asked Mawi-naa hopefully.

Tiig paused, a look of turmoil on his face. "Twelve of us already packed into one humble folliad... what's one more?" He laughed.

Thayliss looked at the two Lii-jit and smiled. "That sounds perfect." He looked around, pointing to one of the few remaining windchargers. "Should we catch a ride aboard one of those?"

"Oh my, no," said Tiig emphatically. "Are you mad? You surely must be mad. Those Masdazii beasts have been known to

feast on the bones of young, virile Lii-jit. We've arranged for...
alternate means of transport." Tiig nodded into the shadows
and several figures appeared, slowly trotting out toward them.
As they entered the light, Thayliss laughed out loud, watching
the pack mule and old, mangy bastik wolf wait attentively for
further instruction.

"I think I know which one is mine," said Thayliss, climbing
atop the wolf's back and grasping the tuft of wiry, gray fur
between its shoulders. "He likes his neck rubbed, you know,"
he said with a smile.

Tiig and Mawi-naa both climbed atop the pack mule, and
the two loyal animals began their journey across the desert,
carrying their passengers back to the serenity of Sani-jai.

Epilogue

Once the eruption within the Bray Ridge ceased, the layers of molten rock coating the whole of the Inner Realm slowly dimmed from bold orange to an ashen gray. As the darkness of night once again yielded to soft morning light, a thick, gray cloud amassed over the center of the desert. Without lightning or thunder, the cloud suddenly began shedding large droplets of rain. A cacophony of violent searing hissed throughout the Inner Realm as cool water struck the glowing sea of stone, casting great, curling wafts of steam and smoke back up toward the sky.

At the very center of the Inner Realm's volcanic wasteland, where a great and sacred tower had risen high mere hours before, there was now a single, tiny ember, glowing red in defiance. Rain droplets struck it, but it could not be extinguished.

Instead, as small pools of water began filling the dips and grooves across the surrounding stone floor, the ground beneath the resistant ember suddenly fractured. The crack delved a full stride into the fresh stone ground, causing a chain reaction of subsequent fissures that surged far below, abruptly terminating on reaching a small pocket of trapped air.

Within it, a dark vapor swirled rhythmically, crackling with a series of minute, shimmering lights. Infused within the formless entity was an intelligence. A dormant consciousness bearing one, solitary thought.

Vengeance.

THE END

About the Author

Erik loves the challenge of creating a story and trying to bring it to life. From suspense/thrillers and epic fantasy to screenplays and health/medical publications, he enjoys delving into a wide variety of different worlds. He lives just outside Vancouver, British Columbia, with his wife and daughter.

www.edbbooks.com.

FANTASY, SCI-FI, HORROR & PARANORMAL

If you prefer to spend your nights with Vampires and Werewolves rather than the mundane then we publish the books for you. If your preference is for Dragons and Faeries or Angels and Demons – we should be your first stop. Perhaps your perfect partner has artificial skin or comes from another planet – step right this way. If your passion is Fantasy (including magical realism and spiritual fantasy), Metaphysical Cosmology, Horror or Science Fiction (including Steampunk), Cosmic Egg books will feed your hunger. Our curiosity shop contains treasures you will enjoy unearthing. If you have enjoyed this book, why not tell other readers by posting a review on your preferred book site.

Recent bestsellers from Cosmic Egg Books are:

The Zombie Rule Book
A Zombie Apocalypse Survival Guide
Tony Newton
The book the living-dead don't want you to have!
Paperback: 978-1-78279-334-2 ebook: 978-1-78279-333-5

Cryptogram
Because the Past is Never Past
Michael Tobert
Welcome to the dystopian world of 2050, where three lovers are
haunted by echoes from eight-hundred years ago.
Paperback: 978-1-78279-681-7 ebook: 978-1-78279-680-0

Purefinder
Ben Gwalchmai
London, 1858. A child is dead; a man is blamed and dragged
through hell in this Dantean tale of loss, mystery and fraternity.
Paperback: 978-1-78279-098-3 ebook: 978-1-78279-097-6

600ppm
A Novel of Climate Change
Clarke W. Owens
Nature is collapsing. The government doesn't want you to know
why. Welcome to 2051 and 600ppm.
Paperback: 978-1-78279-992-4 ebook: 978-1-78279-993-1

Creations
William Mitchell
Earth 2040 is on the brink of disaster. Can Max Lowrie stop the
self-replicating machines before it's too late?
Paperback: 978-1-78279-186-7 ebook: 978-1-78279-161-4

The Gawain Legacy

Jon Mackley

If you try to control every secret, secrets may end up controlling
you.

Paperback: 978-1-78279-485-1 ebook: 978-1-78279-484-4

Readers of ebooks can buy or view any of these bestsellers by
clicking on the live link in the title. Most titles are published
in paperback and as an ebook. Paperbacks are available in
traditional bookshops. Both print and ebook formats are
available online.

Find more titles and sign up to our readers' newsletter at
http://www.johnhuntpublishing.com/fiction
Follow us on Facebook at https://www.facebook.com/JHPfiction
and Twitter at https://twitter.com/JHPFiction